"TO READ A NOVEL BY ANNE TYLER IS TO FALL IN LOVE."
—*People*

THE WORLD ACCORDING TO JEREMY . . .

Jeremy had never left the familiar surroundings of home. His physical world had remained secure and unchanging. Thus it was possible for him to go beyond it, into the world of perception. He could see things at a distance—he had time to sail by—

CELESTIAL NAVIGATION

"ANNE TYLER HAS A WAY OF TRANSCRIBING HER CHARACTERS' PECULIARITIES WITH SUCH LOVING WHOLENESS THAT WHEN WE EXAMINE THEM WE KEEP FINDING MORE AND MORE PIECES OF OURSELVES."
—*New York Times Book Review*

"*One of today's most talented and mesmerizing authors.*"
—*Publishers Weekly*

Books by
ANNE TYLER

Celestial Navigation
Earthly Possessions

Available from
WARNER BOOKS

CELESTIAL NAVIGATION

Anne Tyler

WARNER BOOKS

A Warner Communications Company

WARNER BOOKS EDITION

Published by CBS Inc., by arrangement with
Alfred A. Knopf, Inc.,
201 E. 50th Street,
New York, N.Y. 10022
Distributed by Warner Books.

Warner Books, Inc.,
666 Fifth Avenue,
New York, N.Y. 10103

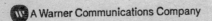 A Warner Communications Company

Printed in the United States of America

First Warner Books Printing: April, 1983

10 9 8 7 6 5 4 3 2 1

Fall, 1960: Amanda

My brother Jeremy is a thirty-eight-year-old bachelor who never did leave home. Long ago we gave up expecting very much of him, but still he is the last man in our family and you would think that in time of tragedy he might pull himself together and take over a few of the responsibilities. Well, he didn't. He telephoned my sister and me in Richmond, where we have a little apartment together. If memory serves me it was the first time in his life he had ever placed a call to us; can you imagine? Ordinarily we phoned Mother every Sunday evening when the rates were down and then she would put Jeremy on the line to say hello. Which was about all he did say: "Hello," and "Fine, thank you," and then a long breathing pause and, "Well, goodbye now." So when I heard his voice that night I had trouble placing it for a moment. "Amanda?" he said, and I said, "Yes? Who is it?"

"I wanted to tell you about Mama," Jeremy said.

That's what he calls her still: Mama. Laura and I switched to Mother when we were grown but Jeremy didn't.

I said, "Jeremy? Is something wrong?"

"Mama has passed on," he told me.

And I said, "Oh, dear Lord in heaven."

Then Laura and I had to make all the arrangements by long distance, had to call the doctor for the death certificate and track down the minister, had to help Jeremy find a funeral parlor. (It seems he had never learned how to work the yellow pages.) Had to catch a train to Baltimore the next day and locate a taxi that would carry us from the station. It didn't occur to Jeremy that at a time like this we might like to be met. What would he have met us *in,* anyway; he had no notion of how to drive. But some men can take things in hand even arriving by city bus, hailing another bus home again and seeing to it their sisters have seats and keeping watch over their bags. Not Jeremy. Laura and I walked out of the station on a rainy cold November noon and found not a single familiar face, not even a redcap in sight, no taxis waiting at the curb. We had to sit shivering on our suitcases with our feet tucked under us and plastic rainscarves over our hats. "Oh, Amanda," Laura said, "that cold of yours will go straight to your chest." For I had been ill for two weeks before this, just barely managing to continue with my classes, as I distrust substitute teachers. I shouldn't have been out at all. And now Laura looked as if *she* were coming down with something. Folding and refolding a flowered handkerchief, blowing into it and then wiping the tip of her nose. She wore her maroon knit, which was supposed to slim her some but didn't. Bulges showed in the gape of her coat. I was in my good black wool with the rhinestone buttons, and my squirrel-collar coat and my gray bird-wing hat that exactly matches my hair. But I might as well not have bothered. The plastic scarf and the Rain Dears spoiled the effect. Wouldn't you think that Jeremy would at least know how to dial a taxi and have it waiting at the station?

Then when we finally did find a cab there was some confusion about where we wanted to go. Laura said straight to the funeral parlor. She was always closer to Mother than I was and had acted much more emotional about her passing, sat up most of the night before crying and carrying on. Well, Lord knows it was a shock to me as well but I am the oldest—forty-six, though people tell me I don't look it—and I have always been the sensible one. I said we would have to drop our suitcases, wouldn't we? And surely Jeremy would be seeing to things at the funeral parlor. He could manage *that* much, couldn't he? Laura said, "Oh, well, I don't know, Amanda." So in the end I told her we would go on to the funeral parlor but just stop off first at the house, leave our suitcases and make sure where Jeremy was. The driver said, *"Now* can we get going?" A put-upon type. But at least he kept quiet, once we were out in traffic. I despise how some taxi drivers will just talk on and on in that tough way they have, giving out their opinions on politics and the cost of living and crime in the streets and other matters I have no interest in.

Our mother's house was smack in the middle of the city on a narrow busy street, one of those thin dark three-storey Baltimore rowhouses. A clutter of leaded panes and straggly ivy and grayish lace curtains dragging their bottoms behind the black screens. The sidewalk leading up to it could break a person's ankle, and yellowy-brown weeds were growing in the cracks. A stained cardboard sign reading "ROOMS TO LET" was propped in the parlor window. The neighborhood was running down, had been for years. Most places had split into apartments and gone over to colored and beatniks, and a few were even boarded up, with city notices plastered across the doors. I told Mother time and time again that she should move but she never got up the energy. She was a *stagnant* kind of person. I hate to say it now she's gone but there you are. She didn't even notice what the neighborhood had turned into. She hardly ever left the house. And over the years all her possessions had piled around her so, her knick-knacks and photographs and her shoeboxes full of bits of string. It would have taken three vans just to move her. When we drew up in front of the door I could see the beginnings of her clutter already: the little scrap of a front yard packed with weeds and spiny shrubs and one great long dead rambling rosebush that had woven itself into everything. That will tell you a good deal about the way she looked at things. She caused no changes; that was Mother for you. She hadn't the courage. If she saw that crack snaking through the mortar or the grillwork fence slowly leaning toward the ground, all she thought was, well, but who am *I* to alter it? I have no patience with people like that.

We climbed the front steps and went into the vestibule, where we found a flowerpot containing a dead twig in a hunk of dry earth. I remembered it from the *last* time we were home, Easter Sunday, and it was dead then. We rang the bell but no one answered. There was a cavelike echo behind the door that gave me a chill. I said, "Evidently Jeremy is out," and Laura said, Out? Out where?"

"Why, at the funeral parlor, I should *hope*," I said.

So we left our suitcases in the vestibule—we hadn't a house key—and went back to the cab. I told the driver the name of the funeral parlor. He said, "Oh, yes, I know it well. They buried my sister from there." Well, I didn't like the sound of *that*. Just what had Jeremy got us into, anyway? "They do good work," the driver said. Laura and I only looked at each other. We didn't say a thing.

Then when we got there—another rowhouse, but some ten blocks away—and had split the fare between us and decided on the size of the tip, I saw I was right to have worried. There was a neon sign in the yard, blinking on and off and crackling. The windows were sooty and a torn awning dripped rainwater down our necks as we bent to take our galoshes off. And inside! I never saw a place so gloomy. It smelled of dusty radiators. The ceilings were high and flaky, the walls that shade you see in hospitals—either a faded yellow or a yellowed white, you never can be sure. The carpet was worn bald. An usher made his way across it with his run-down loafers dragging. "We are Mrs. Pauling's daughters," I told him. He nodded and turned to lead us down a corridor, past a string of rooms where people were standing around looking unsure of what to do next. Laura hung onto my arm. I could feel her trembling. Well, I was quite a bit shaky myself, I admit it. It seemed to me that Mother had allowed herself to slip down yet another rung, continuing even after death and ending up in a place that had decayed even worse than her own. All that sustained me was that Jeremy would be waiting for us—a man, at least, whatever you might say, and our last blood relation, someone to share our trouble. But when we reached the end of the corridor, what did we find? An empty room, a casket sitting unattended. Bleak white light slanting through an uncurtained window. "Where's—" I said. But the usher had gone already. They have no sense of how to do things in these places.

They had laid Mother out in a brass-handled casket, a wooden one. Mahogany, I believe. Her head was on a satin pillow. Her hair, which had stayed light brown but grown thin and dull, was set into little crimps, and for once she wore no net on it. She always used to—a light brown cobweb that I itched to snatch off her. A cobweb and a wispy dress with all the life gone out of it and chintz mules that whispered when she walked. Well, now they had put her into the navy wool that I sent her for her last birthday. "Thank you so much for my pretty new suit," she wrote when she received it, "though as you know I don't go out much and will probably have no occasion to wear it." Her face was set in a faint, sweet smile, with her withered cheeks sagging back toward the pillow and her eyelids puckery. You hear people say, at funerals, "How natural she looks! As though she were asleep." And most of the time they are telling a falsehood, but in Mother's case it was absolutely true. Of *course* she looked natural; why not, when she went through life looking dead? Even her hands were right: crossed on her chest, blue-white, waxy at the fingertips. She always did have poor circulation. She always did keep her hands folded in that meek and retiring way, never so much as fidgeting, boneless and nerveless as some floppy cloth doll. On her left hand was a white gold wedding ring, which any woman of spirit would have thrown away years ago but not, of course, our mother. She kept it on. Inertia. She probably forgot it was there. Now for some reason my eyes got fixed on it, and I stared and failed to realize that Laura was crying until I heard her sniffle. I turned and saw her face curling in upon itself while the tears rolled down her cheeks. "Oh, Amanda," she said, "how will we ever manage now that Mother's gone?"

"Now, Laura. It's not as if—"

"We shouldn't have left her alone so much. Should we? We should have gone to visit her more, and paid her more attention."

"*Jeremy* was the one she cared about," I said, "and he was here all along. We don't have anything to blame ourselves for."

"Jeremy will be just devastated," Laura said. She patted her eyes with her little flowered handkerchief, which was already sopping wet. "You know how attached they were. Oh, what will he do now? How will he get along?"

"Where *is* he, first of all," I said, and I left Laura crying by the casket and went off to find the manager. His office was by the front door. He was seated at his desk, drinking coffee from a paper cup that he hid as soon as he saw me. "Yes!" he said. "May I be of assistance?"

"I am Miss Pauling, and I wonder if you can tell me where my brother is."

He looked over at the usher, who was leaning against the wall. "Brother?" said the usher.

"That would be *Mr.* Pauling," the manager said. "Yes, well, we saw him of course when we came to the house to—but he seemed, he didn't seem—but he did help us pick out the clothing. We like to have a family member do that, I told him, though at first he was reluctant. Family members know what would be most—"

"But where is he *now*," I said.

"Oh, why, that I don't know."

"Hasn't he been by here?"

The manager looked at the usher again, and the usher shook his head.

"Just some ladies," he told me. "From her church, I think they said."

"Hasn't he come here at *all?*"

"Not as I know of."

"Well, for goodness' sake," I said. I turned and left, with the usher suddenly uprooted from his wall and scurrying along behind me. "Oh, leave me be, go see to someone else," I told him. "We are surely not the *only* dead in this house." Then I went back to the room where Mother was, where Laura was just searching her handkerchief in hopes of a dry corner. I handed her a clean one from my purse. "Jeremy has not been here," I told her.

"Oh no, I didn't think he would be."

"Did you ever hear of a son not keeping watch by his mother's remains?"

"Oh, well, you know how—I just expected him to be at home," Laura said. "I hope he isn't in some kind of trouble."

"What kind of trouble would *Jeremy* be in?" I asked her, and naturally she couldn't think of an answer. There are no surprises in Jeremy. He will never go on a drinking spree, or commit any crimes, or be found living under an alias in some far-distant city. "Most likely he is holed up in his studio," I told her. "We should have rung the doorbell longer. Well, never mind." For to tell the truth I was just as glad. It would have been more hindrance than help to have him moping around here. He was even closer to Mother than Laura was. They knew each other so well they barely needed to speak; they spent every evening of their lives together, huddled in that dim little parlor watching TV and drinking cocoa. I have never understood how people can live that way.

We stayed the afternoon in the loveseat out in the corridor and greeted visitors, such as they were. Mother's circle of friends seemed to have closed in considerably. Those who came were mighty brief about it. A moment of silence by the casket, a word to us, a signature in the guestbook, and then they left again. Just doing their duty. Well, I have always said it doesn't cost a thing to perform a duty *pleasantly,* once you are at it, but these people seemed to be thinking of other matters and I could tell their hearts weren't in it. In between visits Laura and I sat without saying anything, side by side. Our arms were touching; we had no choice. The loveseat was very small. I hate to be touched. Laura was all the time twisting her purse straps or fiddling with its clasp, so that her elbow rubbed against my sleeve with a felty sound that made me jumpy. "Sit *still,* will you?" I said.

"Oh, Amanda, I feel so lost in this place."

"Get ahold of yourself," I told her. Her chin was denting. I reached out and squeezed her hand and said, "Never mind, we'll go to the house soon and have a cup of tea. You're tired is all."

"It's true, I am," she said. She has never had as much energy as I.

Two ladies from Mother's church dropped by. I knew their faces but had to cover up that I'd forgotten their names. Then Mother's minister, and then Mrs. Jarrett, who has been a boarder at the house for years. A woman of quality, very gracious and genteel. She always wears a hat. She held out a gloved hand and said, "I shall think of your mother often, Miss Pauling, and remember her in my prayers. She was a very sweet person." Now, why couldn't all boarders be like that? Right on her heels came Miss Vinton, a faded stringy type who rents the south rear bedroom. The smallest room in the house; Mother charged less for it. "I'm sorry about your mother," Miss Vinton said, but if she was so sorry you'd think she would have dressed to show it. She wore what she always does, a lavender cardigan over a gray tube of a dress, baggy mackintosh, boatlike Mary Janes on her great long feet. She shook hands like a man, bony hands with straight-edged nails and nicotine stains. Rides a bicycle everywhere she goes. *You* know the kind. "Well, it was very thoughtful of you to come, Miss Vinton," I said, but meanwhile I threw a good sharp glance at her clothing to show I had taken it in. If she noticed, she didn't care. Just gave me a horse-toothed smile. I suppose she thinks we have something in common, both being spinsters in our forties, but thank heaven that is where the resemblance ends. I have always taken care to keep my dignity intact.

At six in the evening we went home. The streets were black and wet, with no taxi in sight. We walked all ten blocks. Laura was crying again. She kept blowing her nose and murmuring little things I couldn't hear, what with the traffic swishing by and my rainscarf crackling, but I don't imagine that I missed anything. Instead of answering I just marched along, keeping tight hold of my purse and watching for puddles. Even so, my stockings got spattered. The rowhouses had been darkened by the rain and looked meaner and grimmer than ever.

Then to top it off, Mother's place still seemed deserted. The only lit window was on the second floor. There was the same echo when we rang the doorbell. Laura said, "Oh, what if we're locked out? Where will we stay?"

"Don't be ridiculous," I told her. "This house is teeming with boarders, if nothing else, and you can see that someone's been and taken our suitcases in." For the vestibule was bare again. Nothing remained but the flowerpot.

I put my finger on the doorbell and held it there. Eventually a light came on in the hallway, and then we saw a shadow behind the lace curtain. Mr. Somerset, hitching up his suspenders as he shuffled toward us. I knew him by his bent-kneed walk and his rounded shoulders. He was as familiar to me as some elderly uncle, though no uncle I ever asked for. "Now this," I told Mother once, "is what I mean about your boarders, Mother: Mr. Somerset is a depressing old man and I don't know why you've put up with him so long." "Yes, but all he has is his pension, poor man," she said. She didn't mean that. She meant, How will I tell him to go? How will I get used to someone new? Can't we just let things stay as they are?

"Miss Pauling," Mr. Somerset said. "And Mrs. Bates. You've come about your mother, I reckon."

"Why, yes, we have," I said, "and we've been all afternoon at the funeral parlor without seeing a sign of Jeremy. Now, where might he be, Mr. Somerset?"

"He's setting on the stairs," he said.

"On the stairs?"

"On the stairs where your mother passed. He's been there all day."

"We came before now, Mr. Somerset. At noon. We rang the doorbell."

"I must've been out."

"My *brother* was here, you say."

"He don't answer doorbells," said Mr. Somerset, "and he don't move from where he's at. Sets in the dark."

"For mercy's sake," I said. "Jeremy?"

But it was Laura who went to find him, running up the stairs with her galoshes still on. I heard her flick a light switch, start on up toward the third floor calling, "Jeremy, honey!"

"He's not himself at all today," Mr. Somerset told me.

People say that about Jeremy quite often, but what they mean is that he is not like other people. He is *always* himself. That's what's wrong with him. I called, "Jeremy, come down here please. Laura and I have been looking for you."

"He won't," said Mr. Somerset. "He's setting on the step where—"

"She passed on the *stairs?*"

"Yes, ma'am."

"Well, of all places!"

"Way I heard it, he sat by her side till Mrs. Jarrett come home. *Hours* maybe. Nobody knows. It was Mrs. Jarrett dialed your number on the telephone. Otherwise he might never have done so. And then she sent him to bed, for after the fuss with the funeral parlor and the doctor and so on he just come right back to that step up yonder, planning on passing the night there, I believe. Mrs. Jarrett said, 'Mr. Pauling, I think you should lie down on a regular bed now,' and he did. But I noticed this morning he was setting on the stairs again, sat there all day. I told Miss Vinton that. She said let him be. I said how long were we supposed to let him be? 'This is not *natural,* Miss Vinton,' I told her, but she wouldn't—"

"Well, he's come to the end of *that,*" I said, and I took off my Rain Dears and hung my coat and hat in the closet and went upstairs. I crossed the second floor hallway, which smelled of damp towels. I climbed on to the third floor, where Jeremy works and sleeps all alone, seldom letting other people in. There he was, hunched over on the uppermost step, with Laura crouching beside him. She was out of breath; she never takes exercise. "Jeremy, honey, you don't know how worried I was," she was telling him. "Why, we rang and rang! I thought for certain you would be here."

"I was sitting on the stairs," Jeremy said.

"So I hear," I said, climbing till my face was even with his. "The *least* I expected was to see you at the funeral parlor."

"Oh, no."

"Well, you'll have to come downstairs now," I told him.

"I don't believe I feel like it just now, Amanda."

"Did I ask if you felt like it?"

He spread his fingers and looked at the bitten nails, not answering. Speak sharply to Jeremy and you will bowl him over; he can't stand up to things. You'll get further being gentle with him, but I always remember that too late. He puts me in a fury. I don't see how he could let himself go the way he has. No, letting yourself go means you had to be something to start with, and Jeremy never was anything. He was born like this. He is, and always has been, pale and doughy and over-weight, pear-shaped, wide-hipped. He toes out when he walks. His hair is curly and silvery-gold, thin on top. His eyes are nearly colorless. (People have asked me if he is an albino.) There is no telling where he manages to find his clothes: baggy slacks that start just below his armpits; mole-colored cardigan strained across his stomach and buttoning only in the middle, exposing a yellowed fishnet undershirt top and bottom, and tiny round-toed saddle oxfords. Saddle oxfords? For a man? "Pull yourself together, Jeremy," I said, and he blinked up at me with his lashless, puffy eyes.

"She's only concerned for you," Laura told him.

"I'm concerned for all of us," I said. "How would it be if everyone just sat in one place when they didn't feel like moving?"

"In a while I will move," Jeremy said.

"At the funeral parlor they said they hadn't seen a sign of you."

"No."

"Said you hadn't even stopped in to check on how they laid her out."

"I couldn't manage it," Jeremy said.

"*We* managed, didn't we?"

"She looked very peaceful," Laura said. She had leaned forward to grasp both his shoulders. He gave the impression that if she let go he would crumple very slowly to one side with his eyes still wide and staring. "You might think she was just asleep," she told him.

"She fell asleep over solitaire a lot," Jeremy said.

"She looks as pretty as her wedding picture."

Now, where did she get that? Mother looked nothing like her wedding picture. It would have been mighty strange if she had. But all Jeremy said was, "The one in the album?"

"That's the one."

"Her face was kind of full in that picture," Jeremy said.

"Her face is full *now*."

"I suppose they have some way of doing that."

"Her color is good, too."

"Does she have a bit of color?"

"They've put on rouge, I imagine. Nothing *garish*, though. Just enough to—and they've waved her hair."

"*Mama* never waved it."

"Yes, but it looks just lovely, Jeremy. And that dress, it sets off her complexion. Did *you* choose the dress? You did just fine. I think I might have picked the flowered beige, the one she always wore at Easter, but this is nice too, and the color sets off her—"

"The funeral man suggested that," Jeremy said.

"I suppose he knows about these things."

"I had to go looking for clothes in her closet."

"Really. And then the way they've done her—"

"Had to push down all the rack of things in her closet."

"Yes, I know."

"They told me I had to," Jeremy said. "I said, couldn't *they* do it? They said no. They were scared they would get into trouble somehow, be accused of choosing wrong or maybe even stealing, I guess, if any-

thing turned up missing. But *I* wouldn't do that. I
wouldn't accuse them."

"No, of course not," Laura said.

"I had to slide down all the rack of dresses in her
closet."

"Yes, well."

"I had to find some, find her undergarments in the
bureau. Open up her bureau."

"Well, Jeremy."

"Go through her bureau drawers taking things out."

"Jeremy, honey. There, now. There, there."

For Jeremy just then leaned over against Laura, set
his head alongside that pillow of a bosom. And there
sat Laura patting his back and clic**king** her teeth. She
always did pamper that boy. Well, she was only seven
when he was born—the age when you look at a baby
brother as some kind of super-special doll. It never occurred to her that she was being displaced in Mother's
affection. It occurred to *me,* of course. I was the oldest.
I had been displaced years ago. I saw how Mother had
room for only one person at a time, and that one the
youngest and smallest and weakest. I saw how, while
she was expecting Jeremy, she curled more and more
inside herself until she was only a kind of circular hollow taking in nourishment and asking for afghans. In
all other situations Mother was a *receiver,* requesting
and expecting even from her own daughters without
ever giving anything out, but she spoiled Jeremy from
the moment he was born and I believe that that is the
root of all his troubles. A mama's boy. She preferred
him over everyone. She gave him the best of her food
and the whole of her attention, kept him home from
school for weeks at a time if he so much as complained
of a stomach ache, which he was forever doing; read to
him for hours while he sat wrapped in a comforter—oh,
I can see it still! Jeremy on the windowseat, pasty and
puffy-faced, Mother reading him Victorian ladies'
novels in her fading whispery voice although she *never*
felt quite up to reading to us girls. By this time our
father had left us, but I don't believe she truly noticed.
She was too wrapped up in Jeremy. She thought the sun

rose and set in him. She thought he was a genius. (I myself have sometimes wondered if he isn't a little bit retarded. Some sort of selective, unclassified retardation that no medical book has yet put its finger on.) He failed math, he failed public speaking (of course), he went through eighth grade *twice* but he happened to be artistic so Mother thought he was a genius. "Some people just don't have mathematical minds," she said, and she showed us his report card—A+ in art, A in English, A+ in deportment. (What else? He had no friends, there was no one he could have whispered with in class.) This was when we were in college, working our way through teachers college waiting tables and living at home and wearing hand-me-downs, and he was still in high school. When he graduated—by proxy, claiming a stomach ache, not up to facing a solitary march across the stage to receive his diploma—where did he go? The finest art school in Baltimore, with Mother selling off half her ground rents to pay the tuition. And he was miserable for every minute of it. Couldn't stand the pressure. Scared of the other students. Stomach was bothering him. He lost one whole semester over something that might or might not have been mononucleosis. (In those days we called it glandular fever.) And even in good health, he rarely went to class. He would come home halfway through the morning and crawl into bed. What can you say to someone like that? What *Mother* said was, "Those people are just asking too much of you, Jeremy." Then she made him all his favorite foods for lunch. (His favorite dessert is custard. Boiled custard.) Well, they did like his work, it seems. They gave him top grades and let him graduate. But even after that, he had no way to make a living. Can you imagine Jeremy teaching a class? Finally Mother gathered up strength to place a permanent ad in the newspaper: *Trained artist willing to give private lessons in his studio.* His studio was the entire third floor, which she had turned over to him without a thought. It had a skylight. Every now and then some poor failure of a pupil might ring the doorbell—girls mostly, anemic stringy-haired girls that scared him half to death. But they never lasted long.

It seemed all they had to do was get a whiff of his studio to know that he was a bigger failure than they would ever be. Eventually they left and he would be back where he started: working alone, living off Mother. Relying on her insurance payments and her boarders and the last of her ground rents. To be fair I will admit that he *has* sold some of his work for money, but not much. An acquaintance from art school showed the good sense to switch from painting to dealing. Opened some sort of gallery. Fortunately for Jeremy. I often tell him he is lucky to have Brian to give him a hand but Jeremy just stares at me. He takes everything for granted, he tosses what he has made in Brian's general direction and goes on his way without even checking to see if it has landed safely. Well, I suppose we should be grateful he doesn't view his art too seriously. But still, the amount of money he uses up! Not to mention the time wasted. Do you think Mother would have let Laura or me get away with that? Never for a minute. We were always expected to make our own way in this world. For twenty-five years now I have been entirely self-supporting, and so has Laura ever since she was widowed. Does that seem fair? Well, Jeremy isn't as strong as we are, Laura always says. *That's* for sure. Give him a little time, Laura says. She has never seen him as he really is. She just went right along with Mother, coddled and babied him. Sat on the step now with both arms cradling him, saying, "Now, now, Jeremy," while he wrinkled the front of her good knit dress.

"How long are you planning to sit here, Jeremy?" I asked him.

He straightened up then, but he didn't answer.

"We do have things to get done, you know," I said. "First you'll have to change and go over to the funeral parlor."

Laura said, "Amanda—"

"Then we have to make some plans for your future. I don't know whether you've thought yet about what you're going to do."

"Do?" Jeremy asked.

"Oh, why don't we talk about this after supper?" Laura said. "For now we'll just get you off these stairs,

Jeremy. I know you must be ready to come down. Aren't you?"

It was plain he hadn't thought of it, but he let her knead and pull him like so much modeling clay until he was finally in a standing position, and then she guided him down the stairs. I came behind. I arrived on the bottom step to find Mr. Somerset still at the front door, gaping at Jeremy. (In this house, I believe everyone *does* stay just where he wants. As if Mother's inertia were contagious.) I said, "Mr. Somerset, did you put the suitcases in my mother's room?"

"What's that you say?"

"Our suitcases. Did you put them somewhere?"

"I never saw no suitcases."

"Well, *someone* did," I said. I bypassed Jeremy and Laura and went to Mother's bedroom, off the dining room. There were no suitcases there. Only her unmade bed, stopping me in my tracks for a moment. I slammed the door shut again and said, "Jeremy? I want to know where our suitcases are."

"Um, what suitcases are those, Amanda?"

I went through the entire first floor, flicking on lights in the kitchen, the bathroom, the dining room, the parlor. No suitcases. And they wouldn't be upstairs; all the second floor belonged to boarders. "Mr. Somerset," I said, "think, now. Who else has come in while we were out?"

"Why, nobody," said Mr. Somerset. "The two ladies have been gone all day, and Howard left at seven this morning and never come back. I heard him go. I heard him whistling at seven A.M. outside my bedroom door, not a particle of consideration, and nights he comes in from a date eleven, eleven-thirty, twelve o'clock sometimes still whistling, never thinks to—"

"Someone has stolen our suitcases," I said to Laura.

She was just settling Jeremy into a parlor chair, like an invalid. She looked up at me with her mind on something else and said, "Oh no, Amanda, I'm sure they would never—"

"They're gone, aren't they? And no one's been in

that door but us and Mr. Somerset, he says he never saw them."

"It's true, it's true," said Mr. Somerset, and then beat a retreat up the stairs as if I might accuse him of something. Just before disappearing he leaned over the banister to say, "You might ask Howard when he comes in, though as I say I don't believe he—and you might talk to him about making noise. I don't sleep too good as it is. You might mention it to him."

"We've been robbed," I said to Laura.

"Oh, they'll show up. I'm sure of it."

"No, they're gone," I told her. "We've seen the last of them."

Isn't that always the way it is? You would think that in time of tragedy the trivial things would let themselves go smoothly for once, but they never do.

I sat down in an armchair, just crumpled into it. "Imagine!" I said. "Someone who would rob a house in mourning. Oh, I've heard of such things. Burglars who check obituaries daily, they know the bereaved are too upset to take good notice. Isn't it shameful?"

"Oh, I'm sure they didn't do *that*."

"What, then?"

"We could call the police," Laura said.

"They'd be no help. They're paid to keep their eyes closed."

"Well, all that worries me is what will I do for a nightgown," Laura said. "And a funeral dress. Will this be suitable?" She opened her coat wider to show the maroon knit, all creased across the front. "Lucky *you*," she told me. "You wore your black on the train."

People always call it luck when you've acted more sensibly than they have.

I said, "This never would have happened in the olden days. There was a time when our neighborhood was so safe you could walk it at night without a thought, but now look! I don't know how often I told Mother she ought to move."

"One thing," Laura said, "it's not as if we had any valuables in our bags."

"Speak for yourself," I told her, "there are valuables and valuables. *My* suitcase was Mother's graduation gift. The only useful thing she ever gave me."

"We should talk about something more cheerful," Laura said.

"Other times it was sachets and pomander balls and religious bookmarks, but that suitcase was top-quality cowhide."

"Hush, now," Laura said. "Shall I make us a little supper? There's bound to be something in the icebox. Would anyone like an omelet?"

And off she went, still in her galoshes, tugging at her coat. She is the cook in the family—you can tell it by her figure. I myself couldn't have taken a bite right then. I was too sick at heart. I set my feet upon a needlework footstool and said, "What would help me most now is a good long rest. I've walked far more today than I should have." I was talking to Jeremy, but you would never have known it for all the reaction he gave me. "See my feet?" I asked him. "How puffy?"

He didn't answer.

"We couldn't get a taxi from the funeral parlor. It was hard enough to find one at the railroad station, and evidently no one thought to meet us."

But all Jeremy did was lay his hands very lightly upon his knees, as if they would break.

I sat erect in Mother's wing chair and looked all around me. Everything imaginable seemed to be crowded into that parlor. Chipped figurines, a barometer, a Baby Ben that worked and a grandmother clock that didn't, a whole row of Kahlil Gibran, a leaning tower of knitting magazines, peacock feathers stuck behind the mirror. Cloudy tumblers half full of stale water, a Scrabble set, a vaporizer, a hairbrush choked with light brown hair, an embroidery hoop, a paperback book on astrology, an egg-stained shawl, doilies on doilies, Sears Roebuck catalogues, ancient quilted photo albums, a glass swan full of dusty colored marbles, plants escaping their pots and sprawling along the windowsill. On the table beside me, a bottle of Jergens lotion and a magnifying glass and a patented news-item clipper. (How she loved to clip news items! They stuffed all her envelopes, and for years I unfolded them one by one and tried to figure out their relevance to me. I never could. Puppies were rescued from sewer pipes, orphaned rabbits were nursed by cats, toddlers splashed in wading pools on Baltimore's first summer day. Nothing that meant anything. I learned to throw them away without a glance, as if they had come as so much padding for her wispy little notes.) Beneath the clutter, if you could see that far, was scrolled and splintery furniture so scrawny-legged you wondered how it stood the strain. I felt anxious just looking at it. I placed my fingertips to my forehead, warding off one of my headaches. "Well, Jeremy," I said. "I suppose I should hear how this business happened."

Jeremy raised his eyes, not to me but to a point on the wall.

"How Mother went."

"Oh. It—I was—it happened like this."

"You don't have to make a long story of it, just *tell*," I said. I know I shouldn't snap at him that way.

"I had made a new piece," Jeremy said.

"What?"

"Piece. A new piece in my studio."

"*Oh* yes."

That's what he calls them: pieces. He pastes them together and calls them pieces. Well, they're surely not *pictures*. Not even regular collages, not that intricate, mosaic-like way he does them. He has had this drive to paste things together ever since he was old enough for scissors and a gluepot. He started off at Mother's feet, dressing paper dolls, and in grade school he moved up to scrapbooks. Other boys play baseball; he made scrapbooks. One for famous people and another for foreign places and another for postcards. (Photos of hotels, mostly, with X's on minute little windows twelve stories up—"Here's where *my* room is!"—sent to Mother by a cousin.) Then he began his pieces. Mother thought they were wonderful, naturally, but as far as I could see they were just more of the same. More cutting, more pasting. Little people made of triangles of wrapping paper and diamonds of silk. No definite outlines to them. Something like those puzzles they have in children's magazine—find seven animals in the branches of this bush. I couldn't see the point of it. "Then what?" I asked.

"I wanted her to see my piece. I went down and brought her up and at the top of the stairs she just fell down, she fell down and I saw she was dead."

All his eye for detail goes into cutting and pasting. There is none left over for real life. What did Mother say, climbing the stairs? What were her last words? Was she out of breath? Holding her chest? Did she give him any kind of a look when she had fallen? (Maybe she looked at him and thought, Good heavens. Is *this* what I'm dying for? A little paper quilt put together by a middle-aged man?)

"Go on," I said.

He looked blank.

"Tell me," I said (already tired out by the thought of all I would have to ask), "had she been doing any complaining about chest pains?"

"Oh, *Mama* never complained."

That was true, but another person could have read the signs anyway. Whenever she had health problems—gas, indigestion, a little trouble with bowels—she did her own doctoring. Took herb tea and patent medicine and refused all meals. Many's the time I have eaten lunch with her sitting across the table watching, nothing in front of her but a steaming cup and a pint bottle of Pepto-Bismol, eyes following my spoon. "Aren't you eating, Mother?" "No, darling, but pay it no mind. I'm sure I'll be all right." Another sip of herb tea, a tablespoon of Pepto-Bismol. But Jeremy (if he was even at the table, and not off pasting things together and having lunch sent up on a tray) only ate on with his eyes lowered and never appeared to notice. He was so used to being the sickly one himself. I am sure he never changed. Mother could have trailed a line of digitalis tablets clear across to his place mat and he would only have asked for more custard.

Laura came to the dining room doorway and said, "I've laid a little supper on. Will you have some?"

"I'm sorry, I just don't believe I can," I said.

"Oh, Amanda. Try, dear. We have to keep our strength up."

So I came, but while Laura and Jeremy were settling themselves I went out and made myself a cup of hot milk. It was all I felt up to. I stood at the stove, surrounded by dirty dishes and objects out of their proper places, while in the dining room I heard the steady clinking of china. *They* could eat through anything. When I came out I saw their plates just heaped with food, omelets and rolls and several kinds of cake. I said, "Well, don't come to me with your indigestion, that's all I have to say." Which stopped them for a moment; they wiped their mouths and looked up at me with identical foolish expressions. But then they returned to their plates and paid me no more mind. Spreading butter on one roll after another, spinning the lazy Susan to find some new kind of jelly. "Try the gooseberry, Jeremy. I know you've no appetite, but—" Jeremy, who has a sweet tooth, ate half a pineapple upside-down cake. I saw him. And just the bought, gluey kind; Mother never bestirred herself to bake. Laura served it to him sliver by sliver, the politest little portions you ever saw, and he watched each piece arrive as if it had nothing to do with him but when he was finished half the cake was gone. Laura ate most of the other half. Yet she was so dainty about it! She took such tiny bites and set her fork down on her plate betweentimes. Jeremy chewed in a halfhearted way, the same as he does everything. Rolling the food around in his mouth. And then to top it off Laura said, "When this is over I'm going to have to go back on my diet." As if Mother's passing were a picnic! A vacation! Some kind of eating spree! But before I could point it out to her in walked Howard, who has the south front bedroom. "Oh, excuse me," he said, and stood teetering over us. He is a beakish young man with glasses, a medical student. For as long as I can remember his room has been inhabited by medical students. They pass it down from one to another along with a shelf of fifth-hand textbooks and the number of the nurses' dorm scrawled on the wallpaper beside the hall telephone. It is convenient, of course, to know that that particular room will always have an occupant, but the students are generally noisy and untidy and their hours are not at all regular. I would have dispensed with them long ago. And their manners! This Howard, for example, never even troubled himself to offer his condolences. All he said was, "I see you people got here okay."

"Howard," I said, "I wonder if you might have any idea where our suitcases are."

"Me? No, ma'am."

"Well, there went our one last hope," I told the others.

Laura said, "Won't you join us for supper, Howard?"

"Oh, I have a little something in the kitchen," he said. He scratched his head a moment and then left, and I could hear him out clattering around in the silverware drawer. No wonder the kitchen was in such a state. What do you expect, letting people wander in and out like that? I have been trying for years to make Mother lay down a few ground rules. "This is not a genuine *boarding* house," I told her. "You never contracted for them to eat here, they're supposed to take their meals in restaurants." "Oh, well," she said, "I know you're right, Amanda." Yet she never did a thing more about it, and as a result look what has happened: ants in the upstairs rooms where people have carried their sandwiches, roaches in the kitchen, strangers dirtying pans and littering counters and stuffing the cupboards with their various foods. The student before Howard, what was his name? He kept a cake tin in the icebox with a label Scotch-taped to it: CAUTION BACTERIOLOGICAL SPECIMEN DO NOT DISTURB. All a deception, of course; there was only cake inside. But nevertheless it was a disturbing thing to come across as I was searching for an egg or a bit of lettuce, and more than once it's put me off my feed.

Thinking of boarders reminded me; I set my milk down and said, "There's a lot we have to talk about, Jeremy."

He looked startled.

"There's the question of where you will live now."

"Live? Oh, why—won't I just go on living here?"

"In this great house? Nonsense. I suppose you'll have to move in with us."

"But I'd rather, I don't think—"

Whenever Jeremy is upset he has a hesitation in his speech, not a stutter exactly but a jagged sound, as if the words were being broken off from some other, stronger current of words deep inside. It was plain he was upset now, and I couldn't help but feel insulted. Did he think *I* wanted *him*, for heaven's sake? Turning our ordered life topsy-turvy, trailing his little snippets of paper across our carpet? We would have to move to a larger apartment, and give up the one we'd had for nineteen years and grown so used to. But you can't always pick and choose. "We'll put the house in the hands of an agent," I said. "Someone with a talent for selling. Heaven knows he'll need it."

"Oh, but I just, I believe I'll just stay here, Amanda," Jeremy said.

"Jeremy, we are not going to argue about this," I said. Then I rose and went out to the kitchen to get a dab of sugar for my milk. Giving myself a chance to grow calm again, although that turned out to be impossible with Howard standing at the sink eating directly from an ice cream carton. I ignored him. I returned through the swinging door to the dining room and what did I see? Laura and Jeremy reaching simultaneously toward a coconut layer cake, their hands suspended and their faces sheepish when they saw I had caught them. I am always being put in the role of disciplinarian even when I am not at school. It isn't fair. I never ask to be. "Go on then, *eat,*" I told them, and I resettled myself in my chair and stirred my milk, pretending not to care. Inside, though, I felt that I had reached the limit. The headache had descended after all, spreading through my temples and down the back of my neck. I get terrible headaches. No one who hasn't had them can imagine. "Right now, Jeremy," I said, "you are going through a difficult time and I know that you're not thinking clearly. We'll put off discussing

your plans till later. But I'll say this much: I expect
you to come with us to the funeral parlor tonight. It's
the *least* you can do. You would surely not allow your
sister and me to walk alone in the dark."

"Oh, well, Amanda, I was thinking we might stay
home tonight," Laura said.

Which was certainly not what I had expected. I
had thought I would have to drag her away from the
casket. "How would that look to Mother's visitors?" I
asked her.

"There may not *be* any visitors, and even if there
are I'm sure they'll understand."

"You may stay home then," I told her. "Jeremy
and I will go alone."

Jeremy said, "Well, but—"

"You can't refuse to visit your own mother, Jeremy."

"I don't think I want to go," Jeremy said.

And Laura said, "Why don't we *all* stay home?"
With her face bright and hopeful—protecting Jeremy.
Jeremy sat slumped in his chair, mashing cake crumbs
with his fork. His lips were pressed outward. Sometimes I wonder if Jeremy possesses some strength I
have never suspected, some perverse, inner strength
that keeps him an immovable lump in spite of all our
nudges. Wouldn't it be easier just to give up and act
the way he is supposed to? "I don't understand you,
Jeremy," I said. "You did see her on the stairs, after all.
It's not as if you could spare yourself the sight. And this
will be much better, even, now that they have her all—"

"Can't you just let him be?" Laura said.

I set my milk cup down as gently as I could manage. Another person would have slammed it. I said,
"I'll count on you to clear the table, Laura. It was you
and Jeremy who did all that eating. I'll just go and
change the sheets in Mother's room before I leave for
the funeral parlor, shall I?" Then I rose from the table,
keeping a tight hold upon myself. I tried my best not to
notice how my temples were pounding.

We were going to have to stay in Mother's room because all the others were full of strangers. The only

time we ever saw our own room was at Christmas and Easter, when Mrs. Jarrett went off to visit her married daughter in California. And even then we saw it in an altered state, with Mrs. Jarrett's hats stacked in our closet and her dresses shoved to the back of it. Oh, this house had closed over our leavetaking like water; not a trace of us remained. I had never been bothered by it before but I was that night. In Mother's bedroom, which was crammed with half-soiled clothes and wall mottoes and empty coffee cups and pictures of kittens wound up in balls of yarn, there was not so much as a photograph of me at any age. Just Jeremy looking frightened on her nightstand, eleven years old and wearing a Sunday suit that barely met across the front. Beside him our father, in a sterling silver frame. Now *there* is a sample of how Mother did things. Our father was a building contractor who left us thirty-four years ago—went out for a breath of air one evening and never came back. Sent us a postcard from New York City two weeks later: "I *said* I needed air, didn't I?" "Yes, he said that as he left, I remember he did," said Mother, dim-witted as ever. She kept his brushes on the bureau and his shaving mug in the bathroom, never removed her ring, never to my knowledge shed a tear, not even a year and a half after that when he was killed in an auto accident and the insurance company notified her by mail. And look on her nightstand! There he was, big and dashing in an old-fashioned collar and a villain's pencil-line mustache. Handsome, I suppose some might say. (As a small girl I admired my father quite a bit, though not, of course, after he deserted.) And what did he see in Mother? Why, it's written on the bottom of his photograph. "For Wilma, with my deepest respect." She was a cut above him, a storeowner's daughter born to be pretty and frail and useless—which, Lord knows, she was. Spent her mornings tinkling halfway through popular tunes on the piano before she trailed off uncertainly, her afternoons painting forget-me-nots on china plates, her evenings in the front porch swing giving herself the barest ripple of motion every now and then with the toe of her shoe. From a distance I suppose that a building contractor could find her mighty impressive. How was he to know she would stay frozen in china-painting position for the rest of her life?

I stripped the bed and made it up fresh with sheets from the cedar chest. I folded the old sheets and placed them in the hamper. I picked up the clothes that Mother had left scattered everywhere. Meanwhile I could hear Laura clattering dishes and talking on and on—to Jeremy, I supposed. Never a break for breath, even. She thinks she is such an authority, just because she was married and widowed once upon a time. Thinks she is qualified to speak about life. Well, she was only married a year and never had children, and her husband was no more than a boy anyway. A hemophiliac. Died from a scratch he got opening a Campbell's soup can. How does that make her so worldly wise? But there she was just rattling on, handing down her pronouncements. Was it me they were discussing?

Laura used to pull Jeremy around the block in a little red wooden wagon when he was just a baby. He didn't learn to walk until he was nearly two; that's how well she took care of him. He had no *need* to walk. After the ride she would hoist him up by the underarms and lug him into the house, the two of them grunting and red in the face. Then Mother mashed up a little banana for him or peeled some grapes—peeled them!—and set them into his mouth one by one. "You love Jeremy more than you do me," I told her once. I said it straight out. She didn't deny it. "Well, honey," she said, "you have to remember that Jeremy is a boy." I thought I knew what she meant, but now I'm not sure. I *thought* she meant that boys were more lovable, but maybe she was just saying that they took more care. That they were weaker, or more accident-prone, or more likely to make mistakes. Who knows? It doesn't matter what she meant; the fact is she did love him more. And next to him, Laura. The pretty one, who in those days was only slightly plump and had hair that was really and truly golden. Me last of all. Well, I couldn't care less about that *now*, of course. I never even think about it. But I did at one time.

I hung armloads of Mother's clothes in her closet, beside other clothes cram-packed in any old way with their sleeves inside out and their hems half unstitched. They had a used smell, sweet and sickish. Some she had saved for forty years in the hope that they would come back into fashion; she imagined that the rest of the world was as stagnant as she was. "And see?" she would say, draped in some filmy frayed pre-war dress, slumped before the full-length mirror, "people *are* wearing these again, I saw the same hemline in the park only yesterday." The only thing she bought new were shoes, racks and racks of them, top quality. She believed in changing her shoe wardrobe often to safeguard the shape of her foot. As if she pictured herself still soft-boned and malleable, still a child. Which she was, in a way.

I cleared the bureau of whole handfuls of Kleenex filmed with pinkish-gray powder. I collected hairpins from the rug, worn stockings from the seats of chairs. I found her cameo brooch under a corner of the bedspread and held it up to the light, wondering what to do with it. Maybe Laura would like it. It was more her style. Then I thought of Mother's will, so-called—the scrap of paper she always kept in her jewelry box, telling which of her personal objects should go to whom. She revised it year by year, and continually moved the jewelry box to new hiding places. I had to hunt for quite a while—I finally located it on the bottom shelf of the glassed-in bookcase—but sure enough, there was a paper folded into a tiny square below Mother's pearls and her baby bracelet and Grandmother Amory's glove-button hook. A sheet of her favorite stationery, cream-colored, a row of withered-looking wildflowers strung across the top.

> *My dear darling girls,*
>   *Now if I die I don't want to be mourned and grieved over. I want my sweet children to just carry on as usual. I like the hymn "Be Still My Soul" if there is any question about what to use in the service.*
>   *I believe I want Laura to have my personal jewelry, all except the little amethyst finger ring for Mrs. Pruitt at the church and papa's flip-top pocket watch for Jeremy and some small memen-*

*to, I just can't decide which, for Miss Vinton.
Maybe Laura could select something. Amanda
can take the English china and the silver, except
for my teaspoon collection which I think might
go to Mrs. Jarrett. Also she may have the wood-
en rack to keep it in.*

*Perhaps my clothing could be distributed to
the Poor.*

*I hope that my sweet girls won't feel slighted
but I do think Jeremy might like the house and
furniture, and I have had the lawyer draw that up
into a regular will. Also any financial doings are
to go to him. It might seem unfair but I trust that
you will understand, as the two of you have always managed so nicely while Jeremy has his
mind on his art and such.*

Please take care of him.

*Please see to it that he doesn't just go to
pieces.*

*I have thought a long time about what he
should do, and I wondered if he would go to you
girls but I don't suppose he will. He still won't
leave this block, you know. Last July I did get
him to come with me to Mrs. Pruitt's, which is
two streets away, but that's the first time since art
school that he has done such a thing and it didn't
work out. So maybe he will just want to stay on in
this house.*

Please don't let anything happen to him.

Love,
Mother

I took the letter and marched straight out of the
bedroom, past Jeremy, who was slumped in a parlor
chair staring at nothing, and into the kitchen, where
Laura was doing the dishes. She had one of Mother's
old-fashioned flowered aprons pinned to her front,
and who she was talking to was Howard. He was drying plates, if you please. He was saying, "*Next* year,
when I have more freedom—"

"Take a look at this," I told Laura, and I handed
her the letter.

She wiped her hands and started reading, and
right away her eyes filled. I knew that would happen.

"Oh, look," she said, "she's thought of everyone. Even Miss Vinton. Even poor old Mrs. Pruitt at the church."

"Not *that* part."

She read on.

"What, the house and furniture?" she said. "Well, that seems fair to me, Amanda. After all, we have always—"

"No, no. *Jeremy.*"

She looked up.

"See what she says about Jeremy? Where she says he never leaves this block?"

"Yes."

"Did *you* know that?"

"Well, of course," Laura said.

"But not since art school, she says. Art school! Years and years ago!"

But Laura was rereading the beginning of the letter now. She didn't seem concerned at all. I turned to Howard, who hadn't had the tact to leave the room. "Did *you* know?" I asked him.

"Oh, why sure."

Even strangers knew. How could I have let such a thing slip past me? Because Jeremy never stated it outright as a principle, that's why. He gave individual excuses, never the same one twice, whenever we invited him to come someplace. To the park, to take the fresh air: "Thank you, but I'm working on a piece right now." Out shopping at a department store: "Oh, I believe I have a cold coming on." They never visited us in Richmond because Mother was prey to motion sickness. Or so she said. Protecting him again. Is it possible to live out your life within one block? I thought of what this block contained—a café, a corner grocery, and a shoe repair. Church was off-limits. Also moviehouses, pharmacies, barbershops, clothing stores. Funeral parlors. "How does he get what he needs?" I asked.

Laura looked up from the letter with her eyes all glassy.

"Well, there is the mail order," Howard said. "Also, your mother went a few blocks farther afield now and then."

"Has he ever been out of Baltimore? I mean, ever in his life?"

"Not since I've been here," Howard said.

And certainly not while *I* was there. Our father took the car with him when he left.

I snatched back Mother's letter, which Laura had started to read for the fourth time running. "Listen to me," I said. "That is just not *normal*, Laura."

"Oh, Amanda! He'll hear you."

"I don't care if he hears me or not," I said, although as a matter of fact I was speaking barely above a whisper. Laura always thinks I'm shouting when she doesn't like what I'm saying. "You're taking this so calmly," I said. "You let things ride because it's easier, but meanwhile, he's our *brother!* Sitting in one spot like a beanbag. Howard, *you're* a medical student. Wouldn't it be to his own good to make him stop this before it gets worse?"

"Oh, well, I don't—"

"You can't just let it go on indefinitely."

"Oh, well, it's not as if he's hurting anyone."

"I will never understand this world," I said. "More is tolerated every day. Nobody bats an eye."

I left. I went out through the parlor, passing Jeremy, who continued staring into space. Listen here! I wanted to say. Just come *out* of this, jerk yourself up by your own bootstraps, it's all a matter of will. Do you think nobody else has days when he wants to give up?

I went back into Mother's room, squashed the letter inside the jewelry box and slammed the lid. Keep your English china. I yanked the rug straight and folded an afghan, I shook out Mother's shapeless gray gabardine coat and took it to hang in the coat closet. And then, as I was just closing the closet door, I chanced to look again at Jeremy. He sat with his hands pressed flat between his knees as if he were cold. His eyes had an empty look. A man without landmarks, except for the unavoidable ones of getting born and dying. You could imagine that dying was what he was waiting for while sitting in that parlor chair, since there didn't seem to be anything else ahead of him.

I took my own coat from the closet and put it on.

I went over to Jeremy and tapped him on the shoulder. "Come," I said.

He raised his head. "Hmm?" Then he saw me buttoning my coat and he drew back and looked alarmed.

"All I want is for you to come outdoors a minute," I said.

"Um, perhaps I—"

"Surely you're not afraid to do *that* much."

He rose and stood beside the chair, with his knees bent a little like Mr. Somerset. I took his hand to lead him toward the door. As we passed the closet I thought of getting his coat, but that would have made him suspicious. We went out on the stoop. "My," I said, "I believe it's finally going to clear. Don't you? Smell that air. We may have nice weather for Mother's funeral after all." In actuality it was still a bit damp— spray in our faces, the streetlights misty—but I was hardly thinking of what I was saying. And certainly Jeremy was not listening. "Has it been a particularly rainy fall?" I asked him, and he said, "Hmm? No, um —no," meanwhile looking around him nervously, first at the house and then the street and then me.

"We've had *very* nice weather in Richmond," I said.

I heard the front door fall shut behind us. Shut and lock, automatically. Jeremy heard it too and said, "Amanda—"

"Come and look at Mother's poor rosebush," I said. I led him down our walk and onto the main sidewalk. "Do you think there's any life left in it? If it were pruned, perhaps—"

"Yes, maybe pruned," he said. He was so eager to agree, so glad we were only going to look at Mother's rosebush. But I led him on, with my arm hooked through his. I could feel the lumpy weight of his body resisting me, hanging back, although both of us pretended it wasn't happening. We reached the yard next door. "Who does this belong to?" I asked him.

"What?"

"Who lives here now?"

"It's been partitioned up, I believe," he said. He raised his other hand to free his arm from me. I let myself be pried loose, but as he turned back toward the house I took hold of him again. "It's a shame to see these old houses go," I told him. "Why, I remember when those two up ahead were owned by a single family. The Edwardses, remember them? They had so many children they needed two houses to hold them all. Catholic. And *now* look. They've been turned into apartments too, I'll bet you anything. Haven't they?"

"What? Oh, yes."

We had reached the end of the block, where we stopped to wait for a traffic light. Jeremy's teeth were chattering and I wished now that I had brought his coat. Yet it wasn't *that* cold. And he did have his sweater, his limp gray sweater with that single button fastened. I reached over and buttoned the others. Jeremy backed away from me and said, "I really think I should be going home about now."

"Oh, as long as we've got this far," I said, "wouldn't you like to come the rest of the way?"

I took tighter hold of him and led him across the street. The light was still red but there were no cars coming, and I didn't want to delay too long. By now he was resisting more, though still moving forward. "You surely are not *scared* to come," I said.

He didn't answer. I looked over at him. "Not a big grown man like *you*," I said, teasing him. Then he did smile, but just a brief shy unhappy smile directed at his feet. Well, poor soul. There was an *enduring* look about him. He was trudging along so uncomplainingly, with those little saddle oxfords of his squelching in the puddles. "It's for you that I am doing this," I told him. "It's out of concern for you. You know that, don't you?" I could feel my strength flowing from my hand to his arm. Someone should have done this long ago, I thought—expended a little time and energy, that was all he needed—and brought him out of his cocoon.

We had reached the middle of the second block. Jeremy's teeth were chattering so that I could hear them, and he seemed to be shaken all over by great long rolling tremors. I had no idea that he was so susceptible to cold. I said, "Fortunately the funeral parlor is overheated. You'll be all right when we get there."

"How, how far?" he said.

"Oh, just a few more blocks. Now, Jeremy. Please come on."

For he had stopped. I tugged at his arm but couldn't move him an inch. "I think that maybe I, I think that I—" he said. Or I *believe* that's what he said. His voice came out wavery and chopped by the clicking of his teeth. I lost what sympathy I was beginning to feel for him. "Jeremy," I said, "this is getting silly, now."

Then I gave him a prod in the side, just to get him going, and he crumpled up. Just crumpled in upon himself and folded onto the sidewalk, where he sat in a heap and shook all over. Yet I swear I had no more than touched him. It wasn't a *shove* or anything. "Jeremy?" I said. "What's the matter with you? *Jeremy!*" For he was looking odder than I had ever seen him; I can't describe it. His face was yellowish and his mouth hung open. He laid his head down upon his bent knees and stayed that way, shapeless and boneless, and all I could do was call out for help. "Oh, help, someone! Won't someone please stop?" Cars hissed by, not even noticing. Then footsteps came clattering up behind me. "Help," I said, turning. I saw Laura running toward us, her apron a flash of white flowers in the dark. And half a block behind her, Howard, with his shirttails out. "Amanda Pauling, I'll never forgive you for this," Laura said.

"But what's the matter with him?"

Laura bent down and raised Jeremy's head in her two hands. He only stared at her. She fished a handkerchief from her apron pocket and wiped his mouth, and by that time Howard had come up out of breath and bent to peer into Jeremy's face.

"I don't understand," I said.

All I heard was Jeremy's teeth chattering.

"I don't see what's going on. Is he ill?"

"You have no heart at all," Laura told me. "I always thought that of you and now I know it."

"Oh, Laura! How can you say such a thing?"

Laura tugged at Jeremy but he wouldn't stand. It took Howard, bending over him from behind and raising him by the armpits. "There now, fellow," he said. "Come along."

"What did I do?" I asked Howard.

But Howard wouldn't answer either. He gave all his attention to Jeremy; he stood him upright and turned him toward home, and then Laura took Jeremy's other elbow. "Laura?" I said.

"I'm not talking to you right now," Laura said.

Jeremy took a faltering step forward. His head was nodding. I saw it bobbing against the streetlights, up and down, up and down, as if it were out of his control.

I didn't realize. I am not a *cruel* woman, I have never intentionally hurt a person in all my life. I said, "Laura, I didn't *realize*." But Laura just walked on with Jeremy, keeping him close to her, and I had to follow after. Nobody seemed to care whether I came or not. I walked six paces behind, all alone. Well, there are worse things than walking alone. Look at Jeremy, propped up on both sides, beloved son of Wilma Pauling. If that is what love does to you, isn't it possible that I am the most fortunate of us all?

Once we had reached the house, of course, everything settled back to normal. Laura and Howard put Jeremy to bed while I closed up the house, and wrote a note for the milkman, and lowered the shades. I cleared away what clutter I could in the parlor and fixed us two hot water bottles, and when I got to the bedroom Laura was already stepping out of her dress. "Don't let the wrinkles set in that," I told her. (She tends to be careless in her personal habits.) "I suppose we'll just have to sleep in our slips and make the best of it," I said, all energy. And I took my own dress off and hung it up neatly. But then, just as I was sitting on the edge of my bed to roll my stockings down—oh, I can't explain what came over me. Such heaviness, such an exhausted feeling. As if there were no point to moving any more. I looked at my muddy wet stockings and thought, I'll have to wear these again tomorrow. Have to wash them out and wear them tomorrow, but they will never be the same again and anyway they are only lisle, not fit for church. And here I had put that brand-new pair in my suitcase! They hadn't even been taken out of the cellophane yet! Quality hose, with fine seams. (We were raised to believe that no true lady wears seamless stockings, although I must say that nowadays people don't appear to agree.) Now some burglar's wife was probably trying my nylons on. I pictured her lolling on a brass bed in a red lace slip, one leg in the air, smoothing a stocking up her thigh while the burglar sat in an armchair smoking a fat cigar and watching. "Who did these belong to once?" "Oh, some old biddy."

I know what I am. I'm not blind. I have never had a marriage proposal or a love affair or an adventure, never any experience more interesting than patrolling the aisles of my Latin class looking for crib sheets and ponies—an old-maid schoolteacher. There are a thousand jokes about the likes of me. None of them are funny. I have seen people sum me up and dismiss me right while I was talking to them, as if what I *am* came through more clearly than any words I might choose to say. I see their eyes lose focus and settle elsewhere. Do they think that I don't realize? I suspected all along that I would never get what comes to others so easily. I have been bypassed, something has been held back from me. And the worst part is that I know it.

Here are the other belongings I had in that suitcase: my brown wool suit that was appropriate for any occasion, my blouse with the Irish lace at the collar, the lingerie set Laura gave me for my birthday. Also my travel alarm, the folding one that Mrs. Evans sent the summer I accompanied her twins on a tour of Yosemite. *That* was gone now. And my flowered duster that packed so well, and my warmest nightgown and the fleece-lined slippers that always felt so good when I came home tired from a long day at school. You couldn't replace things like that. You couldn't replace the suitcase itself, which our mother chose entirely on her own and lugged all the way to my graduation ceremony on a very warm spring day a quarter of a century ago. It had brass-buckled straps and a double lock; it was built to last. The handle was padded for ease of carrying. Oh, the thought of that suitcase made me ache all over. I felt as hurt as if Mother had asked for it back again. How would I ever find another one so fine?

I was tired, that was all. Just tired and chilled. The next morning I rose as bright as a penny and I handled all the arrangements, every detail. But that one night I must have been at a low point and I lay on my back in the dark, long after Laura was asleep, going over all the objects I had ever lost while some hard bleak pain settled on my chest and weighed me down.

2

Spring, 1961: Jeremy

Jeremy Pauling saw life in a series of flashes, startling moments so brief that they could arrest a motion in mid-air. Like photographs, they were handed to him at unexpected times, introduced by a neutral voice: Here is where you are now. Take a look. Between flashes, he sank into darkness. He drifted in a daze, studying what he had seen. Wondering if he *had* seen it. Forgetting, finally, what it was that he was wondering about, and floating off into numbness again.

Here is his pupil, Lisa McCauley, climbing the stairs to his studio. Jeremy climbs behind her. He has descended to answer her ring, opened the door, greeted her, without once being aware of what he is doing. He has forgotten how he came to be here. All that is on his mind is a circle of blue paper he left upstairs on his drawing table. Is it too bright? Too smooth? No, the problem lies in its shape. A circle; difficult to work with. He will have to cut it into angles.

"It's spring," says Lisa McCauley.

Then the flash, which stops him dead. He stands on the stairs with his mouth open and watches Lisa McCauley's nyloned legs shimmering ahead of him. If he turned the sound of nylon into sight it would make a silver zipper with very fine teeth opening the blackness behind his eyelids. If he touched the gold ankle chain that glints beneath one stocking it would have a gritty feeling; he would keep trying to smooth its echo off his fingertips for a long time afterward. The realness of her is staggering. He could choke on the fine strands of her bones. Her voice seems to displace the air around her, parting it keenly and then slightly flattening itself to separate the halves: "I didn't mean to be late I thought for once I would be on time I said to myself when I got up this morning I—"

The flash fades. Darkness descends in particles around his head. He stands in silence, staring down at the dust from the banister that has coated his fingers, until Lisa McCauley nudges him into motion again and he sets another foot upon another step.

"Purple is my favorite color," Lisa McCauley said. "I've decided to do this entire picture without it, just as an exercise." She cocked her head, shaking long blond hair off her shoulders. "Mr. Pauling? Are you with me?"

"Um—"

"I said, I've decided to do without purple."

"Isn't that purple you're using now?"

"It's magenta."

"Ah."

He sat on the stool beside the easel, holding the blue circle. His thumb slid back and forth over its surface. In a minute he planned to cut it into angles, but for now something else was expected of him. What was it?

"Don't you have any comments?" Lisa said.

She was painting a sad clown. White tears ran in exactly vertical lines down his magenta cheeks. The pain of looking at such an object caused Jeremy's eyes to keep sliding away, veering toward the buckles on Lisa's shoes, although he was conscious of her watching him and waiting for an answer. "What do you think?" she asked him.

Jeremy said, "Well, now."

Her shoes were very shiny but the gilt was flaking off the buckles. Specks of gilt like dandruff were sprinkled across her toes.

When Jeremy was seven he made a drawing of his mother's parlor. Long slashes for walls and ceiling, curves for furniture, a single scribbled rose denoting the wallpaper pattern. And then, on the baseboard, a tiny electrical socket, its right angles crisp and precise, its screws neatly bisected by microscopic slits. It was his sister Laura's favorite picture. She kept it for years, and laughed every time she looked at it, but he had never meant it to be a joke. That was the way his vision functioned: only in detail. Piece by piece. He had tried looking at the whole of things but it never worked out. He tried now, widening his eyes to take in the chilly white air below the skylight and the bare yellow plaster and splintery floors. The angles of the walls raced toward each other and collided. Gigantic hollow space loomed over him, echoing. The brightness made his lids ache.

"I hate to have to tell you this," Lisa said, "but I don't think I'm going to be coming here again."

Jeremy said nothing.

"Mr. Pauling?"

"Oh yes," he said.

"Did you hear what I just told you?"

"You weren't, you're not—"

"My aunt's taking me to Europe, I won't be coming to lessons any more."

"Oh yes, I see."

"We'll make a tour of all the museums. Well, that's what I *really* need, isn't it? Studying the old masters? Learning their technique and brush strokes and use of color—"

She was swirling a slash of magenta unnecessarily on her palette, avoiding his eyes. Telling him she meant no offense. Jeremy had not taught her anything at all about technique and brush stroke. *Line* was where his interest lay. He had given up all painting years ago, didn't even own a set of oils, or if he did they had surely dried up by now in the back of some cabinet. When Lisa's blobs of color slipped out of her control he could only watch blankly, with his mind on something else. It was possible that he had never offered her a single comment. What difference would it have made, anyway?

Now she was glancing at the time, slipping off her spotless Scandinavian smock and carefully folding it.

"We'll start off in Paris," she said. "Have you ever been there?"

"Paris. No."

"That's the place to go, Aunt Dorrie says."

She squatted to replace the tubes of paint in the new raw wooden box they had come in. She tucked in her uncleaned brush, and then stood up and surveyed the studio to see what she was forgetting. Jeremy stayed where he was. He had been through this before. Sooner or later all his students left. They went to college, or got married, or moved to New York City, or found another teacher. Sometimes a student only stayed for one lesson. Sometimes they didn't even bother telling him—just failed to show up, kept him waiting idly on his stool until it occurred to him, halfway through the morning, that things were not going the way they were supposed to be. He pictured himself as a statue in a fountain, sitting eternally motionless while people came and threw their hopeful pennies in and left again.

"I can't take the painting, it will get all over my clothes," Lisa said.

"The—"

"The *painting*. What'll I do? Shall I leave it here?"

"Oh, fine. That will be all right."

"Well, I guess I'll be going, then. I certainly do thank you. I know I'm not a *professional* yet or anything and I appreciate how you've tried to help me."

"You're very welcome," Jeremy said. "And also— and I've enjoyed getting to know you personally, too."

"When I get back," said Lisa, *"if* I get back, and if I'm not married yet or anything, then maybe one of those snotty art schools will accept me this time. I mean, I know this trip will improve me, don't you think? They can't just keep turning me down *forever,* can they?"

She held out her hand, a small tight cluster of fingers. Jeremy stared at it. He was noticing how thick the air seemed. It was pressing against his temples, flattening his eyeballs. Moving would be like swimming through egg whites.

"Well, bye," Lisa said.

Moments later, pulled upward by the fading sound of her high heels, Jeremy rose from the stool. He blinked at the slamming of the front door. The memory of some obligation forced his hand out straight in front of him, and he closed it on nothing and looked at it a moment before he let it drop back to his side.

His boarders were comforting, familiar voices milling around him, automatically allowing for the space he took up as he stood in the center of the kitchen. "Has anyone noticed my bread?" said Mrs. Jarrett. "I've looked all over for it. I was keeping it in the icebox to guard against mold." Yet the open refrigerator seemed to contain nothing *but* mold, row upon row of leftovers in tiny bottles growing green fur, hardened cubes of cheese, doll-sized cans and jars bought for single people's suppers and never finished. "Last week," said Mrs. Jarrett, "I sterilized the sink with household bleach and washed all the dishes myself but now look. I wonder if it might be possible to afford a cleaning lady?" Jeremy said nothing. His eyes seemed fastened to Miss Vinton's lavender cardigan, a restful color. Then when Miss Vinton moved over to the table he scratched his head, searched for some answer he knew he should have given. Nothing came to him.

Mr. Somerset was standing at the stove with a rolled-up copy of *Male* magazine under one arm. He lit the flame below a skillet full of white grease; he flicked out a drowned cockroach with the corner of his spatula and began laying down strips of bacon, but he seemed to be talking about toast. "Know what I've got? Tea-and-toast syndrome. *Howard* will have heard of it. Went in and said, 'Doc, I just don't know what to tell you, seems like nowadays it's all I can do to get out of the bed in the morning.' Tea-and-toast syndrome, he tells me. Common among us older folk. Eat more protein. Now I have to have meat at every meal, not easy for a man of my income, and liver twice a week, which I detest. On top of which food don't taste like it once did, you know. It's these additives."

"It's age," said Mrs. Jarrett.

"It's additives."

"It's age. Your taste buds are drying up, Mr. Somerset."

"And with everything else I got to put up with, it turns out it's no longer possible to get the kind of rest I need in this house. We all know why. I just wish Howard was here and I could give him a piece of my mind. Last night he come in at twelve-thirty. Late even for him. My sleeping is a fragile business, not something you can play around with in such a way. *He* sleeps like a log. He was up at six, whistling in the bathroom. While he's shaving he names over the parts of the anatomy. Tells the mirror all the minor bones of the foot. I just want to say one thing, Jeremy: this is an *older* person's house. Know what I mean? We got no business boarding medical students."

Jeremy watched the bacon crinkling in slow motion. He saw wisps of gray smoke rise toward the ceiling, blurring the kitchen. How long had he been here? Was it for lunch or for supper? Had he eaten yet?

Mrs. Jarrett's plump, ringed hand appeared, bearing a plate. "Have a piece of strawberry shortcake, Jeremy," she said. "Though it's only store-bought." She held the plate out on her fingertips and smiled, fixed in time by a sudden flash of light, imprinted in negative upon his eyelids.

Here is Mrs. Jarrett, all beads and elegance. How gently the planes of her face meet, each meeting prepared for by those little powdery pouches! How perfectly her hair is crimped, how neatly her flowered hat sits upon it! She wears hats everywhere, maybe even to bed. She keeps her cheerfulness even here, even crossing this stained and sticky floor that tries to suck the patent leather pumps off her feet. Mr. Somerset turns a strip of bacon and sighs. Miss Vinton runs the faucet over a tower of jelly glasses in the sink. Mrs. Jarrett says, "A meal is not a meal without dessert at the end," and Jeremy takes the plate, leaving her graciously curving hands up-ended between them. "Why, thank you," he says. "Thank you for offering it to me. I would just like to say—" before the light dies away again and the numbness unrolls itself like a windowshade and he is left holding some cold heavy foreign object that his eyes refuse to focus upon.

He was showing his mother's bedroom to some strangers who must have rung the doorbell, although he could not remember answering it. A man, a very tall woman, and a little girl. "It's not big enough for a family, I don't believe," he said.

"You just said that," said the man. "We just went *through* that."

"John," said the woman. She turned to Jeremy. He sensed the motion even though he was looking at his mother's lace curtains. She said, "Mr. Harris is just a friend. This room would be for me and my daughter."

"Oh yes."

"Is there a downstairs bathroom?"

He couldn't seem to fix his mind to her words.

"Mr. Pauling?"

His sisters had cleaned out his mother's room, but they had not managed to remove her smell. It hung over everything, sweet and damp and dusty. Even the sunlight filtering through the curtains had something of her in it. She had always been translucent, filmy, matte-surfaced like the meshy patterns of light fluttering on the old flowered carpet. There was a lack of body to her that had made him anxious, even as a child, and at any sign of weakness or illness in her his anxiety grew so strong it changed to irritation. ("Jeremy!" she had cried, climbing the stairs, and she laid a veined and trembling hand to her chest while Jeremy climbed on with his heart pounding, terrified and resentful, pretending not to notice. When she fell, there was a soft sound like old clothes dropping. She had not had the weight to roll back down the stairs; she remained where she landed, in a crumpled heap. Jeremy went into the studio and over to the window, where he stood sweating and shaking for a very long time. He chipped at the windowsill with a fingernail, flaking off paint. Then he wiped his forehead with the back of his hand, returned to the stairs, and sat down beside her to lift her by the shoulders.)

"There is plenty of closet space," the woman said. "Come look, John."

"*You* look, Mary. Just tell me if you like it."

Hangers slid down a length of pipe. The child followed her mother, clutching a handful of her skirt. Jeremy was fond of children, and he would have liked to look at this one but she kept on standing too close to her mother. The mother was very beautiful; not someone he wanted to raise his eyes to. Beautiful women made him uneasy. He received his impressions of her from sidelong glances—brown hair worn in a bun, oval face, scoop-necked dress—and the image that he formed was like an illustration in an old-fashioned novel. The man was square-jawed and handsome, a cigarette ad. Only men like that are comfortable with beautiful women.

"Do you supply the linen?" she asked.

He thought of some nineteenth-century linen closet —ivory sheets in stacks, balls of hand-milled soap, a bunch of lavender dangling from a nail.

"Mr. Pauling? Do you supply the linen?"

"Linen. Yes."

"Well, I suppose we should take it," she said.

She was going through a pocketbook of some kind. Jeremy was staring at the nightstand. He saw a photograph of his father, laughing widely from a narrow silver frame. He saw his father lounging on the front stoop, slinging out majestic orders to the scary black men who worked for him. A hand nudged his arm. Crumpled dollar bills were passed to him one by one, as if they were the last of some treasure. He looked down, trying to think what was expected of him. "But the room," he said.

Everyone seemed to be waiting for his words, even the smallest person at the left-hand corner of his eye.

"It's not big enough for a family, I don't believe," he said.

The man made an impatient gesture, turning sharply on one heel. The woman said, "But you don't mind just me and the child here, do you?"

"Child?" he said. He looked back at his father's photograph. He tried to think what his father's voice had sounded like, but it took a long time for him to remember and when he looked up again he found that the strangers had disappeared.

Here is the endpaper from a library book that Mrs. Jarrett carelessly left on the dining room table. It is covered with an intricate multicolored design that caught his eye at once; one edge is a little crooked where he hurriedly snipped it out of the binding with kitchen shears. Will she notice? He paces his studio with it, his crocheted slippers snagging on splinters in the floorboards. The paper crackles in his fingers. With his eyes he traces maroons and blues and browns, a watery yellow, a touch of orange, all flooded with a slow radiance that is soaking into him. Flames and pinnacles and jagged leaves and white rapids swerving around a spear-shaped rock. Feathers of some rich and exotic bird. He sees the bird climbing toward the sun; he watches sunlight coat the wings and gild the head. Downstairs, voices drone on and a radio plays and a clock strikes. Upstairs, Jeremy feels a shimmering joy lighting every crevice of his mind, and he smiles and opens up to it and melts away, leaving no trace.

Now Jeremy sat in his mother's rocking chair, rocking gently in a corner of the dining room. The back of the chair was covered with some sort of quilted material ruffled around the edges, and the ruffle kept making a scrunching sound against his shoulders. To his left was a floor lamp with a pleated shade, a picture of Mount Vernon Place engraved on its ridges. It shed the only light in the room. The rest of the boarders sat in darkness, with their faces flickering blue from the television set in the opposite corner. A very old set, a solid piece of furniture with a tiny screen. On it, a hero in a Stetson hat inched his way from window to window and peered out from behind a cocked revolver. "You can tell there's enemies outside," said Mr. Somerset, "else they wouldn't bother showing you the birdsongs and frog croaks. Want to make a bet on it?"

Mr. Somerset sat at the table with the remains of his supper, a picked-over plate and a shot glass oily from the bourbon it had held. Beside him was Miss Vinton, her neck ropy from craning nearsightedly toward the set; the new boarder, casting glances at her bedroom door from time to time in case her child awoke; Howard, dressed to go out, resting on the small of his back. Mrs. Jarrett was in the other rocker. Her hands worked rapidly in the darkness—knitting, probably, but Jeremy seemed unable to look to either side tonight and he only had an impression of empty movement, as if she were spinning something webbed and soft out of the darkness itself. He was conscious of particles of dark floating between people, some deep substance in which they all swam, intent upon keeping their heads free, their chins straining upward.

A branch crackled outdoors and the hero raised his gun. Every muscle snapped to attention. His face tightened, his eyes swept the sunlit forest. Some people are aware of everything that is going on everywhere at every moment in their lives.

On Jeremy's lap was a clutter of papers in a khaki-colored file—the reason his lamp was on. He was going to try to make some money. The file contained boxtops, coupons, occupant ads, soup can labels, pages torn from magazines, blanks from the grocery store bulletin board. "Can you name our new hybrid rose? Prizes! Prizes! Just tell us why you prefer our brand of bleach. Nothing to buy. Are you already a winner?" Jeremy was almost always a winner. It was one of his peculiarities—a talent you were either born with or you weren't, his mother used to say, and wasn't it lucky he had found something he could do at home this way? Yet he had never *felt* lucky, and he never seemed to win what they really needed. Always tenth prize: a hair dryer, a comb-and-brush set, a movie camera guaranteed to do justice to his speediest action shots. The basement was stocked with a year's supply of cat food. (Jeremy had no cats.) He was the owner of a sewing machine whose value was less than the ten-year service contract he had had to purchase for it. Didn't anyone offer *cash* any more? The gas bill was due, the telephone company had sent their second notice, and if he didn't pay the newspaper soon they would discontinue his classified ad and there would be no more students. On the hall desk was a sheaf of canceled checks from the mail order houses which had supplied his mother with her novelty salt and pepper shakers, her patented corn removers, her Bavarian weather forecaster, her wipe-clean doilies and plastic closet organizers and those miraculous plants that required neither soil nor water; and all anyone wanted to give him was snow tires and ladies' shavers. "Grand Prize! A Trip to Hawaii for Two!!" What did he want with Hawaii? Who did they suppose would go with him?

He gazed down at the blanks, his hands loose on the arms of the rocker, his knees spread. Muddy waters seemed to be clouding his thoughts. When he moved finally to pick up a coupon, its torn edge depressed him, and he dropped it again and went on rocking.

On the television screen, a shot rang out. *"Hot* dog!" said Mr. Somerset. He sat sharply forward, but the searching face of the hero was replaced immediately by a full-grown German shepherd bounding toward a bowl of premium-quality beef bits. "Shoot," said Mr. Somerset. "Wouldn't you know?"

Jeremy set the file of papers on the floor, rose and moved off to the hall telephone. Then he paused, with his hand upon the receiver. What was he doing here? The telephone rang, an irritated sound, so that he knew it had rung before. He picked it up and said, "Hello?"

"Mary Tell, please," said a man.

Jeremy waited, thinking hard.

"Are you there? I want Mary Tell. Your new boarder."

"Oh yes." He recognized the voice now. The cigarette ad man, sounding as crisp as he looked. He laid the receiver down and returned to the dining room, where he lowered himself carefully into the rocker. For a moment he studied his knees, frowning. Then Mrs. Jarrett said, "Was that the phone?"

He looked up. "The phone, yes," he said. "For Mrs. Tell."

"Oh, thank you," said Mary Tell. She rose and

moved out of the room. Her shoes were some special kind that made no sound, or maybe he was just forgetting to listen.

The hero was winged by a bullet. He winced and dropped his gun. "Oh, the poor man," said Mrs. Jarrett, serenely continuing her motions in the dark. Miss Vinton sighed. Mary Tell returned, flowing gracefully into the room, pausing to listen for her child before she sat down. Jeremy raised his head. He looked up at her and blinked, stunned by a flash that came from nowhere to fix her image on his eyes.

Here is Mary Tell, with the perfect oval of her face expressionless and her back beautifully straight, her smooth hands clasped in her lap. She knows how to sit without moving a muscle; she never fidgets. Her mouth is a wide curve and her eyes are very long and brown and level. Tears run down her face in silvery lines. While Jeremy watches, her cheeks grow wet and shiny, but she continues to stare directly at the television and after a minute, when his private flash has faded, Jeremy decides that he has imagined it all and he goes back to studying his knees.

3

Spring and Summer, 1961: Mary

You would think that once he brought me here he would feel responsible in some way. I try not to ask too much of him but having me come to Baltimore was his idea, after all, and for every one of my objections he had some reasonable answer. "But this is just—I'm a *homebody,*" I told him. "This is just not like me." And he said, "Do you always do things exactly in character?" Oh, he knew what would win me. He knew to reach down and pat my daughter's head and say, "Does she, Darcy?" so that Darcy would smile up at him, all trust and confidence. So one day we slid into his red convertible and rode off to Baltimore, with Darcy nestling between us and John's arm lying across the back of the seat keeping a constant contact with my shoulder. We talked non-stop, making plans. His divorce was already in progress and he said mine would be no trouble at all; Guy could sue me for desertion. We talked about where we would live, what kind of life we would have, how many children. Our words tumbled out and stepped on each other's heels, we had so much to get said. I never guessed that this would be the last time he would give me such a block out of his day.

Now I hardly see him. Darcy and I are staying in a shabby boarding house, the only place we could find that would take children. We have a downstairs room. I know every crack and cranny of that room by now, the stains on the wallpaper and the old-lady smell and the roses worn to strings on the carpet. I have spent whole afternoons staring at a ripple in the window glass, waiting for Darcy to wake from her nap. I have polished the furniture until it seems likely to melt away—not because I am such a good housekeeper, I never was that, but because there is nothing else to do. We sit for hours on the edge of the bed, neatly dressed, careful to keep our voices down, like guests who have risen too early. I am often irritable, and I cry a lot for no good reason. When Darcy gets whiny or boisterous I snap at her. I never used to do that. The most I ever did was shout, "Hey, quit that!" but here there is such a dead feeling, we are so much on our best behavior, that I scold her in a low hissing voice that no one else will hear and I threaten her between my teeth. Once I gave her a slap, something so unlike me that I wondered right away if I were losing my mind. She had been fiddling with the bureau knobs and one came off in her hand. I said, "Darcy Tell, if you don't stop that fidgeting I am going to scream. Come over here and sit down." She said, "I don't want to sit down, I want to go out. When is John going to come take us out? He *said* he would." Her voice was high and cracked; it tore at my nerves. I can't describe it. I hauled off and slapped her, and for a minute she stared at me with her mouth open. Then she started bellowing. I shook her by the shoulders and said, "Stop that. Stop it this instant." So she stopped, but she was trembling all over and I was too. I live in fear that she will remember that day forever. At night I go over and over it in my mind. Oh, let Darcy forget all this, please. Let this whole entire stage of her life just fade away and be forgotten, because it *is* just a stage, isn't it? Things are going to get better, aren't they?

We stay in the house so much because I am waiting for the telephone. I seem to be back in my teens, a period I thought I would never have to endure again: my life is spent hoping for things that only someone else can bring about. Some days he calls and says, "I can get away tonight. Be ready at seven." Then I float through the morning singing, I take Darcy out for walks and smile at her a lot although I often fail to hear what she is saying, and far too early in the afternoon I bathe and figure out what dress to wear. I have only three:

the one I came away in and two that John bought me after we arrived. We are going to buy more, but for now I am nearly without belongings—a peculiar feeling. Occasionally I find myself going through drawers— "Now, where is that gold barette I used to wear? Where is my navy cardigan?"—and then I realize that I don't have them. They are left behind. I am free.

On the nights we go out I put Darcy to bed early and ask Mrs. Jarrett to keep an eye on her. Then John and I go to dinner someplace and talk, although half my mind, of course, is always back with Darcy. That is the worst of this new life. The people I love are scattered, there is no way of gathering them snugly together where I can keep watch over them. When Darcy and I are alone I think about John; with John, I think about Darcy. I worry continually about my friends, my neighbors, my mother-in-law. Do they all hate me now? I wonder if Guy is very angry, and how he has chosen to explain the situation. "Here," John says. He leans across the table to pass a hand before my eyes. "Are you with me?" "Of course," I say. I smile at him.

We have no place where we can be alone. His wife left him before we even knew each other, but he is afraid that if he takes me to his house the neighbors will see and that will foul up the divorce proceedings. Sometimes I say, *"Let* them see. How could a divorce get fouled up any more than it already is?" But I know he's right. And he can't afford a house for us, and he knows too many people for a hotel room to be safe. He takes me to dark parking places in his convertible— another thing I thought I would never go through again. Then being out of the reach of a telephone makes me edgy and before too long I always say, "Oh, *please* let's go back. I don't know what Darcy will think if she wakes up and finds me gone." So he starts the car in a bad temper and drives me home, leaves me at the door, and I find Darcy peacefully asleep after all and I regret coming in so soon and I stand at the window a long time looking out at the dark through the ripple in the pane.

Then sometimes he doesn't call at all, not all day, or he does call and says he will not be able to make it.

He has a business crisis, or a trip coming up, or his wife is stopping by for some belongings. I have never seen his wife. I believe that she must be very beautiful, because she works as a model for one of the department stores. When they were first married, John says, she was a homey type. She made all the curtains and cooked and kept house, but then she got restless. She took one of those courses you see advertised in the newspaper and became a model, and after that she was never home at all any more and she got a new set of friends and even her personality seemed to change. "Brittle, sort of," he told me once. "Not at all like the person I married. I wanted a *wifely* wife, someone warm and loving that smells like cinnamon." Which made me feel happy, because he always says *I* smell like cinnamon. But sometimes in low moods I stare at myself in the mirror, I see how enormously tall I am and how busty I have grown since the baby and how even if I lost weight, I would never have that chiseled look that models have. I haven't the bones for it. And I think, Does John regret me? Does he wish I were Carol's type? He did marry her, after all. I take down my hair and fold it under to see how it would look if I cut it. I stand sideways to the mirror and suck in my stomach. It is the days when I know I won't see him that I go through all this. I have nothing else to do. I file my nails or sew on a button, during Darcy's nap I open library books that I can't pin my mind to or I leaf through magazines that I have already worn to tatters. When she wakes up, we go on long walks. I know this street now the way I know our room: every crumple in the sidewalk, every spindly tree, every turret and gable and leaded window of these endless dismal rowhouses. We take Mr. Somerset's toast crusts and feed the pigeons. We go to the library, where Darcy dallies forever in the children's section, choosing books and changing her mind and putting them away again. I never hurry her. What use is time now? We have so much of it. When she has decided on her books we walk very slowly home and then I read them to her, over and over, until my mouth is dry and my throat aches from imitating squeaky mice and growly bears. Darcy nestles under my arm, following the pictures with her great blue eyes. She has started sucking her thumb again. Four and a half is too old for that, I tell her, but I never really try to stop her. I figure she might as well take her comfort from wherever she can.

It was through Darcy that John first got to me. One morning I looked up and there he was, squatting to talk to her and asking her if she knew how pretty she looked. "You've got your mother's mouth," he said. Most people see only Guy in her. "Bright, too," he told me. Then he rose and shook my hand. We had met a couple of times before, but this was the first notice that he had taken of Darcy. After that he spoke to her every time he came by, and often brought her something—a jump-rope, or a set of checkers, and once a little dress-up doll that had a lot of extra costumes they sold separately. He brought her those costumes one by one; in the end I believe she had them all. And meanwhile, of course, he and I were getting to know each other. But Darcy was the starting point. I remember the first time I ever thought seriously about John. It was a few months after we had met. He said, "Now that you have this *one* pretty little girl, are you going to have a whole crowd more?" "Oh, no," I said, "Guy says one is plenty." "He's a fool," John said, and he looked straight at me for a long time and then turned and left. I don't know why that stuck with me for so long. I remember that I went back to the house and started washing dishes, and suddenly I stopped with my hands in the suds and looked out the window after him and got this strange springing feeling in the bottom of my stomach. That was how it began.

The man who owns this boarding house is very odd, and at first I was afraid of him. He reminded me of a slug. You see people like that in the newspaper all the time, caught molesting children or exhibiting themselves on picnic grounds or shooting into crowds; there is something curled and lifeless and out of touch about them. But when I had been here longer I saw that he wouldn't harm a fly, and now I let him talk with Darcy even when I am in another part of the house. You can tell he loves children. He doesn't know what to say to them, really, but he tries hard and he often takes Darcy up to his studio and lets her cut and paste. It does her good to get away from me for a while. When I think he might be growing tired I climb the stairs to fetch her, and I find them bending over separate tables, Darcy chattering away a mile a minute and covered with paste while Mr. Pauling works silently on those kaleidoscope things he seems to like. "I'll take her now," I say, and he says, "Oh, well, oh, no hurry, we were just—she was just—" Then he stands there wringing his hands, the first person I ever saw who truly does wring his hands. He doesn't appear to like me much, or maybe that's just his manner. He makes me feel too tall and too loud and too strong. I never know how to act with him. Evenings, watching TV, which is the only time when we boarders are all together, he is so confused and some of what he says is so out of place—things a deaf man would say, having lost touch with the world —that I have to hold down a laugh. The others are very kind to him. *They* never laugh. They have a habit of bending their heads toward him as they listen, and then straightening to puzzle over what he says, and even if he makes no sense they give him some grave and courteous answer. Because of this all conversation moves slowly, with long pauses, in a sort of circle that is designed to protect him. No wonder the meek will inherit the earth.

Darcy's eyes are blue like Guy's, and her hair is his fine, white-blond color and not much longer—Guy always did wear it long. I remember when I first saw him, he was swimming in Dewbridge Lake and every time he came up for air he had to give his head a sharp flick to get the hair off his face. Wet, it came nearly to his chin. When it snapped back spangles of water flew out from him like jewels. Then he climbed onto this old fallen tree that people used for a diving board. *Other* people used it; I wasn't allowed to, for fear of stobs and hidden branches. I wasn't allowed to do anything back then. I was fifteen, a nice quiet girl who didn't even wear lipstick yet, and I had come with my parents and

we were sitting on an oilcloth with a picnic lunch that
would feed an old folks' home and great quantities of
insect repellent and sunburn ointment and wet cloths
wrapped in cellophane in case of spills. This boy with
the long slick hair (I didn't know his name then)
seemed to have brought nothing but himself, barely
covered by one of those tight satin bathing suits that
I always thought were so tacky. He stood on the far-
thest limb that would bear his weight and then flung
himself up and out, and he cut through the water like
a knife and came up flicking that hair and laughing. I
just stared. I thought he was fascinating. Now I am not
talking about love at first sight or anything like that
—why, he scared me half to death! He and all his
friends, with their horseplay and their great splashing
butterfly strokes and the wolf howls they gave toward
the girls out on the barrel raft. They didn't howl at
me. I was just sitting there in the shade with my parents, watching out for sunburn, shrinking when any of
them came too close. And when my mother said, "This
lake would be right fine if it weren't for the rougher
element," I said, "Yes, ma'am," and meant it. But that
didn't stop me from staring at Guy Tell.

My father was the principal of Partha High School
in Partha, Virginia. My mother was an English teacher.
They were middle-aged when they had me and I was
an only child, which may be why they guarded me so
well—that and their being religious. They were Bap-
tists. My father passed the collection plate on Sunday
mornings. At one point I was religious too, and had
thoughts of growing up to be a missionary and eventually getting martyred, but that all passed away in time.
I don't know why. I just turned out not to be a believer, that's all. But I continued to go to church with
my parents. I sat folding my program into a fan, feeling
chafed inside by some irritation that extended even to
the starchy smell of my mother's best dress and the
way my father kept tugging his shirt cuffs down when
he didn't need to. Yet I loved them. I was very close
to them, especially to my mother. What bothered me
was not my parents or even their way of living, but
the fact that it seemed to be the only way open to me.

I would grow up, of course, and go to college and marry and have children, but those were not changes so much as additions. I would still be traveling their single narrow life. There was no hope of any other. At least, not till Dewbridge Lake.

Is Dewbridge Lake still there? Well, it must be. But after that one summer I have never been back. It's as if the lake had fulfilled its purpose and then vanished from the face of the earth. Its mildewed gray pavilion was erected overnight for me to do the bunnyhop in with my girlfriends, the only dance I was allowed. Its rainbow-colored jukebox was expressly filled with Pat Boone songs so that one day, at the end of a bunnyhop, Guy Tell might step up to me and say, "This here is for me and *you* to dance to, honey," and fold me up in a long walking clinch because I was too scared to say no. That pine forest with its shiny hot floor was grown for the two of us to hide in, leaning against a spruce trunk, Guy perpetually sliding a swim-suit strap off my shoulder while I perpetually slid it back up. His kisses tasted of tobacco. I had never been kissed before and found it tiring; my neck ached and my mouth felt bruised. Drawing back from me, he would smile with his eyes half-veiled as if he had won some contest. I was the loser, and I didn't even know I was *in* a contest. Then we would separate and I would return to my parents, leaving the pine trees shimmering behind me. Now I imagine that the entire forest has fallen, giving off no sound, like that tree they always bring up in science classes. All that will remain of it is a little golden dust floating upward in the sunlight. Yet there is a thirty-nine-cent strawberry-flavored lipstick in the dimestore whose smell can still, to this day, carry me back to the ladies' changing rooms at Dewbridge Lake. Hot pine needles will always make me feel pleasantly endangered and out of my depth. The trashy taste of orange Nehi fills me even now with a longing to break loose, to go to foreign places, to try some adventure undreamed of by my father in his baggy plaid trunks and my mother in her black rayon bathing suit with the pleated skirt. Oh, I would do it all over again, if I were fifteen. Even knowing how it would end up, I would continue to glide across that splintery dance floor with Guy Tell's hand clamping the back of my neck.

He was twenty-two—older than anyone will ever seem to me again. I wouldn't be sixteen till December. (Sixteen was the age my parents were going to let me start dating. And even then, of course, only boys my own age. Only boys from good families. Only in groups.) All that fall, when the Dewbridge Lake Pavilion was boarded over and school had reopened, I continued to see Guy without anybody's knowing. I said I was going to the library, or to visit a friend. Then I stood on a corner of Main Street and waited for Guy to come pick me up in a towtruck, and while he was pumping gas I would sit inside the filling station reading his racing magazines. He worked evenings. Daytimes he was free. Afternoons, as I was walking home from school, he slid up alongside me in his battered Pontiac and plucked me from my girlfriends and bore me off to a country road at the edge of town. While we were continuing our contest—he undoing a blouse button, I doing it up again—I felt lost and uncertain and longed to be safe at home, but once he was gone I forgot the feeling and wanted him back. I remembered the things that touched me: the intent look he wore when I told him anything; his habit of remembering every anniversary of our meeting, weekly, monthly, with some small clumsy gift like a gilt compact or a cross on a chain; the swashbuckling way he dressed and the eagle tattooed on his forearm and the dogtags always warm against his chest. Sitting in church on Sunday morning I called up his kisses, which from this safe distance filled me with a dizzy breathlessness that I thought might possibly be love. My mother sat beside me, nodding radiantly at the reading from Job. My father extended the long arm of his collection plate down the pews. I thought, I am never going to be like them, I have already broken free. I thought, Why aren't they taking better care of me?

On December seventh I turned sixteen. My mother said, "Well, now I suppose you can go out some, Mary." "Yes, ma'am," I said. I went to Main Street to

wait for Guy, and he brought me a charm bracelet hung
with little plastic records to remind me of our first
dance. Then he said, "I reckon we could get married
now if you want. Don't look like I am going to get
over you any time soon." So ten days later we eloped.
I kept expecting my parents to follow me and take me
back, but they didn't. I had to send them a telegram
announcing I was married. And in the motel room,
when I cried, Guy said, "Now *don't* take on so, you're
tearing me up. You want just for tonight I should sleep
in the other bed?" "I'm not crying about *that*," I said.
"Well, what, then?" Why I was crying was that here I
sat, married, and I had never even had a real date.
But it didn't seem the kind of thing that I could tell
him.

Last week I took out a post office box and then wrote
Guy and asked for a divorce. The box was John's idea.
"You don't want him coming after you," he said,
"tracking you down to your boarding house and making a scene." He went with me to the post office, and
afterwards we took Darcy to the Children's Zoo. It was
the nicest day I had had in a long time. Darcy played
in the sand while John and I sat on a bench nearby
in the sunlight, talking over our plans. John said that
someone had seen us together in a restaurant and told
his wife. "I believe it's made her jealous," he said.
"You know how she is." (Although I didn't know, at
all.) "She wants to have her cake and keep another
piece waiting in the tin. As soon as she heard she came
right over to the house all dressed up, sweet as sugar,
asking questions."

"There's no law against your taking someone out
to supper," I said.

"That's what I told her."

"*She* goes out with other people. All the time, you
said."

"Let's not talk about her, shall we?" he said. "It's
too nice a day."

I feel that way when he talks about Guy, too. I
don't like seeing Guy through someone else's eyes.
Then his leather jacket and tooled boots start seeming

ridiculous, and I am aware how his grammar must sound to outsiders and I feel hurt for him and protective. It's *me* that's being insulted as well—six years of my life are tied up with Guy. I changed the subject. I said, "How come you brought your camera?"

"I'm planning to take some pictures of Darcy."

On the days when John can't visit I start hating him, even though I know it's not his fault; but when I see him again he does something like this, thinking up an outing and photographing Darcy, and then I remember why I came away with him in the first place. *Guy* would never do anything like that. Oh, Guy took her picture, of course—with a camera he got for trading off some motorcycle parts—but he always wanted her dressed up first in those pink organdy frills he liked and he would arrange her hair in artificial-looking curls and seat her on the best piece of furniture. He called her his princess. His doll baby. Darcy is no doll baby. She thinks about everything—I *see* her thinking —and if there is a mess around she will get into it and she is never still for a second. I don't believe Guy even knew all that about her. The only time he paid her any notice was when his friends came by and he would show her off like a souped-up car, setting her someplace high and prinking out her skirt just so. "Ain't she a doll baby? You ever seen anything cuter?" Now John goes down on his knees in the sand, fixing his lens on Darcy, who is sugared over with sand like a doughnut, one of her playsuit straps dangling into a bucket. "Keep still," I tell her, but he says, "No, no, let her be." He holds up a light meter, fiddles with mysterious buttons. By profession he is a photographer. He owns a small studio that is still just getting off the ground, which is why it takes so much of his time. Before studying photography he went to college. He is calm and well-ordered and he considers every question from all sides. As far removed from Guy as a man can get. What would have happened if I'd met John before Guy?

I met John when he was shopping for motorcycles. He had just become interested in them. He ran into Guy at some rally outside Baltimore and the following week he came all the way to Partha, looking to see what Guy had in stock. I should explain that by then Guy was managing the filling station, but he had more or less branched out into motorcycles. We lived on the first floor of the house next door, and between the house and the station was a shed that Guy kept filled with spare parts and any used bikes his friends were trying to sell or trade. When John came by I was out in the yard hanging clothes. "Like you to meet a friend of mine," Guy said. "John Harris. He's thinking of buying him a cycle." *Thinking* is right. He was the most well-thought-out man I'd ever seen. For four solid weeks he tested different models, read up on them, asked questions, went off to different dealers, returned to Guy to see if he had anything new. And when he finally did buy it wasn't from Guy at all, but some man in Baltimore. By then he and Guy were friends, though. Not what you would call *close* friends; motorcycles were all they had in common. But they did do a lot of trail-biking together, and sometimes Guy would bring John home with him after a rally. Guy would come in all excited, blaming some fool who'd run him off the road, cursing some flaw in his bike (which *he* had bought in two minutes flat, on impulse, with money he didn't have). He would yank the cap off a beer and chug-a-lug it, stomping around the kitchen. And meanwhile there stood John in the doorway, remarking on how nice my kitchen smelled and searching through his pockets for Darcy's present. Dressed like someone in a sports magazine, in slacks and a polo shirt. *Now* do you see why I say he was so far removed from Guy?

It's as if I have to keep trying different lives out, cheating on the rule that you can only lead just one. I'd had six years of *Hot Rod* magazine and now I was ready to move on to something new. I picture tossing my life like a set of dice, gambling it, wasting it. I have always enjoyed throwing things away.

Darcy said, "Hurry, John, I got to go to the toilet," and John laughed and snapped the picture. Then he rose, brushing off his knees, and I took Darcy to the restroom. There was sand in her scalp; I could look down and see it, glinting under the white of her hair. "When I come out," she said, "I'm going to ride the merry-go-round. Can I?" I said, "All right, baby." I looked back at John. He was smiling after us, turning some knob on the camera that he knew so well he didn't even have to look at it. "Come *on*, Mom," Darcy said, and she reached up and took me by the hand. Her fingers were cool and sandy, and she smelled like sunshine, and she let me bend down and press my face against her hair for exactly one second before she freed herself and danced off again.

Motherhood is what I was made for, and pregnancy is my natural state. I believe that. All the time I was carrying Darcy I was happier than I had ever been before, and I felt better. And looked better. At least, to myself I did. I don't think Guy agreed. He was funny about things like that. He didn't want to feel the baby kick, wouldn't even touch me the last few months, acted surprised whenever I wanted to go out shopping or to a movie. "Won't it bother you, people staring?" he asked. "Why would it bother me?" I said. "Why would they stare?" *He* was the one that was bothered. He didn't even want to come with me to the labor room the night she was born; my mother had to do it. She had thawed out some since I got pregnant. She stayed with me all through the pains, talking and keeping my spirits up, but most of my mind was on Guy. I thought, Wouldn't you think he could go through this with me? He'll worry more, surely, out there in the waiting room not knowing. The doctor had been upset about my age. He had told Guy I was still growing, much too young to have a baby of my own. What if I died? Shouldn't Guy be there holding my hand? But no—"I'm scared I might pass out or something," he said, and laughed, with his face sharp and white. Then he whispered, "I'm scared the pain will make you angry for what I done to you." "Oh, but *Guy*—" I said. Then my mother said, "Never mind, honey, Mama's here." She sat by my bed and rubbed my back, and sponged my forehead, and read aloud from yesterday's newspaper—any old thing she came across, it didn't matter, none of it made sense to me anyway. When it came time to wheel me into the delivery room she said, "I'll be right here praying, honey, everything's going to be fine," but I saw that she was worried. I suppose she had taken to heart what the doctor said. Well, doctors don't know everything they claim to. Having that baby was the easiest thing I ever did. I was *meant* to have babies. Age has nothing to do with it.

When I think back on it—on my mother reading to me from that newspaper, smoothing the hair off my forehead—it seems that starting right there I began to live in a world made up of women. My mother and Guy's, the neighbor women who gave me their old baby furniture and their bits of advice—women formed a circle that I sank into. I suppose you have to expect that, once children come along. The men draw back and the women close in. I thought that things would be different once I got Darcy settled in at home, but then Guy just kept to himself more than ever—acted scared of holding her, couldn't stand to hear her cry, wouldn't help to name her. "Well, I don't know," he said. "Guyette? That would be kind of cute. But, no, I reckon—*I* don't know. *You* name her, you're the one that knows." I named her Darcy, my maiden name. I tried setting her on a pillow in Guy's lap, with cushions all around so that he wouldn't worry about dropping her. When she cried I said, "Now, all that's wrong is she's hungry, Guy. I'll feed her; *then* you'll see." But mealtime was another thing he couldn't stand. I was breast-feeding; he said it gave him a funny feeling. Every time I unbuttoned my blouse he left the room. "Other people use bottles," he told me. "Why go back to this way, now that they've invented something better?" When I got worn out with her nighttime feedings he said, "Switch her to Evenflo. Leave her with Mom and you and me will borrow some money and take a little trip somewheres. You need a rest." I was touchy back then, tired from all those wakeful nights and worried that I might not have enough milk. "The biggest rest," I said, "would be for you to just shut up and leave me *be,* Guy Tell," and then I cried and the baby cried and Gloria came in and shooed Guy out of the house and put me to bed. Gloria was Guy's mother, whom we'd been living with ever since we were married. A peroxide blonde forever in shorts and a halter. Her husband had died long ago, I forget just how, and she had a truck-driver friend who came over whenever he was in town, bringing a bottle of Southern Comfort that they would polish off in one evening over the kitchen table. I know that sounds depressing. See it on a TV screen and it *would* be depressing, but that fact is that Gloria was just wonderful to me and I loved her like a mother. I hate to think what I would have done without her. Before the baby, when Guy had switched to working days and I had nothing to do with myself (there was a rule against married students at school), Gloria was the only reason I didn't go out of my mind with boredom. She talked non-stop, took me shopping, fixed my hair a dozen ways, brought me up to date on all the soap operas we watched and lent me her confession magazines. Why, I was never even *allowed* to watch soap operas, and the most I'd read of confession magazines was the covers, surreptitiously, while speeding past the newsstand with my mother. And after the baby! I'm ashamed to say how much I leaned on her. She didn't interfere, she never tried to take over, but whenever I was feeling lost and too young she was right there handing me hot milk and talking on and on in that airy, fake-tough way she had, appearing not to notice anything was wrong but soothing me all the same. Could a man do that? No man that *I* know of.

I cried when we moved into the house by the station. By then I had no mother of my own any more. I lost both parents when Darcy was still a baby, within six months of each other: heart attacks. I felt as if Gloria was my only strength, and here I was leaving her. "My Lord, honey," Guy said, "most women would be tickled pink to get into a place of their own." He said, "It's *me* should be crying, it's my mama after all." And finally, "Don't you *want* to live alone with me?" "Well, of course I do," I said. But even so, I missed Gloria. I went on seeing her nearly every day,

right up to the time I came to Baltimore. And sometimes even now I think back on how it was when I
was pregnant, still someone's child instead of someone's mother, peacefully floating through those empty
days with Gloria. I remember the books that Guy used
to bring me; he liked to tell his friends he had married
a brain, and almost daily he brought me a paperback
from the drugstore. Sleazy romance novels, beautiful
heroines in anguish. I loved them. I close my eyes and
see myself on the plastic sofa with a book on my stomach, Gloria beside me snapping her gum, great swells
of organ music rising from the television. What does
Gloria think of me now? Has she cut me out of her
mind, now that I have left her son with no more than
a note on the refrigerator door?

If things don't work out with John, I have nowhere to
go. This is the first time I have really thought about
that. I left in such a rush, whipping off my apron,
hanging my wedding ring on a cup hook, giving not a
backward glance to my Corning ware and my potted
plants. I seemed to be drunk with the joy of doing
something so illogical. Now I have hours and days and
weeks to think: I am entirely dependent on a man I
hardly know. I have no money, no home, no family to
return to, not even a high school degree to get a job
with, and no place to leave Darcy if I *could* find a job.
I don't even know if I am eligible for welfare. What if
John stopped loving me? Or if his wife came back—
came walking in with her model's slouch, a mink stole
draped over her shoulder. (Well, not in June, but that's
the way I picture her.) I would be lost, then. I would
be absolutely helpless, without a shred of hope.

　　This is what I resolve: if it works out that John
and I are married, I am going to save money of my own
no matter what. I don't care if I have to steal it; I will
save that money and hide it away somewhere in case
I ever have to be on my own again.

　　Only I won't be on my own, not if it's up to me.
I won't leave anyone else ever. It's too hard. I never
bargained for this tearing feeling inside me. I didn't
know I would be so confused, as if I were in several

places at once and yet not wholly any place at all. I hadn't ever considered Darcy: how bewildered she would be or how her food and shelter would become a problem. You would think *that* much would occur to me. Why, Darcy is the center of my life! And her hair is Guy's, and her eyes; I'll be carrying pieces of Guy around forever. There was no point to my leaving. I can say that even while I am looking straight at John, even crossing to where he stands in the sunlight with his camera slung over his shoulder, smiling at Darcy and me so steadily: I love you, John, but if I were smarter I would have stayed with Guy.

I check the mailbox every day but nothing comes from Guy. I keep trying to imagine what a letter from Guy would look like. He has never written me before. Never had to. If ever he needed to write to someone else—say a business letter, or something—he would ask me to do it for him, and his dictation was full of et ceteras and, "Oh, you know, just put it like you think best." He wasn't too well educated. I would sit there with my ballpoint pen, waiting for Guy to think up a line, wondering what my mother would have said if she could see me. I was supposed to be unusually intelligent. Now look: "Dear Sir, In regards to the used Honda which I seen advertised in the February issue of . . ."

I wonder if maybe he is never planning to write at all. If he is dead, or has left home himself, or is so angry he plans to drive to Baltimore and wait in person beside my post office box until I come looking for letters. The minute I enter the building every day, my eyes fly to the corner where my box is. No Guy. No letter. I take Darcy by the hand and turn away, feeling relieved, but meanwhile there are all these unused words backed up in my throat: "Oh Guy, I wish you hadn't come. I won't go back with you no matter what, you're only wasting your . . ."

It's true I wouldn't go back. It just isn't in me. Even if it doesn't work out with John, even if there is nowhere else to turn. I can't explain why. After all, what did Guy ever do to me? He worked hard, made a home, took good care of us. But I stopped loving him.

I don't know which takes more courage: surviving a
lifelong endurance test because you once made a promise or breaking free, disrupting all your world. There
are arguments for both sides; I see that. But I made my
choice. "Come away with me," John said. "We love
each other, why waste your life? Where is your spirit
of adventure?" The first time he said it, he took my
breath away with shock. The second time it seemed
more possible. He planted a thought in me that grew
when he was not around, so that when he stayed away
a whole week and then returned I was praying for him
to ask me again. It looked as if he might have forgotten.
He played all morning with Darcy, didn't give me a
glance. When lunchtime arrived he stood up, still not
looking at me, not even touching my hand. "Are you
coming?" he asked.

"Yes." I said.

To keep Darcy quiet a while I gave her some blunt-
nosed scissors and a magazine. I sat on the bed beside
her, cross-legged. I pretended that we were in a house
that John had built for us, and he was off at work
but would be coming home shortly for supper. I even
planned what I would cook for him. I love to cook.
Lately we have been living on things from cans, heated
in Mr. Pauling's miserable kitchen, and I am starved
for the smell of herbs and baking bread. I planned the
meal by smells alone: hot dilled biscuits, roast beef, a
fresh green salad. John would open the door and the
smells would curl around him and draw him in. We
would sit down at a table with a white linen cloth, in a
house that was stable, calm, warm, clean, built to
shelter us a lifetime. It would never even occur to me
to run away again.

I cut out squares of paper to make Darcy a dollhouse. I showed her how to Scotch-tape them together.
I cut an oval rug and gave it to her to color, and then
we made curtains from a flowered shopping bag. Darcy
bent over them with her tongue between her teeth, concentrating. The back of her neck was like a little curved
stem, and I kept wanting to reach out and touch it but
I didn't.

You hear a lot about teenaged wives, how they're bound to fail, but nobody mentions teenaged mothers. They are the best in the world; I'm convinced of that. While the neighbor women were nagging their children not to get the house dirty, I was down on the floor playing with mine. I carried her piggyback wherever I went; I dressed up in old clothes with her, read her my favorite storybooks, fixed tea for her dolls. Instead of shipping her off to a nursery school I had other children come visit, and sometimes I felt as if I were running a nursery school myself. Six and seven children would stampede through the kitchen, playing tag or hide-and-seek, with me always It. On rainy days we made picnic lunches and ate them on the dining room floor. Gloria said, "Honey, you spoil that child. She won't know how to amuse herself when her brothers and sisters start coming along." I never told her about Guy's not wanting more children. I kept hoping he would change his mind. But he said, "Ain't this one taking all your time as it is? What you want to go and ruin your figure for?" He said that everytime I brought it up. He never changed.

I would stand in front of the mirror and see how widehipped and expansive I was, how tall I loomed, bigger than life, *full* of life, with not enough people to pour it into. My world had turned out narrow after all— different from my parents', but just as narrow. I looked out the front window and watched the people walking by, and I wanted to climb into every single one of them and be carried off to some new and foreign existence. I pictured myself descending from the sky, all wheeling arms and legs, to sink invisibly into their heads and ride home with them, to see how they arranged their furniture and who their friends were, what they fought about, what made them cry, where they went for fun and what they ate for breakfast and how they got to sleep at night and what they dreamed of. And having found out, I would leave; on to the next one. I wanted to marry a mad genius and then a lumberman and then somebody very rich and cold and then a poet who would dedicate his every word to me and who would have a nervous breakdown when I left him. Which I

would do, of course. As soon as I had been absorbed
into his world, as soon as it stopped feeling foreign; on
to the next one. I didn't guess back then that moving
on would hurt so.

What would Guy have said if he'd known what
I dreamed? His idea of change was to take in a movie
on Saturday night. His greatest joy was attending motorcycle rallies. Hours and hours in someone's hot cow
pasture, with me trying to pick out the cloud of dust
that was Guy from among a lot of other clouds. When
I refused to go any more, he went alone. He was gone
overnight, weekends. "That son of mine should stay
at home more," Gloria used to say, but I didn't mind.
It seemed to be part of the pattern that I had married
into; the other women's husbands didn't stay home
either. They were off bowling, or drag-racing, or playing
billiards. On summer evenings we would pool all our
children and go to Roy's for hamburgers, which we ate
at one of the outdoor tables—a double line of women
and children, not a man among us. All the women
laughing and scolding and mopping spilled drinks, filling every corner of their world. Then when Guy came
home again his boot jarred the house and his bass
voice took me by surprise, and when he plucked Darcy
out from her dolls she squirmed and looked at me for
reassurance, as if he were a stranger.

Which he had been, once upon a time. He was
more a stranger than any boy I'd met. It wasn't his
fault that we finally got to know each other.

I walked with Darcy to the post office and we dawdled
every step of the way. I was hanging back, hunting up
excuses never to arrive at all. And when we got there,
sure enough, a slanted blade of paper was showing
through the window. One of my own envelopes, pale
blue. It gave me a shock to see it. "Now can we go to
the park?" Darcy asked. "No, wait," I told her. We
were supposed to meet John there at noon. I didn't
want him to watch me reading this letter. I leaned
against a counter and tore open the envelope. The letter itself was written in pencil, on several sheets of the
pulpy gray paper I kept for Darcy to draw on. Every

word was smudged over. Guy is left-handed; his hand rubs what he has just written as it travels across the paper. I could picture him at the kitchen table with his hair falling over his forehead, his shoulders hunched with the effort of writing.

Dear Mary,

Now I have never understood you but this time is worse than usual.

I treated you real good Mary always gave you ever little thing you wanted, a house of your own clothes a baby even when I thought we should wait some. I thought you was happy, now I hear it wasn't so. Come home one night to find it wrote out on the icebox door, your going and won't be back and sorry you hurt me.

You didn't hurt me worth a shit Mary I mean that. You could go clear on to California it wouldn't hurt me worth a shit. I am too blasted mad.

We have been married six years now that I could have been playing around in and buying up fast cars instead of cookpots and I could have had me a lot of other women as well let me tell you but never did as I thought you loved me. I stood for a lot from you Mary. First off I near about raised you, you didn't know beans when we were married and had my mama waiting on you hand and foot for years, secondly I let you correct my grammer and my table manners and change my whole way of doing things that you looked down on and drive off all my friends account of you thought none of them was good enough for you. Did you ever invite a one of my buddies to dinner, no. When your mama died you acted like it was my fault it happened to her, also that time your cousin came from Washington you didn't even introduce me but went and ate supper at her motel leaving me a tunafish sandwich. Well I could take all that, what I couldn't take was this, you held my own baby daughter seperate from me. You named her for your family and you raised her like your mother would do and never even let me hold her without fifteen pillows nor feed her nor have any good times with her, you and her just lived your seperate

*lives like I wasn't around. You froze me out.
Don't you think I got feelings too? What do you
think I been thinking all these years? Oh I don't
count I'm just a man. You put me in mind of a
black widow spider, soon as you got your child
then a man isn't no more use to you. For years I
been living a lonely life hoping you would change
and you never did.*

    *NO you can't have a divorce. What is it you
already met a man that wants 20 children? You
can't have a divorce as long as you live and don't
try coming back or I'll kill you, I mean it, I'll
kill you and Darcy both of you don't neither one
mean a thing to me. I mean this Mary I'm glad
you're gone.*

                        Sincerely,
                        Guy

    I put the letter back in the envelope and slipped
it into my purse. I took Darcy by the hand. She said,
"Mom, can I buy a popsicle?" "Maybe later, baby," I
said. I led her down the steps, out into the sunshine
that was baking the sidewalk, but inside I felt cold and
hard and dark like a stone. I looked into a store window and saw my reflection and thought, There goes a
black widow spider taking her daughter to the park.
The whole world looked different. A different set of colors even, and bigger and flatter. When we got to the
park I saw John on a bench and he seemed to have
changed too. He wore a black suit with a white shirt;
he was all black and white. The grass behind him was
such a washed-out shade of green that I hardly recognized it. Some kind of cold white gauze was laid
across everything. "What's the matter?" John said.
"Nothing," I told him. I reached out to touch his
sleeve. I thought, You are my only support. I am certain
I love you. Certainly with *you* I won't fail. "Race you
to that tree," John told Darcy, and they were off like
two jittery birds. I was the only still thing in the landscape. I stood clutching my purse to my stomach, stone
still. Yet when the two of them had touched base and returned to me, and John said, "Shall I take you out to
eat?" I was able to smile the same as ever. I said,
"That would be nice."

We went to a delicatessen where he said they made wonderful sandwiches. It was cafeteria-style—a dangerous place to take Darcy. She always thinks she wants everything she sees. When we reached the cash register her tray was overflowing, and the lady who rang it up said, "Somebody's eyes are bigger than their stomach." Then she winked at me. What would she say if I grabbed both her hands and begged to go home with her?

Once we were seated John started acting nervous, tearing bits of bread off his sandwich and rolling them into balls. I wondered if he had noticed something odd about me. I would have to tell him *sometime*. I leaned forward and said, "I got an answer to that letter today."

John said, "You did?"

"He won't give me a divorce."

John smiled, with the corners of his mouth turned down. "It seems we're beset with troubles from all sides," he said.

"All sides?"

"Carol has moved back into the house."

I looked over at Darcy. She was separating her sandwich to get at the mayonnaise. I wanted to tell her not to waste a bite of it, eat all she could hold, take the rest home in a doggy bag; now we were going to starve. John said, "Well, it's not so bad. You know Carol she'll tire of it soon enough. I couldn't just throw her out of the house, could I?"

"You could move out yourself," I said.

"Well, yes. Yes. In fact I will, but my studio is there. I can't just up and leave my studio. What I'm counting on is her changing her mind, by and by. I'm certain she'll leave again."

"How can you be sure?" I asked him.

"She operates on *whims*, Mary. She goes through fads. She'll get over it. Right now she's taken with the idea of being a homebody again. Says she wants to settle down, have children, grow vegetables. For Carol that's ludicrous, I told her straight—"

"Children?" I said. "You got as far as talking about *children?*"

"*Carol* did, I said."

"You said she couldn't have any children."

"Oh, well, she's talking now about going to a doctor for some tests. Wants me to get tested too."

"What would they test you for?"

"To see if it's me that can't have them."

"That's ridiculous," I said. "It's hardly ever the man."

"Fifty per cent of the time it is."

I stared at him.

"Why, sure," he said.

"I didn't know that."

"Well, I'm not going, don't worry," he told me. He laid his hand over mine. "You'll see, in a week she'll move out again."

"But—what about now? I mean, how are you arranging it? Where is she sleeping?"

"Mary. Look. There's nothing to get upset about. I'm here with you eating lunch, aren't I? I won't let you down. Whatever happens, I think of you as my responsibility. Believe me."

"Responsibility," I said.

"I've been through a lot for your sake, Mary. I'm jeopardizing my divorce, I've given up motorcycle rallies—"

"Well! Are you sure I'm worth the sacrifice?"

"Be reasonable, will you?"

Reasonableness was why I left with him. He was so reasonable and cool; life with him would be so different. I said, "Tell me something. Why did you ask me to come away with you?"

"Now, Mary—"

"No, I mean it. Why didn't you wait till you were divorced, if you were so reasonable?"

"Well, *you* know why. I said we might wait and you said no, we'd better do it now or not at all. You didn't even stop to pack a bag. Once you'd made up your mind you wanted to get going, you said. You weren't the kind to—"

"Oh, never mind." I said. I didn't want to hear what kind I was. I didn't want to learn any more, ever, about how I appeared in other people's eyes.

We took Darcy back to the boarding house because she was cross and sleepy. After I put her to bed we came out and sat in the parlor—I in an easy chair, John perched on its arm. He kept stroking the inside of my wrist. "Don't," I told him.

"This isn't like you, Mary," he said.

"It isn't like me to go out with someone whose wife is waiting at home either."

"In time," he said, "this will all be over. It will seem like nothing. You'll look back on it and laugh."

"Well, it may be over someday, and it might seem like nothing," I told him, "but I will never look back on it and laugh. I don't feel as if I will ever laugh again." Then I looked at his face and saw the boredom and irritation drawn across it like a curtain, removed as soon as he found my eyes on him. His mouth was tugged permanently downward by two acid lines at the corners; that much of his expression he could not remove. Think, I told myself, of the clean cut of him, the precision, the logic and decisiveness. Isn't that why you're here with him? His forefinger chafed my wrist like sandpaper, as if my skin were peeled back and he were stroking raw nerves. I stood up suddenly, pretending to have heard some sound from Darcy, and I went into the bedroom. Darcy was fast asleep. She lay sprawled across our bed, her mouth slightly open, her hairline damp with sweat. I heard John come up behind me and I felt his hand on my hip. "She's asleep," he told me.

"She's tired out."

"We're all alone," he said.

"No, we're not. I'm sure Mr. Pauling is up in his studio."

"Come with me to the couch."

"Are you crazy?"

I moved his hand away but he stayed close behind me. "What do we care about Mr. Pauling?" he said.

"You're crazy," I told him. "I wish you would leave now. Will you go on home to your wife, please?"

"Suit yourself," he said.

He stood there a moment longer but I wouldn't even turn to look at him. I wanted him gone. I wanted to pick Darcy up and sit with her in a rocking chair, just the two of us, shut away from everyone. Yet when he did go (stepping too lightly, as if I were asleep as well), I was angry at him for leaving. I felt abandoned as soon as I heard the front door shut. I sat down on the bed; I took one of Darcy's stockinged feet and held it tight for comfort, while the tears spilled over and came streaming down my face.

A long time later Mr. Pauling came by with a carpet sweeper and a dirty gray dust rag. I heard the sweeper's wheels roll through my doorway and then stop short. "Oh," Mr. Pauling said, "I'm sorry, I thought—"

"That's all right."

"I thought you were still—but I'll come back another—"

"No, please. Go right ahead. Don't let me stop you."

I stood up, digging in my pocket for a handkerchief. Mr. Pauling remained in the doorway. When I sidled past him I could smell the Ivory soap on his white, white skin. I kept my eyes down, hiding the tears, so that all I saw of him was his pale plump chest above a fishnet undershirt. "Please, is there anything at all I could do to help?" he asked me.

That one single piece of kindness shattered me. "Oh, Mr. Pauling," I said, and took a step closer and bent to lay my face upon his shoulder. I don't know why. I felt the shock hit him—a short breath inward, the handle of the sweeper clanging against the door and then dropping to the carpet with a thud. He kept both his arms behind him, like something under surprise attack. Already I was sorry I had scared him so. I thought, Good Lord, I wonder what I will take into my head to do next. I had started trying to smile, to be ready to draw back and face him and apologize, when I felt one of his hands rise up and pat my arm. Little soft pats with the fingers tight together. Little warm breaths stirring a wisp of my hair. "Oh there, oh please," he said, "*please* don't cry, Mrs. Tell." I shifted my face into the crook of his neck. I put my arms around his waist, which felt soft and had too much give to it. "I just can't stand to see you cry," he said. His voice wavered, as if he might start crying himself. Sad people are the only real ones. They can tell you the truth about things; they have always known that there is no one you can depend upon forever and no change in your life, however great, that can keep you from being in the end what you were in the beginning: lost and lonely, sitting on an oilcloth watching the rest of the world do the butterfly stroke.

4

Summer and Fall, 1961: Jeremy

These are some of the things that Jeremy Pauling dreaded: using the telephone, answering the doorbell, opening mail, leaving his house, making purchases. Also wearing new clothes, standing in open spaces, meeting the eyes of a stranger, eating in the presence of others, turning on electrical appliances. Some days he woke to find the weather sunny and his health adequate and his work progressing beautifully; yet there would be a nagging hole of uneasiness deep inside him, some flaw in the center of his well-being, steadily corroding around the edges and widening until he could not manage to lift his head from the pillow. Then he would have to go over every possibility. Was it something he had to do? Somewhere to go? Someone to see? Until the answer came: oh yes! today he had to call the gas company about the oven. A two-minute chore, nothing to worry about. He knew that. He *knew*. Yet he lay on his bed feeling flattened and defeated, and it seemed to him that life was a series of hurdles that he had been tripping over for decades, with the end nowhere in sight.

On the Fourth of July, in a magazine article about famous Americans, he read that a man could develop character by doing one thing he disliked every day of his life. Did that mean that all these hurdles might have some value? Jeremy copied the quotation on an index card and tacked it to the windowsill beside his bed. It was his hope that the card would remove half of every pain by pointing out its purpose, like a mother telling her child, "This is good for you. Believe me." But in fact all it did was depress him, for it made him conscious of the number of times each day that he had to steel himself for something. Why, nine tenths of his life consisted of doing things he disliked! Even getting up in the morning! He had already overcome a dread before he was even dressed! If that quotation was right, shouldn't he have the strongest character imaginable? Yet he didn't. He had become aware lately that other people seemed to possess an inner core of hardness that they took for granted. They hardly seemed to notice it was there; they had come by it naturally. Jeremy had been born without it.

If he tried to conquer the very worst of his dreads —set out on a walk, for instance, ignoring the strings that stretched so painfully between home and the center of his back—his legs first became extremely heavy, so that every movement was a great aching effort, and then his heart started pounding and his breath grew shallow and he felt nauseated. If he succeeded, in spite of everything, in finishing what he had set out to do he had no feeling of accomplishment but only a trembling weakness, like someone recently brushed by danger, and an echo of the nausea and a deep sense of despair. He took no steps forward. It was never easier the second time. Yet all through July, the hottest and most difficult month of the year, he kept attempting things he would not have considered a few weeks ago. He went at them like a blind man, smiling fixedly ahead of him, sweating and grim-faced, pretending not to notice that inwardly, nothing changed at all. He drew from wells of strength that he did not even own. And the reason, of course, was Mary Tell.

Did she know how much courage went into his daily good morning? How even to meet her eyes meant a suicidal leap into unknown waters? "Good, good morning, Mrs. Tell," he said. Mary Tell smiled, serene and gracious, never guessing. He held tight to the doorframe and kept his knees locked so that she would not see how they trembled. Face to face with her, he felt that he was somehow growing smaller. He had to keep tilting his chin up. And why did he have this sensation of transparency? Mary Tell's smile encompassed the room—the dusty furniture, the wax fruit on the sideboard, and Jeremy Pauling, all equally, none given precedence. Her eyes were very long and deep. The fact that there was no sparkle to them gave her a self-contained look. It was impossible that she would ever need anyone, especially not Jeremy.

Yet at night, as he lay in bed, he went over and over that moment when she had put her arms around him. She had needed him then, hadn't she? Like an old-time heroine in one of the Victorian novels his mother used to read to him, she had come in desperation, with no one else to turn to—and out of shock he had responded only scantily and too late. He tied his top sheet into knots, wishing the moment back so that he could do the right things. He tried to recall the smallest details. He took apart each of her movements, each pressure of her fingers upon his ribcage, each stirring of breath against his throat. He turned over all possible meanings and sub-meanings. He wondered if he had made some magical gesture that caused her to think of him in a time of trouble, and what gesture was it? what trouble was it? What made women cry in modern times, in real life?

But most of all, he wondered if it might ever happen again.

Flat on his back in the dark, sleepless after his inactive days, he spent hours constructing reasons for her to turn to him. He imagined fires and floods. He invented a sudden fever for her little girl. Mary Tell would panic and come pound on his door, carrying an antique silver candlestick. He would be a rock of strength for her. He would go for the doctor without a thought, no matter how many blocks from home it took him. He would keep watch beside the sickbed, a straight line of confidence for her to lean against. Her hair would just brush his cheek. What color was her hair? What color were her eyes? Away from her, he never could remember. He saw her in black-and-white, like a steel engraving, with fine cross-hatching shading her face and some vague rich cloak tumbling from her

shoulders. Her clearest feature was her forehead—a
pale oval. In the novels his mother read to him, a wide
ivory brow stood for purity and tranquillity.

Oh, if only he had a horse to carry her away on!

Mrs. Jarrett said, "That poor Mrs. Tell, she
doesn't get out much. Her friend hardly comes at all
any more, have you noticed?"

Jeremy, watching television with the boarders, re-
vived Mary Tell from a swoon and held a glass of
brandy to her lips. He didn't answer.

"I had been hoping he was *more* than a friend,"
Mrs. Jarrett said.

"Who is this we're speaking of?" asked Miss Vinton.

"The gentleman Mrs. Tell was seeing. Remember?
Now he hardly comes at all. Have you noticed him
lately, Mr. Pauling?"

Jeremy said, "Well . . ."

After a while they gave up waiting for the rest
of his answer.

Nowadays his collages filled him with impatience. He
became conscious of the way his eyes tightened and
ached when he looked at them too long. He started
wishing for more texture, things standing out for themselves. He had an urge to make something solid. Not
a sculpture, exactly. He shied away from anything that
loomed so. But maybe if he stacked his scraps, let
them rise in layers until they formed a standing shape.
He pictured irregular cones, their edges ridged like
stone formations on canyon floors. He imagined the
zipping sound a fingernail would make running down
their sides. But when he tried stacking his scraps they
turned into pads, mounded and sloping. He took them
away again. He went to stand by the window, but his
impatience grew and extended even to his physical
position: his moon face gazing out from behind the
tiny clouded panes, his hands limp by his sides, fingers
curled, his feet so still and purposeless, pointing nowhere in particular.

How did people set about courtships? All he had
to go on were those novels. When he thought of court-

ing Mary Tell he imagined taking her for a drive in a shiny black carriage. Or dancing across a polished ballroom—and he didn't even know which arm went around his partner's waist. Yet it seemed as if some edginess were pushing him forward, compelling him to take steps he would never ordinarily think of. He pictured a high cliff he was running toward with his arms outflung, longing for the fall, not even braced to defend himself against the moment of impact. Then maybe the edginess would leave him, and he could relax again.

He returned to the collage. He slid colors ceaselessly across the paper, like a man consulting a Ouija board. Imaginary voices murmured in his ear. Scraps of conversation floated past. He was used to that when he was working. Some phrases had recurred for most of his life, although they had no significance for him. "At least he is a *gentle* man," one voice was sure to say. He had no idea why. Of *course* he was a gentle man. Yet the voice had kept insisting, year after year. Now that he was trying to concentrate, pushing away the thought of courting Mary Tell in an opera box, he absently spoke the words in a whisper. "At least he is a—" Then he caught himself and straightened his shoulders. Other voices crowded in. "If in any case and notwithstanding the present circumstances—" "I don't know how to, don't know how to, don't know how to—" "If in any case—"

Mary Tell sat beside him smelling of handmade lace and fine soap, lifting her mother-of-pearl opera glasses, but her dress was out of Jane Austen's time and the opera she was watching had not been shown for a century.

Monday morning Jeremy got up early, dressed very carefully, and went to Mr. and Mrs. Dowd's grocery store, where he bought a pound of chocolates. They were left over from Valentine's Day—a heart-shaped box, a little dusty, but Mrs. Dowd wiped it off for him with a dishrag. "*Somebody's* found himself a sweetheart," she said. Jeremy was still knotted up from the ordeal of making a purchase, and he only gave a flicker of a smile and kept his eyes lowered. He returned home by way of the alley, so that he arrived in his backyard. There wild chicory flowers were waving among a tangle of sooty weeds, and he squatted and began gathering a bouquet. This was something he had thought out the night before. He had rehearsed it so thoroughly that now it seemed he was picking each flower for the second time. In a shady spot by the steps he found glossy leaves that he inserted between the chicory, making a pattern of blue and green. Then he rose, hugging the candy box to his chest, and went into the house. Through the kitchen, through the dining room, straight to Mary Tell's bedroom, where he instantly knocked. If he gave himself time to think, he would fail. He would run away, scattering flowers and chocolates behind him.

When she opened the door she was wearing a bathrobe and she carried a hairbrush. He noticed that the hairbrush was a wooden one with natural bristles, which gave him a sense of satisfaction. How fitting it was! He could have said from the beginning that she would never be the type to use a nylon hairbrush. But this thought was chosen at random, to take his mind off his embarrassment. He had expected to find her dressed. He had chosen the day and the hour so carefully, knowing that she would be in now and the other boarders out or upstairs; and here she stood in her bathrobe—a pink one, seersucker. Though at least her hair was up. He hadn't wakened her. The brush was apparently meant for Darcy, who sat crosslegged on the bed in a pair of striped pajamas. "Hi, Mr. Pauling!" she called out. Jeremy couldn't manage a smile. "These are for, I brought these for the room," he said. He thrust the bouquet under Mary Tell's chin. It was terrible to see how his hands were shaking; all the flowers nodded and whispered. "I found them by the trashcans."

"Oh! Thank you," she said. She looked at them a moment and then took them. Too late, he thought of the vase. Last night he had decided on his mother's pewter pitcher from the corner cupboard in the dining room, but this morning it had slipped his mind. "Wait," he said, "I'll get a—" but she said, "Don't bother, I'm sure we have something here. My, what a beautiful shade of blue."

They're *your* blue, Mary-blue, he wanted to tell her. The blue from a madonna's robe. He had thought of that last night, but he had known all along that he would never dare to say it. Instead he looked over at Darcy, whose eyes—more chicory flowers—surveyed him steadily. "How come you brought them to *us?*" she asked.

"Why, just, I thought—"

"Never mind, Mr. Pauling," said Mary Tell. "I know why you're here."

Jeremy stood very still, breathing raggedly.

"You just have to understand," she said. "Financially, things are a little difficult right now. Very soon I should be able to pay you, but—"

"Pay me?" he said. Did she think she had to *buy* the flowers?

"Pay you your money. I know that Saturday has come and gone but you see, with Darcy not in school yet I have to find work I can do at home. Till then I was hoping you wouldn't care if the rent was a little—"

"The rent, oh," Jeremy said. "Oh, that's all right."

"It is?"

"Why, of course."

He kept his eyes on the flowers. It was important to see them safely into the water. And then what? Was he supposed to leave? Yes, almost certainly, in view of the fact that she was wearing a bathrobe. Yet that would make the visit so short, and he wanted to be sure he did everything he was supposed to. He raised his eyes to hers, hoping for a clue. The brilliance of her smile took him by surprise. "Mr. Pauling, I just don't know how to thank you," she said.

"Oh, why—"

"You've really been very kind."

"Well, but I believe they should be put in water," he said.

Then she looked down at the flowers and gave a little laugh, and he laughed too. He had not expected that things would go so well the very first time. He watched her fetch a glass of stale water from the night-stand and set the bouquet in without disarranging a single flower, without upsetting his design. When she was finished she turned and smiled at him, apparently waiting for something. He drew in a deep breath. "Now I wish," he said, "that you would call me Jeremy."

"Oh!" she said. "Well, all right."

He shifted his weight to the other foot.

"And you can call me Mary," she said after a minute.

"You can call *me* Darcy," Darcy said from the bed.

That gave them something new to laugh about, only he laughed hardest and had trouble stopping. Mary by then had returned to her smile. It became a little strained and started fading at the corners, and from that he understood that it must be time for him to go. He was glad that he had managed to catch the signal. He held out his hand and said, "Well, goodbye for now, Mrs.—Mary," and she said, "Goodbye, Jeremy," Her hand was harder than his, and surprisingly broad across the knuckles. While he was still holding it he said, "Um, may I come back sometime?"—the final hurdle of the visit. "Well, of course," she said, and smiled again as she closed the door.

Although he had not had breakfast yet he returned to his studio, because it would have been awkward to run into her again in the kitchen. He went up the stairs on the balls of his feet, feeling weightless with relief. Not even the discovery that he still carried the chocolates—a warped cardboard heart plastered to his chest —could spoil his day. He only blushed, and then smiled too widely and sat down on his bed. He could always take them to her on another visit, couldn't he? There were going to be lots of other visits. But while he was planning them he absently opened the box, and he took first one chocolate and then another and then a whole handful. They had begun to melt, and they stuck to the paper doily that covered them and left imprints on his palm, but they tasted wonderful and

the sweetness seeped into every corner of him and
soothed his stretched, strained nerves.

He knew how these things worked. First you set up the
courtship; he had just done that. Then there were certain requirements to be met—holding hands, a kiss—
before he could propose. On television there were a
lot of frills as well, people running through meadows
together and pretending to be children at zoos and fairs
and amusement parks, but he knew better than to try
for anything like that. He wasn't the type. *She* wasn't
the type. And after all, he had done very well so far,
hadn't he? He had completed the first step without any
problems, and now he felt more confident about what
was left.

Only it turned out not to be so easy. For the next
morning, when he had made a pot of percolated coffee
and knocked at her room, she opened the door only
halfway and it seemed as if some veil fell immediately
across her face. "Yes?" she said.

Today she was dressed. (He had deliberately
waited fifteen minutes later than yesterday.) Even Darcy was dressed. Then why did she seem so unwelcom-
ing? "I just made some coffee I wondered if you'd
like some," he said all in a rush.

"No, thank you, I don't drink coffee."

That possibility had not occurred to him. "Tea,
then?" he said.

"No, thank you."

"Well, maybe you'd just like to have a glass of
milk with me."

"I don't think so. I have a lot to do today."

He couldn't leave. He had promised himself he
would see this through. "Please," he said, "I don't
understand. Have I done something to offend you?"

Mary sighed and looked over her shoulder at Darcy, who was peacefully stacking dominoes on the rug.
Then she stepped out of her room and shut the door
behind her. She said, "Come into the parlor a minute,
Mr. Pauling."

Yesterday she had called him Jeremy. He felt like
someone deaf or blind, prevented by some handicap

from picking up clues that were no doubt clear to everybody else. "Is it something I've said?" he asked, stumbling after her. "You see, I just have no inkling . . ."

She led him to the couch, where he sat down while she remained standing. Then he realized his mistake and jumped up again. "Oh, excuse me," he said.

"Mr. Pauling," said Mary, "I realize that I'm behind on my rent."

"Oh. Well, I thought we—"

"We had a talk about that yesterday. You said you wouldn't pressure me for it. But I never suspected that there were strings attached."

"Strings?" said Jeremy.

"Isn't that what this is all about?"

"I don't understand."

Mary looked at him. He had been trying to catch her eye, but now that he had it he seemed unable to face her. He was not used to dealing with angry women. He had never pictured Mary angry at all. He said, "This is so puzzling. I don't see—"

"Yesterday," said Mary, "as soon as it was clear I'd missed paying my rent, you came calling in my room and brought me flowers. Well, I didn't think anything of it at the time but then later I—and today! You come knocking again! Do you feel that now you have some hold over me? Because all I owe you is *money,* Mr. Pauling, and I will be happy to borrow elsewhere and pay you this minute and be out of your house tomorrow. Is that clear?"

"Oh, my goodness," Jeremy said. He lowered himself to the couch again. Horror curled over him like an icy film, followed by a rush of heat. He felt his face grow pink. "Oh, Mary. Mrs. Tell," he said. "I *never* meant to—why, I was just—" Now a picture came to him of exactly how he had looked to Mary Tell the day before. He heard the tentative mumble of his knuckles on her door, he saw his sickly, hopeful smile, beseeching her for everything as he stuck his bouquet under her chin. This was something he was never going to be able to put out of his mind; he knew it. He was going to go over and over it on a thousand sleepless nights, all of them spent alone, for a woman like Mary Tell would never in a million years give a thought to a man like him. He should have guessed that. He felt himself beginning to tremble, the final indignity. "Mr. Pauling?" Mary said.

"But I'm a *good* man," he said. "What I mean to say—why, I never even knew you owed me! *I* don't keep track of that money, the others just put it in the cookie jar."

"Cookie jar?"

If he spoke any more she would notice his voice was shaking.

"In the cookie jar, Mr. Pauling?"

"The cookie jar in the kitchen. Then I take it out to buy groceries whenever—" He gulped, a sound she must have heard three feet away. She came closer and bent over him, but he kept his head ducked. It was the worst moment he had ever lived through. He didn't see how it could possibly go on for so long. Couldn't she leave now? But no, he felt the sofa indenting as she settled down beside him. He saw the edge of her blue skirt, such a calm, soft blue that he felt a flood of pain for those few days when he had loved her and had some hope of her loving him back. "Jeremy," she said. "I feel just terrible about this. Won't you say you forgive me? I wasn't thinking straight. I'm going through a bad time just now and I must have—Jeremy?" She leaned closer and took one of his hands. "Look at me a minute," she said.

Why not? It didn't mean a thing to him any more. He raised his eyes and found the perfect oval of her face level with his. The inner corners of her eyebrows were furrowed with concern. "Won't you accept my apology?" she said. He had to nod. Then he even smiled, because it had finally dawned on him what was happening: They had been discussing an issue as old-fashioned as Mary Tell herself, and here they were side by side holding hands in this second stage of their courtship.

Mornings now he woke feeling hopeful, and getting up was easier. He started being careful of his appearance. He began wearing a pen-and-pencil set in his shirt pocket—a sign of competence, he thought. He practiced smiling with his mouth shut, hiding a dark turmoil of bad teeth. In the bathroom mirror the thought of Mary hung like a mist between himself and his reflection. Her long cool fingers reached into his chest. He carried her image downstairs with him, treading gently as if it might break up and scatter like snowflakes in a paperweight. When the other boarders greeted him he sometimes failed to answer, but that had happened before and none of them thought anything of it.

Then why did his vision of Mary Tell always turn out to be wrong? Oh, not wrong in any concrete way. He had got her nose right, and the set of her head and the shape of her mouth. But when she entered the kitchen, tying an apron around her waist and smiling at Darcy's chatter, there was some slight difference in her which both disappointed and awed him. Her skin had a denser look and the planes of her face were flatter. Her manner of moving was more purposeful. In his mind she glided; in real life she stepped squarely on her heels. Every night he forgot that and every morning he had to learn it all over again.

In the beginning she used to make bacon and eggs for breakfast, but now their diet had changed. She and Darcy filled up on cold cereal. "We *always* have this," Darcy said. "I know, honey," said Mary, and then she told Jeremy, "Yesterday I heard of a job addressing envelopes. Do you think they'd let me do it at home? I'm going to see them today and ask, and if they say yes we'll never eat cornflakes again." But that job fell through, and so did the next one and the one after that, and they continued to eat cornflakes while Jeremy sat at the table with them trying to think up topics of conversation. He kept a glass of orange juice in front of him, although he never drank it. (It was impossible to swallow with Mary watching.) He rehearsed a hundred sentences offering help, what little he could manage: "Could I lend you some of the cookie jar money? Well, then, eggs? Just eggs?" But he never said any of them out loud. He was afraid to.

Rinsing off their little stack of dishes Mary *bustled* so, as if she were daring him to feel sorry for her. Then she said, "All right, Miss Slowpoke, ready to go?" and she and Darcy would set off on their walk. Which was another change: in the beginning Mary waited for her friend to call before she went out. Now she went immediately after breakfast, and the few times the telephone rang it was never for her.

"Going on your walk?" Jeremy would say. "Well now. Have a good time." They passed through the house calling goodbyes, singing out greetings to Mr. Somerset, letting two doors slam behind them, ringing the air like a bell, and then all of a sudden the house would fall silent and the rooms would seem vacant and dead. The only sound was the creak of an old dry beam somewhere. A distant auto horn. Mr. Somerset's papery slippers shambling across the dining room floor.

Jeremy was like a man marooned on an island. Why had that taken him so many years to realize? He was surrounded on four sides by streets so flat and wide that he imagined he could drown in air just walking across them. Yet look, a four-year-old managed it without a thought! Oh, if it weren't for this handicap he could invite Mary Tell to a movie and then bring her home and kiss her outside her door as he had seen done on TV, and that would be the end of all his planning and worrying. It would be so simple! Instead, here it was August now and he had not taken one step toward kissing her and it began to look as if he never would.

Then one morning the telephone rang and no one was in the hall to answer it but Jeremy. Even before he picked up the receiver a knot of anxiety had settled low in his stomach. "Hello? Hello?" he said, and was answered by a voice he had not heard in weeks, but he recognized it instantly. "Mary Tell, please," said the cigarette-ad man.

"Oh! Well, I'll see," Jeremy said.

Then he went into the dining room and knocked on her door. "Someone wants you on the telephone," he called.

She took a minute to appear. She was already

dressed, carrying her apron in her hand, and she looked
startled. "Someone wants *me?*" she said. "Who is it?"

"Why, I believe it's your friend, the young man."

From behind her Darcy said, "Can I talk? If it's
John can I talk?"

"No, you may *not*," Mary said. Jeremy had never
heard her speak so sharply to Darcy. She said, "Keep
her a minute, will you, Jeremy?" and walked off to the
telephone. "Why can't *I* talk?" Darcy asked Jeremy.

"Oh, well . . ." said Jeremy. The knot in his stomach had grown larger. He backed into the dining room
and sat down on a chair, limply, with his hands on
his knees. "How are you today, Darcy?" he asked. Even
to himself, his voice sounded foolish. He made himself
smile at her. "When are you coming to my studio again?
You haven't been all week."

But he was listening, meanwhile, to Mary out
in the hall. She said, "No, no, I understand. You don't
have to call *ever*, John. It's not as if you're obligated."

"But she always let me talk to him before," Darcy said.

"Maybe another day," said Jeremy. He tried a
different smile. Mary said, "Look. I'm fine. *No* I don't
need money."

"Shall we cut out paper dolls?" Jeremy asked Darcy.

"Not right now, Jeremy."

"You don't owe me anything, I'm managing fine.
I'm fine. I still have some of what you lent me," Mary
said. And then, "What's it to you how much is left?
It was a *loan*, you don't have any business asking that.
I'm planning to pay you back. I want to. As soon as
I find a job I will."

"If I go and shout into the phone John will talk
to me," Darcy said. "He likes me. I know he does."

"No, no, Darcy—"

But she was off, skating on her stocking feet into
the hallway with Jeremy at her heels. From this close
they could hear Mary's friend arguing or protesting
or explaining, a thin violent squawk. "—for *Darcy's*
sake," he said, and Darcy gave a little leap. "Hello
John!" she shouted. "Hello *John!*" Mary held up the

flat of her hand, but kept her face turned into the receiver. "All right," she said. "You win."

"Can you hear me, John?"

"Uh, Darcy," Jeremy said.

"All right," said Mary, "but it's a loan, and I want you to know that. I don't want any—Darcy! Look, John, it's hard to talk right now—"

Darcy was tugging at her mother's skirt, and Jeremy was stooped over trying to loosen her fingers. The squawk continued on the telephone, another form of tugging. Mary's skirt had the same cool, grainy feeling that her hands had had, that time on the couch. Why, after all, she was only a collection of textures. Her muscles slanted over her bones exactly as in his anatomical drawing class; her lips were yet another texture, otherwise no different than her fingers had been or this clutch of skirt in Darcy's scampering hands. "No, I mean this," Mary said. "I want you to mail it. *Don't* bring it. You are under no—John?"

She put the receiver down very slowly. "Oh, Mom, *I* wanted to talk," Darcy said. Then Jeremy straightened and looked into Mary's face. Her expression was cheerful and she was even smiling slightly, but tears were running down her cheeks. "I'm sorry—" she said. She started back toward the bedroom, with Jeremy and Darcy stumbling over each other trying to follow. "You must think I make a habit of this," she said in her doorway. She turned, and Jeremy was so close behind her that before he thought, he had found the strength to lean forward on tiptoe and kiss the corner of her mouth. Then he took a step back, and she looked his way for a moment before her eyes seemed to focus on him. "Thank you, Jeremy," she said. "You are a very sweet man."

She wiped the tears away with the back of her hand, giving a little laugh at herself as if they embarrassed her. She shook out her apron and said, "Come along, Miss Chatterbox, let's get you some breakfast, shall we?" Then they went off toward the kitchen, leaving Jeremy smiling so hard that he could barely see. He thought he might just inflate and float away like a balloon at a birthday party.

In magazine cartoons, a suitor proposing marriage always knelt on the floor at his sweetheart's feet. Now, was that an accurate reflection of the way things were done? He suspected not. Nevertheless he kept picturing himself looking up at Mary from a kneeling position, finding her even more frightening at this angle—her sandals the largest part of her, her waist at eye level, the never-before-seen underside of her bosom and the white triangle of skin beneath her jaw. "I don't have much money," he should tell her (the speech owed to her father, he believed, but he had no idea who her father was). "I wouldn't be able to support you in very good style but at least it would be a *little* easier, I do have my pieces and a little from my mother and sometimes I win a contest and I always seem to have enough for groceries." He prepared himself for the way the hem of her dress would loom, and for the difficulty of judging her expression from so far beneath it. Yet every night he went to bed with nothing resolved, feeling thin and strained as if this balloon of hope he had become had been kept too fully inflated for too long a time. He dreamed of losing things—unnamed objects in small boxes, the roof of his house, pieces of art that he would never be able to re-create. He woke feeling anxious, and over and over again read the index card tacked to the windowsill beside him.

In his imagination this proposal always took place outdoors somewhere, although of course that would be too public. Could he be thinking of a park? The nearest park was several blocks from home. He pushed away the outdoor images and in the mornings, while he sat with his orange juice and she poured cornflakes, he tried to think of some natural way to lead in to what was on his mind. He couldn't. Mary talked about her daughter and the weather and library books, nothing more personal. "Now Darcy is shooting out of all her clothes. I've never seen a child grow the way she does. I thought as soon as I got a job I would buy some material and borrow Mrs. Jarrett's sewing machine, but sewing has never been my strong point and I'm not at all sure that I—" How could he bring love into a conversation like that? She gave him no openings. He sometimes thought that she might be sending him some silent warning, telling him not to ask even the simplest things that occurred to him: Where do you come from? Why are you here? Who was your husband? What are your plans?

"At home Darcy used to *beg* for cornflakes," Mary said once. "I've never seen a child so contrary."

"Where was that?" Jeremy asked her.

"What?"

"Where was your home?"

"Oh, well—and now she wants bacon and eggs, wouldn't you know? I believe she just thinks up these things to devil me."

Jeremy didn't press her. He contented himself with the surface that she presented to the world, and it was only inside him that the questions continued. What happened to your husband? Why did you cry with that man John? What is his significance?

Will you marry me?

Now each morning that he failed to propose he saw them to the door, tagging after them in the hope that somewhere along the way—in the dining room, the hall, the vestibule—he might gather his courage. He took to going out on the steps and waving after them. "Goodbye! Goodbye! Have a nice walk!" Turning back afterward was worse than being left in the kitchen. He always felt oppressed by the sudden dark coolness as he stepped inside. He started accompanying them farther—to the second house, to the third. Maybe, given time, he could follow Mary all the way off his island. Gradually: wasn't that the key? Oh, if there were any god he believed in, it was gradualness! If people would only let him go at things his own way, step by step, never requiring these sudden leaps that seem to happen in the outside world! But every day he was overtaken by some magnetic force that seemed to affect only him. It dragged him back with a tug at his spine; it caused him to slow and then to halt, damp with exhaustion. "Goodbye! Goodbye! Have a nice walk!" Mary and Darcy waved and grew smaller. They separated cheerfully at the approach of total strangers, they talked aloud without fear of being heard, they crossed the wide street against the light. Dogs with enormous grinning mouths sniffed at Mary's skirt and she never even noticed. Oh, he had undertaken too much. He could never keep up with a woman like that. He turned and trudged homeward, stumbling over cracks in the sidewalk and muttering words of encouragement to himself, and before he started the day's work he had to lie on the couch in his studio a while catching his breath and trying to still the twitching of his leg muscles.

It seemed to him that his sisters were always calling him on the telephone nowadays. "What are you doing, Jeremy, why haven't we heard from you? Are you getting out more? Are you eating right?" They no longer phoned only on Sundays but occasionally on weekday evenings as well, on Saturdays and in the middle of lunch. Then one morning they called so early that he was still in the kitchen with Mary and Darcy. "Jeremy, honey, this is Laura," he heard, and although he had always felt close to Laura he was conscious now of a sudden impatience tightening his fingers on the receiver. In the kitchen Darcy said something and Mary laughed. There was no telling what he was missing. "Is there something—what seems to be the matter?" he asked her.

"Matter? I was just worried about you, dear. You haven't answered our last letter."

"But I don't believe I received any letter this week," he told her. Then, too late, he remembered the flowered envelope that he had absently stuck in his shirt pocket on the way upstairs the other day. It was probably in the bathroom hamper. "He says he didn't *get* any letter," Laura told Amanda. To Jeremy she said, "Honestly, they can fly to Europe but they can't get a simple note from Richmond to Baltimore. Well, I knew there was *some* explanation. Now here is Amanda to say a few words. Amanda?"

"How do you seem to be getting along, Jeremy," Amanda's voice said very close to his ear.

"Oh, fine, thank you."

"I *told* Laura there was no need to call but she said she had a funny feeling, she gets them more and more these days. Any fool should know you can't trust the U.S. mail."

Jeremy stood up straighter. It always occurred to him, when talking on the telephone, that to people at the other end of the line he was invisible. Except for the thin thread of his voice he did not even exist. "Jeremy!" Amanda said sharply, and he said, "Yes, I'm here"—reassuring both himself and her.

"Labor Day is coming up, Jeremy."

"Oh, yes, is it?"

"Maybe you could make the trip to see us."

"Well, Amanda . . ."

"Now I don't want to go over three minutes here but I'm sending you a train schedule. Let's not hear any excuses, Jeremy. Why, you'll just *love* travel, once you catch on to it. And you don't want to spend your life just sitting home now, do you. Mother wouldn't have approved of that at all, she would have wanted you to get out and enjoy yourself."

He knew that his sisters were all that was left of the world he had grown up with, his only remaining connection with his parents, but sometimes when Amanda spoke of their mother it seemed she meant someone he didn't even know in passing—someone stern and rigid, not his own sweet-faced mother with her soft, sad smile. "Well, you see," he said, "I do try to—"

"I have to run, Jeremy. Do please answer our letters, you know how Laura worries."

"All right, Amanda."

He laid the receiver carefully in its cradle. There was a damp mark where his hand had been. He went back to the kitchen and found Mary just sponging Darcy's face, with breakfast finished. He had missed everything. His chances were over until tomorrow. "I'm going to the grocery," Mary told him. "Do you want anything?"

His despair was so enormous that it gave him courage. He said, "Oh, why, several things. Perhaps I should come along."

Mary only nodded. She was frowning at a stain

on Darcy's collar. "Oh, Darcy, look at you, it's your last clean dress," she said.

"I don't care about an old stain."

"Well, I do. Come along then."

Words kept rearranging themselves in Jeremy's head. May I have the honor—? Could you possibly consider—? Is it asking too much for you to marry me? But once they were descending the front steps the only conversation he could think of was an exaggerated squint toward the sun, implying a remark about the weather. Mary didn't look up. She was reading her grocery list. "I'm going to get a gumball," Darcy said. "Am I going to get a gumball, Mom? I'm going to bet a penny for the gumball machine."

"I wasn't aware they had a gumball machine," said Jeremy.

"Oh yes," Darcy said. "Perry's does."

Would you think me forward if I—?

Perry's? Why, Perry's was two blocks away; it was where his mother used to go for soupbones. And no sooner had it hit him than sure enough, they came to Dowd's grocery and passed it by, with neither Mary nor Darcy giving it a glance. Jeremy did. He gazed longingly at the crates of oranges and peaches and pears slanted toward him behind the fly-specked plate glass window. The tissue paper they nestled in seemed a particularly beautiful shade of green. He thought with love of Mrs. Dowd's gnarled old hands spreading the tissue just enough, rescuing a runaway peach and setting it back in place with a little grandmotherly pat. Mary and Darcy walked on. "Wait!" he said. "I mean—have you ever tried Dowd's?"

"They're more expensive," Mary said. She went on studying her list. Darcy took Jeremy's hand in both of hers and swung on it—a clamp on his index finger, another on his little finger. What could he do? He set one foot in front of the other, doggedly, barely managing each step. For Mary Tell's sake he was slaying dragons, and yet to keep her respect it was necessary that she never even guess it. He wiped his face on his sleeve. They came to the end of the block, where a red light stopped them. Cars whizzed back and forth, but what he was most afraid of was the street itself. Then the light turned green. "Wait!" he said again. Mary looked up, in the act of putting her grocery list in her purse.

"Could we—I mean I don't believe I—"

"Hurry," Darcy said, "we'll miss the light."

He stepped off the curb. All the comfort he had was Darcy's grip on his hand, but now Mary said, "Darcy, don't *swing* on people. How often have I told you that?" One of Darcy's hands fell away; only his index finger was secure. He reached out blindly and found Mary's arm, the crook of her elbow, which he hung onto as he had seen men do on the late show. Did she notice that it was she supporting him and not the other way around? "I certainly wish the price of tomatoes would go down," Mary said.

Then they had reached the other sidewalk. The air on this block was different. He could have told it with his eyes shut. It was hotter, more exposed, and old Mrs. Carraway's wind chimes were not tinkling. What was that flat-faced cement building? He didn't like the look of it. He noticed that the rowhouses ran only in twos and threes, which gave the block a broken-up look. A mean-eyed woman watched him from her front stoop. He saw a commercial printer's whose black and gold sign must have been here years ago, when he was a boy walking to school. Its sudden emergence in his memory made him feel strange. He lowered his eyes again. Pretend this is only a corridor leading off from the vestibule. Pretend it is just an unusually long room. It will all be over in a while.

Then they reached Perry's. "*Here* we are," said Mary. He looked up to find a window full of dead things stacked in pyramids—tinned vegetables, Nabisco boxes, paper towels. No fruit. "I'll wait outside," he said.

"Outside?"

"I'll just—I do my shopping at Dowd's."

Mary seemed about to ask him a question, but then Darcy said, "Can I have my penny now?"

"What penny?" Mary said.

"You said you would give me a penny for the gumball machine. You *said* you would. You said—"

"Oh, for mercy's sake," said Mary, opening her pocketbook. "Here." Then she went in, and Jeremy chose a place outside the door. First he watched the street, but the unfamiliar buildings opposite made him feel worse. He looked behind him, toward the glass door, and saw Darcy just coming out with a gumball. "Look. Pink," she said. "My favorite color."

"Is that right?" said Jeremy. He was glad to see her. He turned outward again, so that he was facing the street. Darcy stood beside him. "They have charms and things too," she said. "You can see them in the machine but they never come out. Do you think I might get one someday?"

"Perhaps so," Jeremy said.

"Or are they just to fool people. You think that's what it is? You think they're just trying to get your pennies from you?"

Jeremy had a terrible thought. He felt that he might become marooned beside Perry's Grocery. How would he ever get home again? He imagined himself dipping the toe of one shoe into the street, then drawing it out and turning away, unable to cross. "I'm sorry, I just can't," he would have to say. He thought of the time he had climbed the crape myrtle tree in his back yard when he was three. He had climbed only to the first fork but then had found it impossible to get back down. Every time he tried, his hair stood on end and the soles of his feet started tingling. "Let him stay," his father said. *"He'll* come down." Then at night, when he still hadn't managed it, his father took three long strides to the tree and lifted him off roughly, one arm around his waist, causing Jeremy to scream in that single dizzying moment before his feet touched solid ground again. Now Mary would take him in hand, nudge him out, coax him into one step after another. "Come on, you can do it, you'll see, when you get to the other side you'll look back and laugh at how easy it was." Only he wouldn't. He would have to back away, and now he was too big to be carried bodily. He imagined spending the rest of his life on this new island, exposed for all the world to see, propped against the wall like a target. "Would you like half of my 'gumball, Jeremy?" Darcy asked him.

"No, thank you, Darcy," he said.

"I don't have a knife, but I could *bite* it in half."

Dread rose in him like a flood in a basement, starting in his feet and rapidly filling his legs, his stomach, his chest, seeping out to his fingertips. Its cold flat surface lay level across the top of his throat. He swallowed and felt it tip and right itself. Nausea came swooping over him, and he buckled at the knees and slid downward until he was seated flat on the sidewalk with his feet sticking out in front of him. "*Jeremy,* you silly," Darcy said, but when he couldn't smile at her or even raise his eyes she said, "Jeremy? Jeremy?" She went screaming into the grocery store; her voice pierced all the cotton that seemed to be wrapped around his head. "Mom, come quick, Jeremy's all squashed down on the sidewalk!" Then he was surrounded by anxious feet nosing in upon him—Darcy's sneakers, Mary's sandals, and a pair of stubby loafers almost covered by a long bloody apron. "It's the heat," the apron said. Mary said, "Jeremy? Are you ill?"

"Sick," he whispered.

She set a rustling paper bag beside him, bent to lay a hand on his forehead and then straightened up. Her sandals were the largest thing about her. The hem of her skirt was so close he could see the stitches, he saw the underside of her bosom and the triangle below her jaw. "Will you marry me?" he asked her.

She laughed. "No, but I'll see you home and into bed," she said. "Can you stand? You need some air." And she raised his head herself, and then propped him while he got to his feet. She said, "Walk a ways, now. It'll clear your head. Here, take this." From her grocery bag she brought out a navy blue box, and while he swayed against her she tore the wrapper off and handed him a cinnamon graham cracker. "Sometimes it helps to eat a little something," she said.

"No, no."

"Try it, Jeremy."

He only clutched it in his hand. He felt that opening his mouth would cause his last remaining strength to pour out of him. Inch by inch he headed homeward, shaky but upright, leaning on Mary's arm. The bloody apron receded behind them. Darcy danced ahead. They came closer to the street while Jeremy prayed continuously to the traffic light: oh, please turn red, turn red, let me at least have time to get my bearings. But it stayed an evil green, and Mary led him without a pause off the curb, across a desert of cement, up the other side. They were home. They were on his own block. He straightened and let out a long slow breath. Mary said, "You're just like Darcy, whenever you don't eat breakfast you get sick to your stomach. Isn't that what happened?"

"I meant it seriously, I asked you to marry me," Jeremy said.

"But you both say no, you couldn't eat a thing, you don't want a . . ."

She stopped walking. She turned and stared at him across a silence that grew painful, while Jeremy waited with his head down. "Oh, Jeremy," she said finally. "Why, thank you, Jeremy. But you see, I *can't* get married."

"You can't?"

"My husband won't give me a divorce."

"Oh, I see," Jeremy said.

"But it was sweet of you to ask, and I want you to know how flattered I am."

"That's all right," Jeremy said.

He stood there a minute more, and then they both began walking again. Up ahead, Darcy leaped and skipped and twirled. Her hair made him think of something metallic falling through the air, catching the sunlight and ducking it and catching it once more. He fixed his eyes on it and stumbled along. When they were within sight of home he lifted his cracker without thinking and took a bite. Mary was right; it helped. His head cleared. His stomach righted itself. He felt cinnamon flowering out of his mouth, taking away the tinny taste, leaving his breath as pure as a child's. Like a child he let himself be led home while all his attention was directed toward the cracker. Crunching sounds filled his head and tiny sharp crumbs sprinkled his shirt front. He felt limp and exhausted, and something like relief was turning his bones so watery that he could have lain down right there and gone to sleep on the sidewalk.

Now he no longer came downstairs while Mary was making breakfast. He lay in bed late and rose by degrees, often sitting against his pillow for as much as an hour and staring vacantly out his window. The index card lost its tack and fell behind his bed; he let it lie. He sat in a sagging position, smoothing his sheet over and over across his chest, and if he wanted a change of scenery he raised his eyes from the screened lower portion of the window, which was open, to the closed upper portion where two sets of cloudy panes dulled the morning sunlight. Maybe someday he would wash them. The floors had a frame of dirt spreading out from the baseboards, thinning only where his traffic pattern had worn the dust away. There were little chips of paper everywhere, some so old that they seemed to have become embedded in the wood. If the light was right he could look out toward his studio and find a long glinting red hair snagged on one of the floorboards. It had belonged to a student from two' years ago, whose name he had forgotten. He neither swept the hair away nor made any special effort to keep it. It was just there, something he registered in the mornings without considering the possibility that there was anything he might do about it.

When he had finally struggled out of bed there was the bathroom to face—a chilly place even in summer, with all its fixtures crazed and rust-stained and the swinging naked lightbulb pointing out every pore of his skin in the watery mirror. He shaved for hours. He cut one small path across his cheek and then stood looking into his own eyes until it occurred to him to lift his razor again. Even before the mirror he did not bother rearranging his expression. His muscles sagged and the soft skin of his throat pouched outward. He noticed, and disliked what he saw, but only in the

detached way that he might dislike a painting or some
scene that he witnessed on the street. Then when he
was tired of shaving he left, often without rinsing off
the last traces of soap, so that his skin felt itchy and
dry. He wrapped himself in a bathrobe and put on his
crocheted slippers and shuffled into his studio, where
he sat on a stool for a long time looking at his latest
piece. Too many browns. Not enough distinctions. More
and more now he was adding in actual objects—thumbtacks and washers and bits of string and wood, separating the blur of colored papers. Brian hadn't seen
these yet. Jeremy didn't care whether he saw them or
not. He pulled off a piece of twine that was in the wrong
corner, leaving a worm of dried white paste behind. He
dropped it to the floor and then noticed, beside one
leg of his stool, the tin top off a box of cough lozenges,
and by the time he had figured where to paste that he
had forgotten about dressing. He snipped things apart
and fitted things together. He rummaged through the
clutter in a bureau drawer, meanwhile holding his
bathrobe together by its frayed sash. Till Mrs. Jarrett's
clopping heels mounted laboriously to the second floor
and she called up to the third, "Mr. Pauling? I don't
see your dishes here, have you not had breakfast?
We're getting worried about you. *Please* come." If he
were too absorbed he merely shuffled his feet on the
floor, showing he hadn't died in his sleep. Other times
he sighed and laid his scissors down and went to his
bedroom for clothes. Most of his clothes seemed to be
falling apart nowadays. He kept having to throw away
shirts with long rips and trousers with the zippers
broken and shorts with the elastic gone, but he didn't
bother sending to Sears for more. He tossed them in
the wastebasket almost gladly. Later he would listen
with a sense of satisfaction while the garbage men came
clanging trashcans and bore his belongings away with
them. It felt good to be done with things. He thought
of the New Year's Eves he had sat up for—the relief
that came from putting away another year and brushing
off his hands and knowing that there were twelve
months less to get through. Or of all his life—the hun-

dreds of memories he had closed the files on, the years assigned to him that he had dutifully endured, waiting to reach the bottom of the pile.

His breakfast was other people's lunch. Mrs. Jarrett ate in the dining room with everything just right, dishes set on one of his mother's linen placemats and a matching napkin in her lap. Mr. Somerset wolfed a lacy fried egg straight from the skillet. Miss Vinton, home from the bookstore on her lunch hour, read publishers' brochures while she ate health bread at the kitchen table. "There's a new Klee in, Mr. Pauling," she might say, without looking up. "I put it on the sideboard."

"Oh, why, thank you, Miss Vinton."

He ate whatever took the least trouble—a box of day-old doughnuts or a can of cold soup. After every mouthful he wiped his hands carefully on the knees of his trousers before turning a page of the Klee. It would have to go back with Miss Vinton, spic and span, before her boss noticed it was missing. The cover of the book was a glossy white, promising him something new and untouched and wonderful. At the beginning there was a long jumble of words, a résumé of Paul Klee's life, which Jeremy skipped. What did he care about that? He plunged into the pictures; he drank them up, he felt how dry and porous he was, thirsty for things to look at. At every page he wanted to pause and spend hours, even when he had seen the pictures before in other books, but he felt a pull also to turn to the next one quickly so that he would be sure to finish in time. Sometimes he said, "Miss Vinton, I wonder if I might—?" "Oh, why surely, Mr. Pauling," she said, refolding the bread wrapper. "I can always take it back tomorrow. Mr. Mack won't notice." She had never once hurried him or shown any concern over his handling of the books, although Jeremy knew that Mr. Mack was unreasonably strict about such things. And for all of August, when Jeremy's life seemed duller and sadder than he had ever noticed before, she managed to bring a new book for him almost every day, as if she guessed that he needed comfort. Klee, a collection of impressionists, Miro, Renoir. A book of American primitives whose dollhouse landscapes and lack of perspective filled him with a kind of homesickness. If only he could just step inside them! If only he lived in a place where a man could go any distance and yet never grow smaller! Miss Vinton brought him Braque, a man he disliked. He sat through her lunch hour testing the anxiety that each picture called forth in him, the discomfort caused by some clumsiness in the shapes. Years before, when he was in high school, an art teacher explaining cubism had made Jeremy's class copy one of Braque's paintings line for line. Jeremy had felt sick all the while he was doing it. It seemed that he might melt away to nothing, letting himself get absorbed into another man's picture that way. Now he found the picture again—a still life involving a musical instrument —and stared at it until he couldn't stand it any more and had to turn the page. "Would you care to keep it till tomorrow?" asked Miss Vinton, rising to rinse her dishes. "You seem to like him."

"What? No, no," Jeremy said, "please, I don't want it, take it back with you." Then he was ashamed of his rudeness, and he blushed and looked up at her. In the summertime, stripped of her lavender cardigan, her bony freckled arms gave her a vulnerable look. White strings stood out along the inside of her wrist when she turned the faucet off. "But I'm grateful to you for bringing the book," Jeremy said. "I'm sorry, I didn't mean—"

"Oh, *that's* all right, I never much liked him myself."

She turned, cheerful as ever, to hang up her dish-towel and take her purse from the table. Meanwhile Mrs. Jarrett ate fruit cup in the dining room, the lady-like clink of her spoon sounding at perfectly spaced intervals. Mr. Somerset put his skillet down silently and gravely, making certain that it sat in the exact center of the circle of the burner, ready to be used at another meal. Was there anyone gentler than old people? Could he ever feel as much at rest as he did sitting in this triangle of muted gray voices?

Then here came the second shift, as if in answer— Darcy slamming the door and pounding down the hall-way with a bucket full of dandelions, Mary laughing and calling out warnings and threats and promises, and maybe if it were a weekend Howard's high-pitched whistle and the squeak of his sneakers. "Where's the milk I left here?" "Who wants a dandelion?" "You're going to bump *into* someone, Darcy!"—which Darcy would almost surely do, as if she had to depend on someone else to break her speed for her. *Flunf!* into Miss Vinton's middle. "Oh, Darcy, say you're sorry." "No harm done," said Miss Vinton, and Darcy spun on through the kitchen, ending up with her arms around Howard. "Howard, make me flapjacks, Howard." "Let him be, Darcy." "Oh now," Howard said to Mary, "you're just jealous because I won't make *you* flapjacks." Then the kitchen splintered into bits of laughter, and Miss Vinton smiled and left while M. Somerset turned slowly from the stove, dazed by the laughter, baffled by frivolity. "What?" he said. Mary folded Darcy into the circle of her arms and said, "Milk or apple juice, young lady?" "Both," said Darcy. "Or wait. Is apple juice what I want?" She turned toward Jeremy as if she expected him to answer, but Jeremy was looking at Mary. He saw the curve of her cheek against Darcy's tow hair; he noticed how her nearly unarched eyebrows calmed and rested him.

Why hadn't he been granted the one thing in life he ever hoped for?

At the beginning of September, Darcy started kindergarten and Mary found a job. It was something she could do at home: making argyle socks on a knitting machine. In the morning while Darcy was at school Mary worked alone in her room, but Darcy returned at lunchtime and was in and out all the rest of the day, leaving the door open behind her, and the sock machine soon became part of the household. It consisted of a circle of vertical needles, which first had to be threaded one by one. Threading was the time-consuming part. Then Mary cranked a large handle a prescribed number of times, after which she paused to rethread in another color. Jeremy, passing her doorway, had a glimpse of her huddled in a C-shape and frowning at metal eyes that seemed far too close together. She reminded him of old photographs of life in a sweatshop. But when the threading was done she could straighten up and stand back, and the cranking was so easy that sometimes she let Darcy do it while she herself counted the strokes. Numbers rang out and floated through the house—"Thirty-six! Thirty-seven!" After the tense silence of the threading, her voice and the circular rattle of machinery seemed like an outburst of joy. Wherever he was, Jeremy would raise his head to listen, and he noticed that the whole house appeared to relax at those times and the other boarders grew suddenly talkative, as if they too had held tense during the threading.

At the end of her first week of work, Mary packed the completed socks in a cardboard carton. She left Darcy with Mrs. Jarrett and caught a bus to the factory, where she was supposed to deliver them. "Why can't I come too?" Darcy asked. "Because it wouldn't be any fun," Mrs. Jarrett told her. "The place where Mommy is going is the factory section, all nasty and dirty." Jeremy felt something shrink in him. As if her absence were one long threading period, he held himself rigid in a parlor chair, scarcely breathing, silently turning the pages of a book of old masters that his mother had given him. "Goodness, don't you have anything to do?" Mrs. Jarrett asked once. "I thought Saturday your students came." Jeremy looked up, still turning pages. He had lost his last student a month ago and no others had called yet, but before he could put all this into words his thoughts trailed off again and he forgot to answer.

Mary returned just before lunch, bringing a new carton of yarn. When Darcy heard she came running out of the kitchen with Mrs. Jarrett close behind, and Jeremy stood up holding his book to his stomach. He thought that now the shrunken feeling would leave him, but it didn't. Mary's face was gray and her shoulders sagged. "How's our career woman?" Mrs. Jarrett asked, clapping her hands together.

"Oh well, I'm all right."

"You seem a little tired."

"I had to wait in line a while," Mary said. "There are a lot of other people doing this work."

"Is that right? And just think, I never even heard of it before. Did you meet anybody interesting?"

"Oh, trash mostly. Just, you know. Just trash." She set her carton on the coffee table and sat down. "I didn't make as much money as I thought I would," she said.

"Now be sure they pay you what they owe, you hear?"

Jeremy, back in his armchair now, kept nodding his head to show that he agreed. He felt as tired and sad as Mary. He wanted to offer her something—a cup of coffee? She didn't drink coffee. In his mother's old books a rich gentleman would come now to rescue Mary from life in the sweatshop, but Jeremy was the only gentleman present and he wasn't rich and he didn't believe that Mary had even noticed he was in the room. She spoke solely to Mrs. Jarrett. She said, "Oh, they paid me what they owed. But I had made a few mistakes, and also I'm still slow. Some of these people just whip them out by the dozen, but I don't. I don't know why. I thought I was going so *fast*. I thought I could make up the rent and the grocery and Darcy's school clothes, all in just a few hours a day."

"Now, now," said Mrs. Jarrett. "Give yourself time."

Jeremy went on nodding. He kept his eyes fixed on the label at the end of the yarn box—a rectangle of glaring yellow, a color he had always disliked. The brightness of it made his eyes ache. He imagined himself winning twenty-five thousand dollars from some soap company and offering it to her, watching her brow slowly smooth and lighten as she looked down and saw what he had put into her hands. "No, no," he would tell her, "no strings. You don't even have to be my friend, just please don't thread those needles any more . . ." Yet if she had that much money, wouldn't she leave him?

Well, but hadn't she left him already? Had she ever really been there?

"Now can we have our ice cream?" Darcy said.

She had been promised a treat. Mary had told her she would come home rich. Mrs. Jarrett said, "Not yet, Darcy, let Mommy rest a while," but Mary said, "No, I'm all right. Let's go." She picked up her pocketbook and they went out the front door. This time there were no slams, no voices calling back and forth outside. The house felt the same when they were out as when they were in, bleak and dark and tired. Mrs. Jarrett settled with a sigh onto the creaking springs of the couch. Jeremy turned a page and smoothed the edges of a Rubens. "It's a shame, it's just a shame," Mrs. Jarrett said. "Do you think they'll have to go on welfare?"

The word stabbed him. He looked up, open-mouthed.

"And she's bright as a button. I don't care what you say. A high school diploma isn't everything."

"Welfare?" Jeremy said.

But Mrs. Jarrett was talking to her needlework.

"I said, 'What you want is a husband, my dear.' 'I do, don't I,' she said, and just laughed, didn't take me seriously, but I meant what I said. Now I don't know what happened there, widowed or divorced or what, but she is a *young woman* still and on top of that she has that child. Have you noticed how out of hand that child has gotten? She used to be a real little lady. She needs a father, and you can tell it by the number of times that she says a thing over again. Shows she isn't listened to enough, her mother has worries on her mind and can't pay attention. Not that I blame her, of course, I realize what a—"

Jeremy blinked down at the Rubens, a fat naked blond lady laughing. He felt that Mrs. Jarrett's words were twining around him like vines, rooting in the sad darkness inside him. The fat lady reminded him of a student he had once had, a girl named Sally Ann something who had wanted to learn portrait painting. She weighed two hundred pounds; she had told him so herself. She seemed proud of it. Once she asked him, "Would you like a nude model? I could do it." And then she had come very close and laid a hand on his arm, smiling at him but looking, for some reason, only at his mouth. "No, no," he had said. He was unprepared. He backed off, shaking his head, and stumbled over a tin can full of brushes. "No, that's all right, I don't paint at all, really." But afterwards he had lain awake regretting his answer, and Sally Ann, whom he had not liked, gained importance in his mind and he began to see that there could be something compelling about a person who was dimpled all over. Only the next time she came to the studio he found that he still disliked her, and he kept himself at a distance even though she never offered again to be his model. Then what happened? Did she stop coming? He couldn't remember. He stared down at the Rubens, who laughed directly at him with her eyelids lowered, and he felt some sort of wasted feeling, as if he were a very old man realizing for the first time how little was left to him.

". . . and then my very own sister was married four times," said Mrs. Jarrett. "Well, some claimed that was carrying things too far, but I don't know. I don't know that I blame her at all, to tell the truth. We do need someone to lean on. I imagine I'll spend the rest of my life feeling naked on my street side every time I take a walk, and I am sixty-four now and been a widow longer than a wife."

Jeremy sank lower in his chair, letting the book fall shut, and closed his eyes. He kept them closed for so long that Mrs. Jarrett thought he had gone to sleep. Anyway, she suspected he had not been listening.

In the middle of the night he woke with the feeling that he had just heard his name called, but he found it was a dream. He couldn't get to sleep again. First he was cold, and he had to kneel in his bed and tug the window shut. Then he discovered he had a headache. He felt his way to the bathroom, found an aspirin tin, and washed two tablets down with a mouthful of lukewarm water from the faucet. In the mirror his silhouette was gilt-edged with moonlight. He studied how his shoulders sloped. He reminded himself of a low hill. There seemed to be no good reason to move any more,

even to go back to bed. He stood rooted at the sink.
Then far below him he heard a whirring sound, so
faint he might have imagined it. He cocked his head,
trying to place its source. With his hands stretched
before him like a sleepwalker he guided himself out of
the bathroom and into his studio, toward the open rear
window, where the sound became louder. Even there he
took a minute to identify it: the cranking of Mary's
sock machine. He placed both hands on the windowsill
and lowered his head, forming a clear image of her
in some long flowing flannel nightgown, a shawl around
her shoulders, working away by the light of a smoky
lantern. Then he turned and went back to his bedroom.

Still in the dark, he opened drawers and slid
hangers down his closet rod and rummaged through
his shoebag. He found the one dress shirt he possessed,
easily recognizable in its crackling cellophane envelope
from the laundry. It was limp and sleazy and the collar was frayed, but he thought it would do. He knotted
a tie, fumbling a little, trying to remember the complicated set of motions learned from Mr. Somerset's
predecessor many years before. Then his suit—a three-
piecer, ordered by mail back in the fifties but it still
fit fairly well. Socks that might or might not match
—he couldn't tell for sure and it seemed important not
to turn on the light. Pinchy black shoes, also mail-order.
A handkerchief tucked in his breast pocket the way his
mother had taught him. Then back in front of the
bathroom mirror he combed his hair, puffing up the
little moonlit cloud skimming his scalp. He set the comb
down on the edge of the sink and walked very slowly
out of the room and toward the stairs. Every step made
him sicker, but he didn't let himself feel it.

All the doors on the second floor were closed and
dark. The only sound was a ragged snore from Mr.
Somerset's room. On the first floor, street lights shining
in picked up the shapes of the furniture but not its
colors. Everything was a different shade of velvety gray,
like what he had imagined a color-blind man must see.
Jeremy had often tried to picture color-blindness—the
worst affliction he could imagine next to blindness itself

—and now, as if this were the only reason he had dressed up and come downstairs, he stood for a while letting his eyes blur and swim. Then the whirring sound started up again. He straightened his shoulders and passed through the parlor and into the dining room, where a knife blade of light shone beneath Mary's door. His first knock was not heard, but at the second knock the machine stopped. There was a moment of silence. Then, "Is someone there?" she asked.

"It's me, it's Jeremy."

"*Jeremy?*"

"I'm sorry to bother you at this—"

The doorknob rattled, so loudly and so close to him that he started. Light flooded the dining room and screwed his eyes up, and Mary stood before him in her blue dress with her hair still knotted as if this were daytime. "Was I disturbing you?" she asked him. "I thought while Darcy was sleeping I might turn out a few extra pairs."

"No, no."

Darcy lay sprawled in the double bed, taking up more than her share of it. She was shielded from the light by a blue paper Woolworth's bag that Mary had fitted over the lamp bulb. Now that Jeremy's eyes were adjusting he saw that the room was actually dim. He couldn't imagine how anyone would be able to thread a needle here. "I should have thought," he said. "You don't have to keep the machine in your bedroom, you can set it up anywhere. No one will mind. I didn't guess that you would be doing this while Darcy was asleep, you see—"

He whispered, taking care not to wake Darcy, but Mary spoke in a normal tone. "Why, that's very nice of you, Jeremy," she said, "but I don't believe it bothers her. She's a very sound sleeper." They both looked at Darcy, who seemed pale and waxy, with her eyes sealed and her arms and legs still for once. "Thank you for thinking of it, though," Mary said, turning back and giving him a bright, social smile. She thought that was what he had come for—to offer her space. She expected him to go now. "Maybe I'll quit for tonight anyway," she said. "I do feel a little tired."

"But nobody *knows* you're still married," Jeremy said suddenly.

She stopped smiling.

"They think you're widowed, or divorced. *They* don't know you're not free to remarry."

"Jeremy, really I—"

"Please listen. That's all I'm asking, if you say no I won't ever trouble you again. Listen. You see how well you fit in here. Sometimes we have had new boarders come in one day and leave the next, they just don't seem to like it. But you didn't do that. You've stayed a whole season with us."

"Yes, but you see I really didn't—"

"You fit in here. Everybody wants you to stay. And you know it has a lot of advantages, kitchen privileges and Mrs. Jarrett babysits. As far as money goes, why, I do make a little money from time to time, not very much I know but enough so that you could stop knitting argyles, and besides Darcy needs a father, they say she's getting out of hand without one—"

"*Who* says that?" Mary asked, so loudly that Darcy stirred and murmured.

"Mrs. Jarrett does."

"Well, I'm very surprised at her."

"So this is what I was considering," Jeremy said. "Couldn't we just *pretend* to be married?"

Mary stared at him.

"Oh no, please don't be angry," he told her, stumbling to get the words out. "I know how it sounds. But you see, to me it *would* be marriage. It isn't as if there were any other way we could do it. We could go out one morning all dressed up and then come in and tell the others we'd been married at City Hall. That's all we'd have to do. Then we would be married in the eyes of everyone we know, and I would take care of you and you would start another life instead of going along on tag ends the way you are now, you could give all your time to Darcy and have more children if you wanted and never have to leave them to go out and work in sweatshops—"

"Jeremy, dear," Mary said, "I'm sure you are saying all this with the best of intentions—"

"I am," he said sadly. He understood now that she would refuse, but still he had to go on. "I am proposing, not propositioning. I mean only the deepest respect," he told her, and he looked up to find her nearly smiling, no longer so severe but kind-faced and amused, gently shaking her head. "Besides," he said, beginning to mumble, "I love you."

"Thank you, Jeremy. I do appreciate it."

"What hope do you have for a better life, if you keep on saying no to everything new?"

But he was speaking mainly to himself now, offering himself consolation, and he had already turned to go. He saw the dining room lit into color from Mary's doorway, a clump of dusty strawflowers turning orange on the table. Then her face appeared in his mind as it had looked at the moment of his turning—the smile fading, the eyes suddenly darker and more thoughtful. He turned back again. Mary took a breath, and he knew from the sudden shock and panic flooding through him that she was about to say yes.

5

Fall, 1968: Miss Vinton

The way it used to be, I stayed home with the children while Jeremy took Mary to the hospital by taxi. This was before I had bought my little car. Mary would wake me in the night just to let me know I was in charge—"Now don't get up!" she always said, but of course I *did* get up, I wouldn't have missed the excitement for anything. I put on a bathrobe and ran downstairs to say goodbye, only then it would turn out that they weren't quite ready to go yet. Mary was waiting at the front door with her overnight case and Jeremy was off trying to locate the house keys or change for the taxi. I kept Mary company. We just stood there smiling at each other. We *beamed*. Never mind that I am an old maid; I can still recognize a happy occasion when I see one. When Jeremy arrived, all worried and shaky, I would find his coat for him and help him into it. "Hurry now," I'd say. "I hear the taxi. Don't let him leave you." I slid back bolts and flung open first the inner door and then the outer door, I burst into the frosty night air ahead of them. I wanted to shout out a fanfare: "Make way! Make way! We have a pregnant woman here! A baby is being born!" Instead I opened the door of the taxi, meanwhile holding my bathrobe collar shut with one hand. "You get in first," I would tell Jeremy. He always had this moment of hesitation just then, but when I gave him a pat he would climb on in. Mary laid her cheek against mine, leaning across a whole table's width of stomach

113

and overnight case, which made us laugh. We would have laughed at anything, I believe. Mary glowed all over, lighting up the sidewalk. "Take care of Jeremy for me," she always whispered. And then, aloud: "I'm off!" She climbed into the cab. She rolled down the window and leaned out, waving. "Goodbye, Miss Vinton! And thank you for getting up! I'm off! Goodbye!"

I bought my little car when my knees grew too rheumatic for bicycling. I chose a '51 DeSoto, not much to look at but very steady and reliable. This was when Mary was well into her fourth pregnancy. (Her fifth, counting Darcy.) "One thing," I told her. "You can go to the hospital in style this time. Well, maybe not *style,* exactly, but at least you won't have to depend on the Yellow Cab Company." Secretly I was a little nervous. I must have checked the route to the hospital a dozen times, although it wasn't far and I had often been before. I kept reminding Mr. Somerset, "Don't go anywhere in November. Promise me, please." He was supposed to watch the children while I was away. Now, Mr. Somerset had not been gone overnight in the fourteen years I'd known him, so you can see how edgy I must have been. I kept wishing that Julia Jarrett were still alive. Or that they had replaced her, at least —found another grandmotherly type for that room instead of turning it into a nursery. What kind of babysitter was an old man with a fondness for bourbon? By October, before Mary had even packed her suitcase, I had laid out a dress on the chair beside my bed and put a pair of shoes beneath it, all ready to hop into. I took to sleeping in tomorrow's underwear. I kept dreaming that my car ran out of gas halfway to the hospital.

But it was mid-November, about four o'clock one morning, when the knock came on my door. I had been expecting it for so long that it hardly seemed real. I ran downstairs still fastening buttons and carrying my belt looped over my wrist, and there was Mary as calm as always, smiling up at me. She had on the blue maternity dress that she'd worn day in and day out for the majority of her married life, and over that the old black coat that didn't meet across her stomach. "Are you all right?" I asked her.

"I'm fine."

"How close are the pains?"

"Every four minutes."

"Jeremy had better hurry," I said.

"Oh, he's not coming."

"Not *coming?*"

"I didn't wake him."

I stared at her.

"Well, I do have *you* to help," Mary said. "It's not as if I have to manage the taxi any more."

"Mary, he wouldn't want to miss being with you now for all the world," I told her. If there was one thing I was sure of, that was it. Why, that man would move heaven and earth for her! You have only to look at him to see how much he loves her. But there stood Mary shaking her head, planted squarely in front of me like little Abbie when she has made up her mind about something. "You don't know how hard it is for him," she said.

I did know. I probably knew better than she did, but I also believe that everyone has a right to take his own leaps. Of course, I didn't tell Mary that. She has her rights too. And there might be other reasons I had no inkling of, so all I did was nod and bend to pick up her overnight case. "Suit yourself," I said. "You got everything?"

"I think so."

"Let's go, then," I said. It wasn't even necessary to call Mr. Somerset—not with Jeremy at home.

But I felt that we were making a mistake, all the way to the hospital. Mary didn't, apparently. She just looked out the window and talked about ordinary things—the house, the children. I have to admit I was relieved about *that*. I don't like hearing too much of people's personal lives. Sometimes she stopped speaking and her face would flatten and her eyes would get fixed on a point far away. That was the only sign she gave of being in labor. It wasn't at all like in the movies, thank God. Then after a minute she would relax and go on with what she was saying before. "I wanted to get Pippi's snowsuit out. That nylon jacket she has is not—"

"I'll see to it."

"I believe it's in the trunk. It's that old one of Abbie's, you remember."

"Yes, yes."

I had never realized how long some traffic lights can take.

"And Darcy needs a note of permission, she's going on a field trip."

"I'll write her one in the waiting room."

"But how will you sign it? How will they know who Miss Vinton is?"

I had assumed I would simply forge Mary's name, but since that didn't seem to have occurred to her I came up with another answer. "I'll give it to Jeremy to sign," I said.

"Oh, yes," Mary said. She turned and looked at me. Why did she suddenly become so beautiful? The corners of her mouth lifted, and she brushed her hair up off her neck and tipped her head back until it rested on the back of the seat. "Jeremy can do it," she said. Then she closed her eyes, and the light changed to green. I nearly stripped all the gears, I was so anxious to get us moving again.

At the hospital they whisked Mary away in a wheelchair, and I went into a waiting room I found at the end of the hall. It was huge and barren-looking, with linoleum floors and vinyl furniture and a stiff bouquet of hothouse flowers on a coffee table. On one couch a bald man was stretched out asleep. I took a chair at the other end of the room from him, turned on a lamp, and wrote a note on the back of a shopping list: "To whom it may concern, Darcy Tell has my permission to go on a field trip today. Signed," and I left a blank space for Jeremy's signature. Then I sat back and stared at the blank space. I kept wondering if I should just go and phone him. Wouldn't Mary be glad, after all, once he had come? I know that Jeremy is supposed to be the weak one in that couple but he might surprise some people: if you are so scared of so many things, sometimes you turn out even stronger than ordinary men. I took a dime from my purse, but then I reconsidered. I haven't lived fourteen years on the edges of other people's lives for *nothing*. I could never interfere like that. So I stayed in my seat. I spent the next hour chain-smoking and reading torn *Life* magazines whose photos seemed very dim and long ago, the way they always do in waiting rooms. Then someone said, "Miss Vinton?" and I looked up to find a doctor dressed in green standing in the doorway. "Are you Miss Vinton? Mrs. Pauling sent me to tell you," he said. "She has a boy."

I said, "A boy? Are you sure?"

Which made him smile, but you can't really blame me. The first three babies were girls: Abigail, Philippa, and Hannah. They'd been planning for an Edward so long that the name was getting stale. I think all of us had given up hope. I said, "My, won't Jeremy be surprised? I can't wait to tell him!" but the doctor held up his hand and said, "That was the rest of her message. She'll call her husband herself, she says. She wants to."

"Oh, of course," I said. "I didn't think."

I watched him walk off again. Then I looked down at the warm dime in the palm of my hand. Other people save dimes for weeks. They spend hours in the phone booth as soon as the baby is born, telling grandparents and aunts and uncles and friends. Who could I tell? As far as I knew Jeremy had one solitary sister left from all his family—Amanda, who kept her distance. (She never did get on with Mary.) I couldn't see waking her at five-thirty in the morning. The only friends were the women Mary sat in the park with, behind a row of strollers. I didn't even know their last names and possibly Mary didn't either. So in the end I put the dime away again, and got up to leave. The bald man was still asleep on the couch. I hadn't seen a single husband pacing the floor in his shirtsleeves. Things rarely work out the way the magazines would lead you to expect.

By the time I got home it was almost light, and the children were up. They keep the most amazing hours. Darcy was in the kitchen fixing cereal for the little ones, Abbie and Pippi were quarreling in the parlor, and Hannah was sitting in her high chair sucking her thumb. "Heavens," I said to Darcy. "Who's watching over you? Where's everyone else?"

"In bed, I guess," Darcy said.

"Didn't Jeremy tell you you have a baby brother?"

"No."

She was eleven at the time—a silent age.

"Well, you do," I said.

"Well, nobody told us."

"I believe they're naming him Edward."

"I knew that," she said. "I'm the one that chose it."

I'd forgotten. They let her choose *all* the names, to make her feel a part of things. It's lucky they didn't end up with a pack of Hepzibahs and Lancelots. I said, "Well, I think that's a very fine choice, Darcy."

"When do we get to see him?"

"In a few days."

She poured milk into the cereal bowls and I went out to the parlor to separate the two who were quarreling. "All right, what's going on here?" I said. It was something to do with a pack of bath salts. I put the pack on the mantel, wiped Pippi's tears, and buttoned Abbie's pajamas. Meanwhile, I was wondering who was in charge. I seemed to be the only grownup around. I still had my mackintosh on. I was stained with tears and pink bath salts, and in two hours I was due at the bookstore. Not that I would have *minded* staying with the children. I have offered to, for every birth. "Let Jeremy go on with his work," I always tell Mary. "I'll take some of my vacation time." She says, "No, goodness, he can manage." Now I couldn't see a sign of him. I got the two girls seated with their cereal and then I went into the dining room and tapped on Jeremy's door. He and Mary share his mother's old room. But there was no answer, and finally I looked inside. All I found was an empty bed, unmade. Bedclothes trailing across the floor. I shut the door and went back to the kitchen. "All right, children," I said. "It looks like we're the ones holding the fort," I passed out paper napkins, and fixed them hot cocoa while they sat eating around the kitchen table. They made quite a picture—Darcy so blond, the others brown-headed and round-faced and solemn. The younger ones were fairly close together in age—six, four, and two—and that morning it seemed to me that the littlest was much too little to have a new baby coming in. She was drinking from one of those training cups with a spout. Every time she took the cup out of her mouth she replaced it instantly with her thumb. Abbie and Pippi continued to fight. Darcy started bossing them around—a bad habit she has. Meanwhile Buddy came through, our current medical student, and grabbed an apple on his way out, and Mr. Somerset appeared but left when he saw the crowd. "Mr. Somerset! Wait," I said. "Have you seen Jeremy?"

"Nope."

"I bet you he's in the studio," Darcy said.

So while they were busy with breakfast I set off for the third floor. I took Darcy's teacher's note with me. I held it in front of me, like a ticket of admission, while I knocked. "Jeremy? It's Mildred Vinton," I said. No answer. I knocked again. They put a door on his studio when they moved the first two girls upstairs, to his old bedroom. It used to be that the whole house showed signs of his working, scraps littered everywhere and the smell of glue and construction paper, but the better his pieces get the more he shuts them away from us. Someday, I believe, Jeremy is going to be a very famous man, but it is possible that no one will be allowed to see his work at all by then, not even strangers in museums.

I said, "Jeremy? Are you in there?" Then I said, "Well, I'm not going to disturb you, but I do have to know if you'd like me to stay with the children today."

Footsteps creaked across the floor. The door opened and there stood Jeremy, unshaven, in a round-necked moth-eaten sweater and a pair of baggy trousers. It was years since I had seen him looking so awful. The funny thing about Jeremy is that he never seems to age, he always has the same smooth plump face, but today that made it all the worse. He looked shocking, like a baby with a hangover. However, I pretended not to notice. "Morning, Jeremy," I said. "Congratulations."

"Thank you, Miss Vinton."

When we heard they were married (and after we got over the surprise), and the house warmed up and we started using first names more, I asked them to call me Mildred but apparently that proved impossible. I am doomed to be Miss Vinton forever.

I stuck out my note, along with a ballpoint pen. "Could you sign this, please?"

He signed, but without even reading it so far as I could see. Then he handed it back. "You didn't call me," he said.

"Well, I—she asked me not to, Jeremy."

"She didn't even want me with her."

I couldn't think what to say. I looked off down the stairs, so as not to embarrass him. Finally I asked, "Would you like me to take care of the children today?"

"You think that I'm not up to it," he said.

He startled me. I said, "Why, no, Jeremy, I know you are."

"I can do things like that."

"Of course, but—if you're working on something."

"I'm not working on anything at all."

He shut the door again. What could I do? It seemed he was too abstracted for me to leave the little girls with him, but in the end that's what I did— bathed and dressed and went off to the shop. At noon I couldn't get away, but I called. The phone rang seven times before he answered. "Jeremy?" I said. "Is everything all right?"

"Why, yes."

His voice sounded more like himself, and I could hear Pippi singing in the background. It seemed I had worried for no good reason.

In the afternoon I took off from work early and went to visit Mary. As you can imagine, I was an old hand at hospital visits by that time. I knew enough not to bring her flowers (extravagance makes her anxious) and to stop off at the nursery first so that I could tell her I'd seen the baby. (She always has me promise that everything is fine, no doctor has drawn me aside to whisper anything dire.) After I had looked at Edward a proper length of time I went down the hall to her ward, where I expected to find her chattering and smiling the way she always was after a baby, but she wasn't that day. She was lying flat on her back, crying. All up and down the room were women with bows in their hair and lace on their bedjackets, talking softly to their husbands, and there was Mary crying. Well, I nearly left. I *would* have, if I could. When people cry I back off to give them privacy. But then she saw me and I was trapped. "Oh, Miss Vinton," she said. She sat up quickly and darted her index fingers underneath her eyes, getting rid of the evidence. I pretended not to notice. "Got quite a son there," I said. I wished I *had* brought flowers. Then I would have had something to fuss over, give her time to get her bearings. I said, "Were you asleep? Because I only stopped in for a moment. Wasn't planning to stay. I'll be back at the next—"

"I've upset Jeremy," she said.

"Oh. Well, I'm sure he—he'll get over it."

"You were right. I should have told him."

"I really don't know much about such things," I said. "I'm sure it will all get straight in the end."

"I thought I was helping. All I did was hurt his feelings so badly I don't know *what* he'll do. I've never seen him so hurt. I called him and—"

Then she started crying again. She couldn't even talk. I said, "Oh, well. Oh, well." I spent a long time getting my mackintosh unbuttoned and draping it just so over the back of a chair.

"I called," Mary said, getting hold of her voice, "and I told him—and he waited a long time and then he said, 'I see.' Then he—then—"

Her voice gave way. I felt helpless. I just knew she would lie awake hating herself for exposing her secrets this way. Could I make believe I hadn't heard? That was ridiculous.

"Then he said, 'Didn't you *want* me with you, Mary?' "

"Well, of course you did," I said, pulling down my sweater cuffs very carefully.

"I *tried* to make him see. 'I *always* want you with me, Jeremy,' I said, 'but it's not as if this is my first baby after all and I know how hard it is for you to—'"

Honesty: her one fault. There is such a thing as seeing too deeply, and then telling a man too much of what you see, but I don't know when she's going to find that out. "Look," I wanted to say, "the biggest favor you can do for him is to take him at face value." But I managed to keep quiet. I just handed her the tissue box and watched her blotting her tears. "This is a postnatal depression, I believe," I told her finally. Mary laughed and then went on crying. "Shall I come back later?" I said.

"No, Miss Vinton, don't go. Please don't go. I promise I'll stop this."

It seemed unlikely that she would keep her promise, but I couldn't think of any decent way to get out of the room. I settled back in my chair. "Now, I've been to see the baby," I told her. "Seems quite healthy, I'd say from the looks of him."

"Did you see him, Miss Vinton?"

"I told you. I've just been by the nursery."

"I meant Jeremy. Did you see him?"

"Yes, this morning I did."

"How did he look? Was he all right?"

"He was *fine*," I told her. "Just fine."

"They won't let me use the phone again until I'm up and about," Mary said, "and that won't be till tomorrow. It's out in the hall. All I want to do is ask how the children are, and get this misunderstanding straightened out. I can't stand just lying here thinking that—"

"The children are managing beautifully," I said.

"Are they doing what he tells them to?"

"Of course."

"He doesn't always know quite how to handle them, you see, and I worry that—"

"They're *fine*," I told her.

"He said he wanted to come visit me."

"Oh, good, good," I said. I thought that was a

wonderful sign; before he had always left the visiting to me.

"I told him not to."

"Mary Pauling! Why ever not?"

"It's so hard for him," Mary said. "I told him not to bother."

Some people take a terribly long time learning things.

I went home and found everything in chaos—Buddy cooking spaghetti, Jeremy changing Hannah's diaper, Mr. Somerset stroking the carpet with an old bent broom. There is something so pathetic about men trying to figure out the way a house works. "Here," I said to Jeremy, "let me do that." He had laid a clean diaper on the floor but he seemed to be having trouble getting Hannah to set herself down on it. I said, "At eight o'clock it will be visiting hour at the hospital. I'll stay with the children while you go."

"She doesn't want me to," he said. He looked at me with his eyes very wide and steady. It nearly broke my heart.

"Jeremy," I said, "are you *sure* she doesn't?"

"She asked me not to come."

Then Hannah started wandering off toward a stack of blocks. I grabbed her. "Now listen, young lady," I said, "this has gone far enough, do you hear?" Only Hannah, of course, was not really who I was mad at.

It is very difficult to live among people you love and hold back from offering them advice.

I have never been married and never planned to be, never had the inclination to be. Yet I don't believe I am an unhappy person. I had a normal childhood, good parents, five fine brothers and sisters. I had the usual number of young men to come calling when I was the proper age. Still, I did not once consider the possibility of marrying any of them. If you were to ask my vision of the future back then, my favorite daydream, it was this: I would be reading a book alone in my room, and no one would ever, ever interrupt me.

I realize how antisocial that sounds. But it seemed to me that my life was so *crowded,* when I was young. There were always so many people around. Everyone knew everyone's secrets. And then later, when my father died and my brothers and sisters married and moved away, I was the one who nursed my mother through her final illness. I chose to; it wasn't a case of the put-upon spinster daughter. And my mother was never one of those querulous old ladies. She was kind and cheerful, right to the end. But the *sharing* we did! The five years of meals shared, house shared, news shared, plans and worries and money problems, even the plots of *books* shared. I knew everything about her, because I had to: the state of her bowels and the foods that disagreed with her and the thoughts that kept her awake nights. And she knew about *me* because there was no escaping me; I was perpetually with her. Toward the end I even slept on a cot in her bedroom. When she died I was awakened merely by the silence —the stopping of a breath that I had lived with continually for five long years. *Solitude* shocked my eyes open. I was alone. I went through her funeral fully composed, and the only thing that disturbed me was the noise of all those brothers and sisters and nieces and nephews that had gathered for the occasion. "Oh, Mildred," they said, "we know how you feel: you can't believe it yet." That was how they explained my not crying. Then Carrie, the sister closest to me, said, "I guess it must be almost a relief to you, her going. None of us would be shocked to hear it." But it wasn't the kind of relief she meant. I wasn't relieved to be free, or to be rid of the work; I was relieved to have my privacy. If you were to shake me awake in the middle of the night and say, "Quick, without thinking: What is the most important thing in the world?" I would say, "Privacy." I *know* that's not right; you don't have to tell me. I know that the true answer is probably love, or understanding, or feeling needed—even for me. But I am telling you what comes to mind first, and that's privacy. Sitting alone in a room reading a book, with no one to interrupt me. That is all I ever consciously wanted out of life.

When I first came here, immediately after Mother died, I announced my requirements from the doorstep. "I see you let rooms," I said. "I'd like one that's cheap and quiet. No noise, no people in large numbers. Can you provide that?" At the time, I had no way of knowing that everything I said was unnecessary. Jeremy Pauling and his mother were more private than I had ever thought it possible to be. That front door might as well have had a curtain of cobwebs across it, like the Sleeping Beauty's palace gate, with the two of them inside trying to make as little noise as possible and the rest of the world outside—some large cold frightening force waiting to pounce, something certain to win, superior to them in every way. Mrs. Pauling, going to the grocery store, wore several layers of clothing no matter how hot the weather was, as if she wished for armor. She stopped outside the house and looked all around her with a timid blue startled gaze, checking on what the enemy had in mind for her. She returned pushing a wire tote cart so packed with non-perishables that it seemed she was expecting a siege, and she would scurry inside with them and line them up in rows in her cupboards and then stand back to stare at them a long time, moving her lips as if counting. After one of those trips she might not go to the store again for weeks— or anywhere else, except church occasionally. She and Jeremy stayed inside and drank hot cocoa. Was there any other door in the world so suitable for me to knock upon? Originally I was going to live here only a few months, until I found a job and had saved the money for an apartment. Then I could be *truly* alone. But the years passed and I just never got around to it, and now I suppose that I never will. I like it here. If you want my opinion, our whole society would be better off living in boarding houses. I mean even families, even married couples. Everyone should have his single room with a door that locks, and then a larger room downstairs where people can mingle or not as they please. For I do like *some* people. I'm no hermit. I like to watch Jeremy's and Mary's children growing up, and the medical students turning into doctors, and Mr. Somerset shuffling through his pension. For such a good life, isn't it fair that I should have to pay some price? The price is silence. Keeping silent when I am moved to speak, staying out of other people's affairs, holding back my advice, giving them the privacy I have asked for myself. Often I wonder if I am making a mistake. I think: Am I missing something? Have I forfeited too much? Is there a time when people I love might not *want* to be left alone? But I resist; I climb the stairs to my room. I turn the key in the lock. One sad thing about this world is that the acts that take the most out of you are usually the ones that other people will never know about.

Mary stayed in the hospital five days, and believe me those were five mighty long days. At home the disorder grew worse, and the children got cranky and the house didn't feel right any more. Daytimes Jeremy pottered around looking helpless; nights he worked in his studio till nearly dawn, and came to breakfast so tired and pale he could hardly speak. He never did go to the hospital. *I* went. I went every afternoon and every evening and watched Mary cry. Oh, I don't mean that's all she did. She had her cheerful moments, particularly when she'd just been with the baby. She made friends with the mothers in her ward, she received other visitors (Buddy, Buddy's girlfriend, a few of the women in the park once word seeped out), and she wrote little notes for me to take home to the children. But at least once on every visit she would break down and cry. "Oh, why can't I just go home to him?" she said once, and then, "Do you think I shouldn't have had this baby?" One evening she was telling me why she'd wanted such a big family. "I was an only child," she said (the first mention she had ever made to me of any kind of past), "and I always promised myself I would have at least a dozen children when I grew up. Well, I'm keeping my promise, aren't I?" Then her eyes glazed over with tears. I wasn't at all prepared, right then. "But sometimes," she said, "I feel that every new baby is another rope, tying me down like a tent. I don't have the option to *leave* any more. I'm forced to depend on him. He's not dependable."

"Hush, now, my goodness," I said.

"I love him more than I ever loved anyone, do you believe me? But sometimes I start falling in love with my doctor or even the children's doctor, they're both so sure of what they're doing. Even the furnace man, who knows exactly where the leak is, or the man who delivers my groceries. He whistles cheerful songs and slams that big box of groceries on my kitchen table."

"You're just upset," I said.

I went home upset myself, and lay awake hoping that she would forget she had ever told me such things.

In the beginning, when they were first married, she asked so much of him. It was plain that she didn't realize he was different from anybody else. "Come with me to pick out curtains," I heard her say once. And another time, "Why don't we ever go to movies, Jeremy?" Of course none of us had discussed the subject with her. Julia Jarrett always believed that for Mary's sake he would change, and you might say that in a sense he did. He does go out more now. Why, presumably he had to go off this block for his wedding, and then there were those trips to the hospital and three years ago he went to Darcy's school to see her play a flower in Red Riding Hood's forest. (She gave Red Riding Hood a warning in a silvery little voice—I was there. "Be careful, little girl, remember what your mother told you." Jeremy walked seven blocks to hear that and applauded all alone the minute she said her line, which naturally made Darcy furious. But I admired him for that. There are other kinds of heroes than the ones who swim through burning oil.) But no, he has never gone to Hecht's to pick out curtains. He has never taken Mary to a movie. How does she explain that to herself? When did she put two and two together and realize that he never would? I really have no idea. All I can say is that bit by bit, it seemed she stopped asking him. It seemed she grew quieter, older, stronger. There was something more loving in the way she treated him. Then I heard her talking with Buddy, back before she knew us well. He was telling her about a play that she and Jeremy shouldn't miss. "Oh," she said, "Jeremy has nearly stopped going to plays. His eyes have been bothering him." And I knew the pieces had finally fallen into place for her, she had stopped expecting him to be like other people. Still I worried. I realized, of course, that it was none of my business. Yet I was so anxious for Jeremy, so quick to imagine him in all possible scenes of failure with her. During the first few weeks of their marriage I sent her silent, invisible messages: If you are unkind it will be a *sin*, the worst you've ever committed. Don't forget that this is a very special man you are dealing with. A genius. Not some run-of-the-mill insurance salesman. It wasn't that I disliked her, you see; I was fond of her even that far back. But in some ways Mary is an everyday kind of woman, and this marriage was as odd for her, as distant from her main road, as it was for Jeremy. Look at the telephone pad in the hall! Her doodles are minute line drawings of steam irons and tricycles and Mixmasters. She adds to their incomes by sending household hints to ladies' magazines. Is it any wonder I worried? All for nothing, as it turned out. She remained her serene and contented self, while Jeremy seemed ready to burst out of his skin with pride and happiness. I remember one morning she wore a new dress to breakfast, practically the only one I have ever seen her in. She looked just beautiful. I said, "My, that's attractive. Isn't it, Jeremy?" But Jeremy was in that mood he gets when he is about to start a new piece —a thousand miles away. He gave her a wide, blank smile and said nothing. I said, "Jeremy? Doesn't Mary look pretty?" Because now it seemed he *had* to answer, for Mary's sake. Jeremy said, "What?" He stood up and left. Now, a thing like that can seem important to some women. But when I looked over at Mary I saw that she was laughing, and she said, "Don't worry, he loves it. I know because last week he cut a patch from inside the hem and used it for one of his pieces. He thought I wouldn't notice."

I was so relieved when I heard that. I thought, "Well, at least she understands him." I never dreamed she would grow to be *too* understanding.

On Thursday evening Brian came by for Jeremy's new batch of work. Brian's visits are quite an event in this household. He himself is so impressive, in the first place—a handsome kind-faced man with a square-cut beard—and then too it is always the first glimpse we have of what Jeremy has been up to lately. The things they brought down that night were the best I'd yet seen. It's strange how over the years Jeremy's pieces have grown up. I mean physically, literally. They have doubled in size, and they are so deeply textured that they are almost sculptures. Ordinary objects are crowded into them—Dixie cups and bus tickets and his children's plaid shoelaces, still recognizable—and his subjects are ordinary too, the smallest and most unnoticed scenes on earth. I found a man with a rake, a woman ironing a shirt, a child strapping on a roller skate. Their features were gone and they were bare of detail; they were layered over with the Dixie cups and the bus tickets. They made me sad.

Have you ever seen a television show that ends with stills from the scenes you have just finished watching? Music plays and the titles roll over them. The effect is of distance. Moments that you just witnessed are suspended forever while you yourself recede from them with every breath you take. The moments grow smaller, and yet clearer. You see some sorrow in them you had never before suspected. Now, does it make any sense when I say that Jeremy's pieces affect me in the same way? This man with the rake, slightly stooped and motionless, reminded me that life is nothing *but* motion and passes too swiftly for us to observe with the naked eye. At least, for me to observe. Jeremy has no trouble whatsoever. He sees from a distance at all times, without trying, even trying not to. It is his condition. He *lives* at a distance. He makes pictures the way other men make maps—setting down the few fixed points that he knows, hoping they will guide him as he goes floating through this unfamiliar planet. He keeps his eyes on the horizon while his hands work blind. Am I the only one who sees this? Surely Brian never has. Brian merely tapped the pictures with his knuckles and nodded, chewing his pipe. "Good work, good work," he said. Then he went on to talk about a boat he had bought. "In the spring I'm going to try a real trip on her," he said. "I'm going to do it old style. I'll eat what I catch, I'll sail by celestial navigation." Jeremy listened with his eyes wide, his expression awed and admiring. He stood beside his very best piece and forgot it utterly. Oh, Jeremy, I wanted to tell him, you too sail by celestial navigation and it is far more celestial than Brian's.

But, of course, I didn't say it out loud.

On Friday I went to visit Mary and she said they were letting her come home Saturday. She didn't seem as happy as you'd expect. "Why, that's wonderful!" I said. "I have Saturday off this week. I'll drive everybody over at ten o'clock or so, shall I?"

"Oh well," Mary said, "this time I think you might just come by yourself if you don't mind."

"What, alone?"

"It's simpler that way."

"Who asked it to be *simple?*" I said.

Ordinarily I wouldn't have spoken out like that, but I could tell this new arrangement wasn't really what she wanted. She was twining a wisp of hair very slowly around her fingers and not meeting my eyes when she spoke. She looked limp and uncombed. "Look," I told her. "There's no law that says you can't change your mind. Call him up. Tell him you want him to come for you after all."

"I never told him I *didn't* want him to come," she said.

"Then what's all this about?"

"I've been waiting for him to offer, but he hasn't."

"You know it would be hard for him to offer."

"I mean that he won't even speak to me on the phone."

"He won't?" I said. I hadn't realized that.

"When I telephone, one of the children always answers, and if I ask to speak to him they go off to call him and come back and say he's in the middle of changing Hannah or frying eggs or something. He's angry."

Jeremy angry?

"No, he's hurt, Mary," I said.

"Well, I'm hurt too. I've been waiting all this time, thinking surely he would give in and call me. I lie here just for hours. Don't you think I would say yes like a shot if he called and asked to visit me and take me home?"

"Of course. Yes, I know. But *you* could call, Mary."

"I spend my life calling!" Mary said. She sat up in bed, and a few of the other women in the ward turned to stare. "It's always me," she said more quietly. "Never him. I make the first move every time. I'm tired."

"Yes, now, I know," I said, trying to hush her. And after that she did grow more reasonable. For the rest of the hour we talked about ordinary things. But when finally I rose to go, when I turned in the doorway to say goodbye, the last thing I saw was Mary sitting with her hands folded and her eyes lowered and her face sad and wistful. She reminded me of a girl waiting for an invitation to dance. Even her lace-trimmed nightgown had a pathetic look, like a ball dress carefully ironed by some loving mother who had imagined her daughter waltzing all evening, and never dreamed it could be otherwise.

For bringing home a new baby there is a ritual in this house, and I am part of it. I go along in the taxi, to stay with the children while Jeremy is inside the hospital. We are all packed into the back seat, and up front the driver is grumbling over the noise and the crowding and the cracker crumbs. While we wait I take the children to a concrete space beneath Mary's window. I point it out to them. "See? There it is—the one with the shade pulled all the way up." "Where? Where?" When all the children have located it, they start shouting. "Mama!" they call—even the littlest one. It is against our rules for Mary to be watching for us. She must stay out of sight, and wait to hear their voices. Then she comes to the window. Dressed, finally, all set to go. First she waves and blows kisses, then she play-acts her impatience to come down. She pounds silently on the windowpane, she sets her fist against her forehead. The children laugh, too shrilly. They sound a little hysterical. It occurs to me that for the smallest ones, this may be exactly how they have imagined her absence: they suspect she is being kept prisoner somewhere, forced to leave them in the fumbling care of their father. For she would never desert them of her own free *will*, would she? Then another face appears beside hers—Jeremy's, round and blurred. Mary flings up her hands in joy, showing that the rescue squad has at last arrived. She turns and throws her arms around his neck. The two of them are framed in the window like heroes at the end of a romantic movie—wrapped together, touched with sunlight. We go back to the taxi. This will be our longest wait, while they collect the new baby and settle the bill. To pass the time we play "I Spy," and we become so absorbed that Darcy is the only one to see her parents emerging. "Ta-taaa!" she says, like a trumpet. We look up to find them coming across the driveway, flushed and smiling. Mary carries the overnight case. She has read somewhere that if it is the father who introduces the new baby there will be less jealousy, and although I can't see what earthly difference it makes she has given the baby to Jeremy. He holds it stiff-armed, at a distance, with his entire self concentrating on getting his prize safely to the car. He reminds me of little Pippi carrying a very full glass of water. "Here we are!" Mary says. Then the taxi is a flurry of hugs and kisses, and the baby is passed from one grimy set of hands to another. Even the taxi driver must have a turn; no one will be satisfied until he does. "Well now," he says. "Yes sir. What do you know." He gives it back, grins and shakes his head, and starts the motor. The ceremony is over. All requirements have been met. The rules are stashed in the back of our minds until two years from now.

I thought we would be collecting new babies that way forever. I didn't realize the ritual could be abandoned so easily.

Early Saturday I went to the dimestore and chose a small toy for Mary to bring each of the children. Usually she tells me exactly what they have been wanting, but this time she didn't seem to know. "Oh, anything," she said. "You probably have better ideas than I do." I entered the dimestore feeling uncertain—I had no idea at all—but then I began to enjoy myself. I had been watching those children more closely than I suspected. I knew that Darcy would like something she could do with her hands—an embroidery set—and that Abbie had a yen for costume jewelry. The jewelry on the toy counter was not very satisfying. All I saw were pop-it beads and plastic bangles. But then in the grown-ups' section I found a wealth of glitterly rhinestones and great multicolored teardrop earrings. They were more expensive, but I could always chip in a little money of my own. I felt as proud of myself as if I had discovered them in a pirates' chest. Who else would think of looking here for a child's gift? I chose green glass earrings shaped like peacock tails and purple ones like huge bunches of grapes. I held one of each to my ear and looked in the mirror that sat on the countertop. Then I froze, with jewels dangling ridiculously below my great long earlobes.

For there I was, against a background of crêpe-paper turkeys and pilgrim-shaped candles and sheaves of plastic Indian corn: my bony face all lit up and feverish and my pupils enormous and my fingers a little shaky, clutching those earrings. Like some tacky trite cartoon: old maid preparing for the arrival of the troops, or waiting for the meter man. Only it wasn't any soldier or meter man that had lit my eyes so; it was the prospect of what I was going to do today. Choose the children's surprises on my own, check Mary out of the hospital, carry that new baby home the way Jeremy used to do. Why, I could *see* myself carrying him! It was as if, without realizing it, I had spent all of the night before imagining every detail! I saw myself climbing the front steps holding the baby exactly right (much better than Jeremy would have, much more securely). I saw the children crowding around me, all anxious to share my treasure. I saw myself dispensing gifts. "Open that bag, will you, Darcy? See what you find. There are surprises there for all of you, I chose them myself." They would scatter brown paper bags and cash register slips, all excited over gifts I had selected that Mary would never have thought of. Mary faded. Jeremy faded. I was left alone with that baby wrapped in powder blue and that circle of little faces.

I picked three toys in haste and went directly home. In the front hall I found Pippi, wearing frayed underpants and nothing else. She was shivering. Tears had made little gray streamers down her cheeks. "Miss Vinton, Abbie *hit* me," she said. I gave her a pat on the head and walked on by. I went straight to the kitchen, where I found Jeremy trying to get Hannah to eat her egg. That was what he had been doing when I left, an hour ago. Hannah was in her high chair with her lips clamped together, and Jeremy was saying, "Pléase, Hannah. Won't you consider taking another bite?"

"Jeremy, here are some things I'd like you to give Mary," I told him. I set my shopping bag on a chair. Jeremy looked up quickly. "Me?" he said.

"I won't be going to the hospital, but I'll be happy to stay with the children."

Jeremy set the spoonful of egg down and opened the bag, as if he expected to find some answer inside it. "E-Z Do Embroidery Set," he said.

"Hush, it's supposed to be a surprise."

"I don't quite see," he told me. "Have I—is there something the matter, Miss Vinton?"

"Nothing's the matter."

"I had thought perhaps Mary wanted *you* to bring her home."

"No, I think she would prefer you to do it."

He started smiling. He nodded several times and his face grew pink. "Oh, well, then, certainly," he said. "Thank you, Miss Vinton! I certainly do—"

"Any time," I said. "Here, give me that," and I reached for Hannah's bowl of egg. "Now you'd better hurry. She was due to be released at ten and it's already five of."

"Oh yes," Jeremy said. He rose and held out his

hand. For a moment I couldn't think why, but then I saw that he was beaming at me and I set the bowl on the table and shook his hand. "It's certainly—it's just wonderful of you to watch the children this way," he said. "I really don't know how to—"

"Oh shoot. Run along, now."

He picked up the bag of gifts, which I had forgotten all about, and left the kitchen. I heard him in the hallway, scattering hangers and stumbling over rubber boots in the coat closet. A minute later I heard the front door slam. "Where's he going?" Darcy said, coming into the kitchen. "I thought you were off getting Mom."

"Jeremy's doing that," I told her.

"He is? Then can't we all go too?"

"Not this time."

"But Miss Vinton! We always *used* to!"

"That's no reason to keep on doing a thing, is it?" I said.

I lifted Hannah out of her high chair and then I went into the parlor, to the front bay window. The lace curtains hid me. I watched Jeremy for as long as he stood waiting there—a radiant, dumpy man holding a paper bag. He leaned forward from time to time and looked for a taxi, first in one direction and then the other (although we live on a one-way street). He kept shifting the bag higher on his stomach. He wore no coat or jacket, nothing but his gray tweed golf cap and that sleazy sweater he had been in all week, but I held back from rushing out to him with an armload of wraps.

Then a taxi stopped for him, but instead of getting in immediately, Jeremy turned and looked back at the house. His face was so open, so happy and hopeful. I saw him take in a breath, maybe planning to call out something. Yet I know that he couldn't see me. I stayed far back in the room. Finally he climbed into the taxi, and I sat down on the windowseat and reached for Pippi. "*You* think she hit just a little," Pippi said. "But she hit me hard, smack in the stomach. She really hurt." "I know, I know," I said, barely listening. I put her on my lap and set my face against her head. Her hair had a clean sharp smell. I took a breath of it and felt it fill me like an ache, and I closed my eyes and held on to her for as long as she would allow.

Darcy made a poster: WELCOME EDWARD. We Scotch-taped it to the window. The four girls sat beneath, freshly dressed and combed, making four steamy o's on the glass. Then Abbie said, "Here they are! Here they come!" The taxi pulled up, the door opened, out stepped Mary. After her came Jeremy, with the baby in his arms. "See, how little?" I said, but I was talking to an empty room. The children were already fighting their way to the door. "*I* open it, because I'm the oldest," Darcy said, but Abbie said, "You *always* get to do things!" "Hush!" I called. They paid me no attention. I stood alone at the window and smiled down at Jeremy and Mary, who came up the walk side by side, laughing, surrounded by a sea of bobbing heads and small hands waving in celebration.

6

Spring, 1971: Jeremy

"I have something to tell you," Mary said. "Jeremy? Are you listening?"

He wasn't. He was making a statue. He stood before a circle of tin children, waist-high; he wrung his hands. Like a man in a well, he heard Mary's voice only dimly. It was necessary to find red. Where was the right red? But then he detected some urgency in what she said, something different from the Muzak of her discussions of washing machines, report cards, DPT shots. "What?" he said. He struggled up from under layers and layers of thought. There was a dry feeling at the back of his throat, as if he had been buried in cotton. He fixed his eyes on Mary but saw, instead, the exact shade of red he needed—very bright, a little fuzzy. It seemed familiar. He turned away from her and dumped out a carton of scraps. Nothing there. He went across the room nearly at a run, bent-kneed. He flung open shelves and pulled out drawers and turned over a wastebasket. There was a red lace heart and a red geometric design from a magazine and a piece of red construction paper that smelled like the inside of his grammar school forty years ago. He held the paper to his nose and closed his eyes and took a deep breath. Now children's voices came singing through his head, over all those decades:

> She'll be wearing red pajamas when she comes,
> (Scratch, scratch)
> She'll be wearing . . .

Red flannel. He saw it clearly now. He even saw the microscopic dots of lint left from laundering. He plowed through the wastepaper and out of the door, across the hall to the girls' room. "Jeremy?" said Mary. "What are you doing? You said you wouldn't use their things any more, you promised!"

"I'll get them new ones," Jeremy said.

"New what? What are you looking for? You *always* say that, Jeremy."

He paused in the middle of a drawer, up to his elbows in pink and white. "Where are their red pajamas?" he asked.

"What red pajamas?"

"Don't the children wear red pajamas any more?"

"*They* never had any red pajamas."

He straightened up from the drawer and went over to the closet. Scattered across the floor were dirty socks, blouses, stuffed animals—you would think that somewhere in here would be a tiny piece of red flannel. He opened the closet door and scanned a rack of dresses all different sizes and colors. "I have something I want to tell you," Mary said.

Like a string pulling him, some strong piece of twine pulling him away from the picture in his head. Even before he turned to her the red flannel had dissolved and the circle of children had stopped spinning, dropped their hands, and crumbled away. He opened his mouth to protest but saw, suddenly, how the curve of her cheek fitted so exactly to the curve of Rachel's head—the latest baby, nestled into her mother's neck like a piece in a jigsaw puzzle. Mary's hair had come undone and was tumbling down her back, lit by the sun in the window. The three faint lines beginning at the corner of each eye were lit as well, radiating as precisely as a cat's whiskers, giving her a look of constant, gentle puzzlement. "What is it, Mary?" he asked.

"Are you really listening to me?"

"Yes, yes."

But up came the sound of feet, pounding on the stairs. An interruption to the interruption. Was this how life progressed? If he traced his way back through the chain of interruptions, looking for the first act someone had tugged him from, wouldn't he find himself ten years in the past? In came Pippi, out of breath. "Mom? Where's Mom?"

"Why, here she is," said Jeremy.

"Guess what, Mom?"

Mary's face took on that change that always happened when her children spoke. She bent her head, her eyes grew instantly opaque with concentration and every muscle seemed tensed to listen. "Some men are bringing in a refrigerator," Pippi told her.

"A refrigerator?"

"They say Jeremy won it in a contest."

Mary raised her head and looked at him. "You should have let me know," she said.

"But I—how could I? This is the first I've heard of it."

"They say he got a letter," said Pippi.

"Oh, Jeremy. Are you not opening letters again?"

"Why, I *thought* I was. I can't imagine what—"

"They say you have to come down, Mom," Pippi said.

"All right, I'm coming."

She descended the steps without hurry, unruffled as ever, behind Pippi's clattering shoes. Rachel's face bobbed over her shoulder. Jeremy followed, wiping his hands on his trousers. He felt pulled in too many directions. Pieces of the statue still crowded his mind along with Mary's listening face, the thunder of furniture moving downstairs, the news she had never managed to tell him. "Um, Mary," he said, "can't they take it back again? This house is getting so full. We surely don't *need* another refrigerator."

"Oh, that's all right, Jeremy, we'll put it in the basement."

"We put the last one in the basement."

"Well? There's still room. You know how much food this family eats."

"But it feels so cluttered," Jeremy said. "Mary, there are so many *things* in this house. I just feel so—"

They arrived in the downstairs hallway. Two men in leather jackets were rolling an enormous pink refrigerator along a path they had cleared through the parlor, steering their way between rocking chairs and tricycles and hordes of children. "Look!" said Mary. "It's a side-by-side refrigerator-freezer, the kind I've always wanted."

"Kitchen?" said one of the men.

"No—well, yes, why not. Then we'll send the old one down to the basement. Could you move the old one first?"

"Look, we ain't *moving* men."

"I'll pay you," Mary said.

"Five dollars is what we would ask for it."

"Jeremy?"

Everyone looked at him. He felt embarrassed, as if he were there under false pretences. He wasn't the one who handled the money. "Well, actually," he said, "I don't believe we want this item."

"Jeremy!"

"You should've told the contest people that," one man said. "All we do is deliver them, like they ask us to."

"It appears I must have mislaid the letter. Actually I—we *have* two refrigerators."

"What you go and enter the contest for, then?"

"I thought I might win money," Jeremy said.

"Jeremy, you know we can use another refrigerator," Mary told him. "Especially for this summer, when watermelons come in. Leave the gentlemen alone, Hannah. And you know the boarders need shelves of their own, they don't want to get—"

"Do we move it or don't we, lady?"

"Yes!" said the children, and jumped up and down, and clapped, and made Jeremy's head ache. Mary said, "Of course you do. Empty the old one, will you, children? Everybody help; just put the food on the counter." She herded them into the kitchen and Jeremy followed. He would feel awkward left alone with the delivery men. He watched from the doorway while children stacked endless cartons of milk on the drainboard, relayed heads of lettuce to the table, tossed an arc of oranges across the room. "Quite a family you got there," a delivery man said behind him. Jeremy smiled too widely and ducked his head.

Did anyone guess how his children baffled him? He didn't understand them. He had trouble talking to them. All he could do was watch: drink them in with such speechless, open-mouthed amazement that he was accused of being off in a daze. Mary watched too, but for different reasons. She was checking for danger and germs and mischief; she was their armed guard. What Jeremy was doing was committing them to memory, preparing for some moment far in the future when he could sit down alone and finally figure them out. He knew the exact curl of Abbie's eyes when she laughed, the way Hannah rubbed the down on her upper lip when she sucked her thumb, the dimples like parentheses in Rachel's cheeks. It seemed to him that all of his children were miniature Marys. He could find no physical resemblance to himself. He thought that was natural, for Mary's pregnancies appeared to be entirely her own undertakings. It was she who discovered and announced them, took her calcium tablets, disappeared behind those closed swinging doors at the hospital to give birth. But then he looked at Darcy—still blond and blue-eyed, nearly as tall as her mother now but with someone else's frail bones. *Her* father had not been eclipsed. Her father's genes must have been as recessive as Jeremy's, all pale and slight; yet they had won out. How come? He turned a puzzled stare on his own children, brown-headed and dark-eyed. He watched his son Edward, who at two and a half wore faded Levis dangling below the pot of his stomach and little cowboy boots. He had not known they made boots as small as that. He had never had boots when *he* was a boy; and if he had he would not have known how to walk in them with that jaunty swagger or how to hook his thumbs through the belt loops of his Levi's. Where had Edward learned? Where had *all* of them learned to march so fearlessly across the teeming streets, to brave their way through the city schools, and shout and cheer and throw oranges without a trace of self-consciousness?

Sometimes he said, "Don't you think we should see to their last names?"

"They *have* last names," said Mary. "Yours. It's on their birth certificates."

"Yes, but if anyone were to check or anything. If they asked for proof."

"Why should they do that?"

"Yes, well."

He had the feeling that the children were some new type of boarder, just louder and more troublesome. They were not entirely of this house, they were visitors from the outside world. When he was most deeply absorbed in his work, children came seeping up the stairs like the rising waters of a flood, and their noise— strange clangs and hoots and the unbearable pitch of their quarrels—would soak into him slowly, at first unnoticed, then so exasperating that he would fling down his scissors and throw open the door and stand there trembling. "Why are you doing this to me?" he would ask. "Why must you make this noise? Why do you keep, why do you—" Their faces would all be turned up to him. There was something pathetic and yet irritating about their fallen socks, their patched jeans, the damp gray underpants drooping beneath some little one's dress. They were utterly silent. Silence brought Mary more quickly than any shriek could. She was there in an instant, running up the stairs already asking, "What is it? What's happened?"

"Mary, I was just trying to do some work here—"

"Yes, all right. Come on, children, Jeremy's working."

"It's just that they keep making so much noise, you see."

"You can play in the kitchen," Mary told them. "I know what. Shall we make cookies?"

There was no way to win. He felt depressed at the way she herded them down the stairs, shielding them from him with her back; he felt lonely and guilty now that the third floor was silent again. How could he have scolded them like that? He knew them so little, couldn't he have let them stay a while? He looked around the hall and saw the traces they had left behind —one roller skate, a homemade doll, a chalky handprint on the newel post. At his feet was a paper covered

with purple writing: HANNAH 4 YR OLD I AM
HANNAH. A fire engine with a key in its back wound
itself down, its little red light blinking more and more
slowly and the sound of its engine growing weaker.

Now a child tossed him an orange and he caught it by
accident, astonishing himself so much that he dropped
it again. He fell in with a parade that followed the old
refrigerator down to the basement, which was dark and
dank and smelled of mildew. The basement walls were
lined with case lots of Mary's household goods. There
was an entire cabinet of sneakers, waiting to be grown
into. Another of toilet paper. A barrel of detergent big
enough to hold two children. Was this necessary? He
felt that she was pointing something out to him: her
role as supplier, feeder, caretaker. "See how I give?
And how I keep on giving—these are my reserves. I
will always have more, you don't even have to ask. I
will be waiting with a new shirt for you the minute the
elbows wear through in the old one." A delivery man
knocked over a stack of flowerpots, bought on sale in
preparation for spring. Somebody stepped on a cat.
"Damn it all," said the other man, "will you please get
those kids of yours *out* of here? Will you get them out?
They ain't giving us room to step."

The children vanished, but their giggles lurked in
all the corners. The men went upstairs to bring in the
new refrigerator and Mary followed, giving instructions.
Jeremy came last. He felt old and tired. By the time he
reached the kitchen, puffing and wiping his forehead,
the refrigerator was already moving into place. It
stuck out too far into the middle of the room and it
blocked four inches of doorway. "Isn't it too big?" said
Jeremy. "Mary, I feel so—it seems so *crowded* here."

But Mary said, "You'll get used to it."

Then she turned and smiled, and in front of everyone she threw her arms around him and said, "Oh,
Jeremy, *don't* be a grump. Isn't it nice that you keep
winning us things? Aren't you glad you're so lucky?"

With people watching he couldn't hug her back,
but he smiled so widely that it seemed his face was
melting.

He and Mary went to the gallery to see his one-man show—just the two of them, in Miss Vinton's car. Mary drove. She wore a hat, also Miss Vinton's, the first Jeremy had ever seen her in. Jeremy wore his golf cap. He was feeling a little sick. He held tight to the edge of the seat every time they turned a corner, and he kept swallowing. "How are you, Jeremy?" Mary said.

"Oh, fine, fine."

"It isn't far now."

She had been to the gallery before. She had been visiting it for years, checking on how his pieces were arranged every time Brian took in a new batch. But Jeremy had never set foot in it, and only the importance of this occasion—an entire show devoted only to him, already bringing in more money and comment than he had ever imagined—made it impossible for him to refuse to go. Not that he hadn't tried. "I've seen it," he said. "It's my own work. What's the use of looking again?" But they left him no escape. Mary and Brian and the others had set things up among them. Miss Vinton lent her car; the boarder Olivia babysat. Mary said, "We'll go on a weekday when the place is not packed," and Brian said, "No one will know you, Jeremy. And you might even learn something! It's been years since you last saw some of your pieces." That was the argument that won Jeremy over. He thought of all the work he had produced—objects he had looked at for so long that he couldn't see them anymore, things that had worn him out and sickened him until he handed them to Brian merely to get rid of them, to free himself to go on to something new. What would they look like now?

So here he was, in Miss Vinton's dusty-smelling car on this clear cold afternoon in April, gazing around him at what appeared to be some sort of bomb damage in the middle of Baltimore. Whole blocks were leveled; nothing but rubble remained. Beyond were caved-in tenements showing yellowed wallpaper, tangles of pipe, crumbled understructures of something like chicken wire. "Mary? What seems to be the trouble here?" Jeremy asked. Mary only gave the scene a glance. "Oh, they're rebuilding," she said, and drove on. Jeremy shrank back further in his corner of the car.

He and she looked at different things. They might have been taking two separate rides. *"There's* an interesting place," she said. "It's a shop for hippies; they sell tie-dyed denim that would make wonderful curtains for the children's rooms." And later, "That's a new office building without any windows, but they say you don't notice that once you're inside." Sometimes she explained things to him that he had known for years. Did she imagine he was deaf and blind? "Look, there's a girl with a bush. Isn't it amazing? They call it 'natural.'" He had been seeing girls with bushes for years, in magazines and TV commercials and on the sidewalk before the bay window. He had probably seen more from that window than Mary saw on all her trips to stores and schools and obstetricians. He had observed the world steadily swelling and involuting, developing new twists and whorls and clusters like some complicated cell mass—first inch by inch, then faster, so that now it seemed that after the briefest holing-up in his studio he could come back to find everything changed: people stranger, cars more vicious-looking, even the quality of light altered in some indefinable way. But he had kept up with things. He knew what was going on in the world. Mary underestimated him.

The gallery was a narrow white building with an awning that extended across the sidewalk. It sat on a quiet street among other buildings very much like it, out of sight of the bomb damage. "Well, at least it's not too big," Jeremy said, but as he stood on the sidewalk waiting for Mary to put a coin in the parking meter he had the feeling that this gallery out-classed him somehow. Certainly, if he had been a mere passerby, he would have been intimidated by that great glassy door with its gold grillwork. He would never have gone in on his own. "Mary," he said, "are you sure that this is a proper time for us to come?"

"I told you, Jeremy. People are never here on weekdays."

"Why do they keep it open, then?"

She didn't seem to have an answer for that.

In the foyer, lit by a yellow light, was a piece that Jeremy remembered from three or four years ago: an old man going through a wire trashbasket. The man himself was made of dull brown wrapping paper, crushed and reflattened. The basket was a network of all the glittery things he had been able to lay his hands on—small skewers for trussing poultry, a knitting needle, a child's gilt barrette, a pair of Abbie's school scissors with "Lefty" on the blade. Within the basket was a cluster of bright colors formed from postage stamps and cigarette packs and an old bandanna handkerchief that Mr. Somerset had left lying on the couch one day. "Haven't they done it nicely?" Mary asked him. "I told Brian, it's the perfect keynote for the show. I'm glad they set it up at the beginning this way."

"Yes, yes," said Jeremy. But he was uncomfortable. He had never seen his work in such a setting before, among thick red carpets and hushed sounds and golden light. From some hiding place in the back of his mind a picture leapt forth of the model for this piece—an old man he had seen from the bay window, rummaging in the trashbasket one cold November day. He remembered the dry grayness of the man's skin, nothing like this warm brown wrapping paper, and the claw-like fingers and silently moving lips. None of it was caught in his piece. He sighed. "Jeremy?" Mary said. "Aren't you happy with it?"

"Oh, yes," he said, and moved on.

Past the hallway, behind the wall where the old man was displayed, stretched a larger room flooded with light and carpeted also in soft deep red. Five or six people were moving around it, stopping before each piece. He noticed the people before anything else. All but one were women, and they were whispering together about his work. *His.* He felt like rushing up and flinging his arms out, shielding what he had made. Two fat ladies stood in front of one of his old collages, one that was still two-dimensional; a girl made her way too quickly down a row of his statues. His smallest statue, the first he had ever made, sat on a wooden column: a woman hanging out washing. A curve of tin among stiff white billows that he had formed by spraying canvas with clear plastic. He remembered conceiving the idea and then wondering how he could set it in a frame. It had taken him weeks to think of making it a statue. He had worked fearfully; he had felt presumptuous, using up so much vertical space. But now a tag beside it read "From the Collection of Mrs. Herbert Lee Cooke"—one of the richest women in Baltimore. She had bought the statue the first day it was shown. And there were tags or "Sold" stickers beside most of the other pieces as well—each statue taller and more solid than the one before it. He wandered among them, dazed, holding his golf cap and chewing the tip of his index finger. He had never realized that he had produced quite this many things. Why, some people might consider him an actual artist, by profession. Was that possible? He pictured all those hours spent alone in his room, patiently fitting together tiny scraps, feverishly hunting up the proper textures, pounding in a row of thumbtacks until the back of his neck ached—all that drudgery. It wasn't the way he pictured the life of an artist.

Brian appeared beside him and set a hand on Jeremy's shoulder. "Hi," he said. He wore a double-breasted suit that made him appear untrustworthy. Jeremy was used to seeing him in sweaters and corduroy trousers. His beard was trimmed too neatly. "Well, Jeremy," he said. "What do you think of your show?"

All the visitors looked up, their faces startled and avid. Brian's voice had carried everywhere. "We've got them set up well, wouldn't you say?" he asked. He smelled of some bitter spicy aftershave. He smiled not at Jeremy but at one of the statues, ignoring the visitors as if it were accidental that they had overheard.

Jeremy freed himself from Brian's arm. "You said, but you said—you told me there wouldn't be people here."

"Well, Jeremy, it *is* relatively—"

"You broke your word."

"Oh, now—"

"I want to go home, Mary," Jeremy said. He turned to find her and saw, behind her worried face, all the spectators looking pleased. Of course, they seemed to be saying, this is what we expected all along. Brian *told* us. Had he, in fact, told them something? Did Jeremy have some kind of reputation? He pulled his golf cap on with shaky fingers; he turned on his heel, making Mary run to catch up with him. Yet immediately he sensed that he had done something else they expected. There was nothing he could do they would *not* expect. He stumbled across miles of deep treacherous carpet, trapped still in their image of him. His breath came rustily. He flailed one hand behind him and encountered Mary's strong fingers. Then she had caught up with him and was hugging his arm close to her side and helping him through the glass door. "Never you mind," she whispered. "It's all right, Jeremy." Out on the sidewalk she raised her other hand to cup his face and she kissed him on the cheek. "There now," she said. But she only troubled him more. Was it expected of him also that he would stand here being kissed like a child? He wiped away the damp equal-sign left by her lips, and he pulled his coat more tightly around him and trudged off toward the car.

They had no medical student now. Buddy had married and moved to an apartment, and before a successor could be found Mary came home one day with a girl hitch-hiker she had picked up while driving Miss Vinton's car. A hippie named Olivia. Her hair was like spun glass, colorless and straight, long enough to sit on. She was so thin she seemed translucent and she wore jeans studded with silvery stars and a shimmering white trenchcoat. When she held out a hand to Jeremy, her fingers felt like ice. "I found this child thumbing rides," Mary told him. "Can you imagine? Why, you must be no older than Darcy!"

"I'm eighteen," said Olivia.

Mary said, "I don't care, *any* age is too young," and she went off to find the girl some food. Olivia trailed her, the way one of Mary's children might. She had a watery, boneless way of walking. From the dining room, where Jeremy sat with a cup of tea, he could hear her questions: "What is this for? What are you doing now? Is it all right if I have one of these crackers?" Later Mary told him that she had persuaded Olivia to stay in the south front bedroom. "What?" said Jeremy. He mentally placed the house on a map, set down a star for the compass points, found south. "But that's the students' room! We have always had students there!"

"I'm sorry. I didn't know it mattered," Mary said.

"Well, no, of course it doesn't matter. It's just that—"

"I worry so, seeing a child out in the streets that way," Mary said.

It seemed to him that every year she was becoming more motherly. She had six children now and she was six times more motherly than when she had had only one. Was it a quality that grew by such mathematical progressions?

Last month, going to Dowd's grocery store for milk, they had been approached by a teenaged boy asking for money for a meal. "Why, you poor soul!" said Mary. "Haven't you eaten?" It was six in the evening; all her own children had been fed an hour ago. "Wait here," she said. "They sell sandwiches at Dowd's." "Well, money is what I *rather*—" the boy said. "Don't go away," said Mary. "Stay with him, Jeremy." She went alone into the store. The point of her kerchief fluttered behind her, her family-sized handbag swung at her side, her unstockinged legs flashed white in the twilight and her scuffed oxfords beat out a businesslike rhythm. The eternal mother, scandalized, indignant, interfering, setting everyone straight. "Money is what I *rather* have," the boy told Jeremy. Jeremy only nodded and swallowed. He couldn't think of anything to say. Then Mary returned with a sandwich in waxed paper and a cellophane tray of oranges and a carton of milk. "You eat every bit of this, you hear?" she said. "Look," the boy told her, "you didn't have to go to all this trouble. Look, what I could really use is—"

But she had pressed the food into his hands and turned to go into the store again. "Don't gulp it, now," she said. "Not on an empty stomach."

"Well. Thank you, ma'am."

Then he and Jeremy had stood looking at each other, bemused, unsmiling, across the knobs and angles of Mary's gifts.

At night, colors and shapes crowded his mind, elbowed each other aside, quarreled the way his children did: "Let *me* speak! No, let *me* speak!" He traced outlines in the dark with his index finger. He pressed his thumbs against his lids to erase images that disturbed him— cones rising in a tower, the base of one resting on the point of another in a particularly jarring way; yellow and blue appearing together, a combination he could not tolerate. Meanwhile Mary slept soundly beside him, and her breaths were so soft and even that they might have been no more than the sound of his own blood in his ears.

Were women always stronger than men? Mary was stronger, even when she slept. Her sleeping was *proof* that she was stronger. In Jeremy's insomnia there was something fretful and nervous; he felt the presence of thoughts he would rather not look at, nameless fears and dreads. Yet Mary, who could name *exactly* what she feared and whose worries came complete to the last detail—Was Abbie's tonsillectomy really necessary, when anesthesia could backfire and kill you? Should Edward have had a tetanus shot for that cat bite?—lay peacefully on her back with her palms up, her fingers only loosely curled, open to everything. She didn't even believe in God. (Jeremy said he didn't either—how could he, knowing how carelessly objects are tossed off and forgotten by their creators?—but he was haunted by a fear of hell and Mary was not.) Mary was more vulnerable than any man, the deepest pieces of herself were in those children and every day they scattered in sixty different directions and faced a thousand untold perils; yet she sailed through the night without so much as a prayer. There was no way he could ever hope to match her.

He sank back through time until he encountered the faded, powdery face of his mother—a woman who had prayed all day every day, every breath a prayer.

("I don't have to say my prayers at bedtime, Jeremy,
I've been saying them since I got up this morning. I
said them all last night in my sleep. It's you I pray
for.") He saw her pouring tea at his tenth birthday
party, which he and she had celebrated all alone in the
parlor. "Just us would be more fun," she said, and of
course she was right, because his classmates disliked
him and if they spoke to him at all they called him
Germy. *"We* don't need those other children," she said.
She smiled at him over the teapot, with the corners of
her mouth trembling slightly the way they always did,
making her look uncertain of the smile, uncertain of
what she said, uncertain that there was anything less
than God Himself that she might have confidence in.
The smile grew pale and then transparent. The teapot
vanished. He saw her from even longer ago than the
birthday party, some distant point in time when hats
were covered with starched cloth roses and her limp,
watery dress was the height of elegance—the dress that
looked exactly like her, its tracery of flowers so faint
you could almost wonder if she had put it on inside
out. She was taking him to the dentist. She stood in
front of a receptionist whose hair seemed to be coated
with black shoe polish. "I don't care what you
thought," the receptionist said, "the appointment was
for an hour ago and you've missed it. You kept the
doctor waiting. He had to go on to another patient."

"Well, perhaps there was a misunderstanding. Because I couldn't have made it for an hour ago, you see,
Jeremy would still have been in school then. Perhaps
we—"

"Are you questioning my word?"

"Please, oh please—"

In front of all those people—a waiting room full
of watching people on needlepoint chairs. The receptionist bent her head to the letter she was writing, putting an end to the conversation. Her fountain pen dug
angrily into the page and sparks of black ink flew out.
"Come, Jeremy," his mother said finally. Then she gave
a little trembling sigh and took his hand to turn him
around, to lead him out of the room. On the sidewalk
she said, "Don't feel bad, darling, we'll get you another

appointment." She patted his cheek, where a muscle was jumping. "We mustn't waste our lives feeling cross with such people." But it wasn't the receptionist he was angry at; it was his mother. Why had she waited there so foolishly, the center of attention, twisting her ridiculous little taffeta evening bag around and around in her hands? Why had she pleaded that way? He imagined the receptionist leaping up suddenly, overturning her chair behind her and stabbing his mother with that sputtery fountain pen. "Take that, you worm! Die!" His mother would only cower lower, and keep that tentative smile on her face. She would crumble into the floor, ground down to powder by the receptionist's heels, not even raising her arms to protect herself. He felt flooded suddenly with grief and horror and a deep, anguished love. "Jeremy, darling," his mother said, "shall we go home and have a cup of cocoa?" And he said, "All right, Mama," but it hurt to speak, even; he had clenched his teeth so hard that his jaw muscles ached.

That was long ago. It was all in the past. He was through with that.

He turned his pillow to the cooler side, lowering his head again very gently so that he would not wake Mary. He began reconstructing his favorite night game. In this game he possessed a sauntering, slaphappy courage that no one else suspected. He was given to acting on impulse. Driving down a city street one day on an errand (never mind that he didn't know how to drive, and had no car; he would work that out later), he was suddenly taken with the urge to leave town. He would speed along for block after block, at first just toying with the idea and then giving himself over to it as the buoyant feeling of freedom swelled in his chest. All the traffic lights were green and all roads led directly out of Baltimore, without so much as another car to slow him down. The sky was dull and sunless, the best weather for his eyes. He could travel for hours without squinting or straining. He would stop when he got tired. Maybe never. If he ever settled down again it would be in a small, bare, whitewashed cubicle, possibly in a desert. He would change his name—a one-syllable first name, a one-syllable last name. Something crisp. His art would change as well. That would happen automatically. If he changed his name his work would be totally different. He would be childless, wifeless, friendless—all alone, like that silent golden period between his mother's death and Mary's arrival. Only this time, of course, he would know enough to appreciate it. Back then, he hadn't. He had felt then that his life was running out too quickly, and that he should have something more to show for it. Was that what caused *all* major events in the world? He had felt compelled to take desperate steps before it was too late, but now it seemed that life would stretch on forever and grow more tangled and noisy every day. There had been no need for such a plunge.

He had waited for love like a man awaiting salvation. The secret, the hidden key. Was it love that failed Jeremy, or was it Jeremy who failed love? Was there anything to hope for *after* love?

The baby started crying, working up to it with sharp little noises that broke into Jeremy's thoughts. Mary rose from the bed and stumbled over to the crib, maybe still asleep, already murmuring words of comfort. "There now, Rachel. There now, Rachel." She picked the baby up and Jeremy felt the jolt of the mattress as she returned to bed. "It's that tooth, I believe," she said. She spoke without looking at him, taking it for granted that he would be lying awake. She propped her pillow on the headboard, sat back against it and undid the buttons of her nightgown. When Jeremy looked over he found the baby's shadow blended into Mary's, and all that emerged clearly was one moonlit breast. "Where is Edward's old teething ring?" Mary asked him. "I'll have to find it in the morning."

The baby gulped softly. Jeremy laid a hand over his eyes.

"The drugstore has something you can rub on their gums but I don't believe it really works," Mary said.

Once, one of the few times she had ever referred to her life before she met him, she told him that when Darcy was born she had worried about feeding her. "I thought I wouldn't have enough milk," she said. Then she laughed; nursing came as naturally as breathing now, and he had often seen her walking around the house or even cooking with a baby glued to her breast. He tried to imagine her worrying over Darcy. He constructed a scene in which she might worry again—in which she would come to him, on the edge of tears, asking him what he thought was wrong. "Never mind, you're just tired," he would tell her. "You must leave things up to me for a while." He would arrange cushions around her, bring her tea, shepherd the older children to the other end of the house. "Quiet now, leave your mother alone. She needs her rest." He would form around her a nest of love and safety, and later when he tiptoed in to check on her she would ask him, "What would I do without you?" He had been picturing that for years now. He had ordered a book before Abbie was born, a book for prospective fathers; he had read and memorized all the forms of support that he might offer her. Lighten her load, the book told him. Try to help out as much as you can, shoulder all the burdens that distract her, be prepared for unreasonable tears. None of that advice had come in handy. Mary made her *own* nest. She sat beside him now relaxed and warm, and the baby gave soft mmm's of satisfaction on the tail of every swallow.

Then Mary said, "This thing I've been meaning to talk to you about—"

The baby stopped nursing and protested, giving away some tension in Mary. Jeremy opened his eyes. He had been aware all day of this news hanging over his head. He even thought he knew what it was. "You're pregnant," he said.

"What?"

"I thought—"

"You know I can't get pregnant when I'm nursing."

"I was afraid that might not have worked this time," he said.

"You were *afraid?*"

He kept quiet. He didn't know how to take it back.

"Jeremy?" Mary said, but then she let it rest. "Well," she said, "I seem to be divorced, Jeremy."

For a moment he thought she meant divorced from *him,* and his heart gave a lurch. Just for that one little imaginary game he had played? He hadn't *meant* anything by it. But they weren't even married! What was she talking about?

"Guy has divorced me."

He had asked her, once, what her husband's name was. It was the least of what he wanted to know, but he had never dared bring up the *real* questions and he had thought that maybe, having started with his name, she might go on to tell him more. She hadn't. "Guy Tell," she said. "Guy Alan Tell." After that, nothing. Not even chance clues—not even mention of a trip on which her husband, incidentally, had accompanied her, or reports of some adventure in which he happened to be included. That single fact, "Guy Tell," had become embedded in him, and he had layered it over with a thousand attempts at forgetfulness, with a literal squinching shut of his eyes whenever any thought of her husband recurred. Now her saying the name stunned him. It was as if she had suddenly entered into some hidden fantasy of his—named, out loud, a product of his most private imagination. "What?" he said. She seemed to understand that she didn't need to repeat it. She waited, calmly.

"You're divorced?" he said.

He sat up. He noticed how the air waves seemed to shiver, recoiling from a shocking word: divorce. Such a hard, ugly sound. Nothing like this warm-breasted shadow beside him. "Who was—how did you find out?" he said.

"The lawyer wrote me. They got my address from Gloria."

"From—? I don't quite see."

"From his mother."

"Ah," he said. This secret husband had had a mother, then. Also a father, and perhaps a grandmother who knitted him winter scarves. He had friends who called out greetings on the streets, he paid visits to people, he no doubt drove a car and made purchases and worked in some place of employment. He had once lain beside this very same woman, perhaps waiting for her to finish nursing the baby before he reached out for her with absolute, cool confidence. A lump of something like clay, thick and soft, rose up in Jeremy's throat.

"He divorced me on grounds of desertion," Mary said. "That's allowed when he hasn't known my whereabouts for so long."

"Well—" said Jeremy. He coughed. "I mean— how did *she* know your whereabouts? His mother."

"Oh, that's just lately. I wrote her a letter."

"You did?"

"Just a note, really. I wanted to find out how she was getting along."

"I see," Jeremy said.

"I was very close to her, you see. She was always very kind to me. And the other day I was thinking, 'It's Gloria's birthday right about now. Couldn't I send her a card to tell her I still think of her?' "

She still thought of her. When was that? At what point in her cheerful, bustling day, behind that tranquil face, did her thoughts turn to her old life? Really, he didn't know anything about her. She might be thinking about her husband constantly; she might be full of discontent; she might be planning some new love affair far away from him. He suddenly remembered a night last week when she had been braiding Pippi's hair in front of the television. Some celebrities were appearing on a panel show, among them a movie hero with deep, shadowed eyes. "Why does everyone think that man is so attractive?" Mary asked. Jeremy had been filling out contest blanks, ignoring the program. "What man?" he asked. "That one on the left," she said, "that tall attractive man beside the blonde." Jeremy looked up then, puzzled, but Mary had not heard her own words and she merely snapped a rubber band on Pippi's braid and gave her a pat. "Off you go now. Bedtime." But it wasn't until now that he thought to wonder: Was she longing for something more? When she read those romantic novels she liked, with the distraught pretty girls on the covers, was she wishing that she too had a man who would carry her up castle stairs or defend her with his sword or even, perhaps, frighten her a little with his dark, mysterious gaze?

As if she had guessed at all the cracks of uncertainty running through him, she turned to look at him over the baby's head. In the dark her face seemed like a piece of felt. The baby made sucking noises in her sleep, lying on Mary's arm as limp as a beanbag. Only Jeremy felt some brittle crumbling sensation inside him that kept him sitting upright.

"Jeremy? I guess maybe we could be married now," Mary said.

"Well, if you wanted to."

"Do you?"

"I do if you do," he said.

"You don't sound very sure."

"Of course I'm sure."

"We'll have to do it in secret, then," she said. "And I'm afraid you'll have to come with me, Jeremy. For real, this time."

"Oh, certainly. Anything you say."

"But I'll make all the arrangements. Would you like to get married this Thursday? Olivia's home on Thursdays, she can babysit."

"All right," he said.

The crumbling sensation went on. Bits of him kept breaking away and falling, but Mary didn't seem to notice.

All through the next day, while he sat in his studio filing down the metal edges of a statue, he kept thinking about this mother-in-law whom Mary still remembered after so many years. He saw her as fat, blowsy, good-natured—an open-hearted woman who could give Mary some indefinable quality that he was not up to. He pictured her holding Mary's letter in enormous, motherly hands. He tried to imagine what Mary would have written. It was polite, it was almost obligatory, to ask a woman about the welfare of her son. "How is Guy doing? I think of him often." Oh, he could almost see those words in Mary's round, looped handwriting.

"I live with someone else now but Gladys (or Dolores or whatever her name was), it's not the same at all, he's so wishy-washy and spends so much time in his studio, and at first he wanted to make love too often and now he doesn't want to hardly ever." Jeremy winced and dropped a bolt and picked it up again. He imagined the mother-in-law's answer. "Guy has a divorce since he gave up hope but you could come back any time, any time at all, Mary. Things have never been the same here since you left."

He knew that was what she would say. Things would never be the same *any* place that Mary left.

At noon one of the children climbed the stairs to tell him lunch was ready, but he called through the door that he was too busy to come. In actual fact he was finishing the ring-around-the-rosy statue. He was working slowly, as he always did near the end of a piece, putting in small touches with long pauses for deliberation. He could easily have stopped for lunch. It was just that the thought of going downstairs made him feel so tired, somehow. All that noise! That tumult of emotion, rising in billows around him as he tried to swallow his food! Even from here he could hear the clatter of silverware, the children's endless contests for their mother's attention and the sudden clamor over some domestic accident—as if, overturned, those peanut butter glasses painted with nursery rhyme characters had spilled forth shouts and laughter and scoldings instead of milk. Above it all Mary's voice rode, like a ship on waves. He could not understand how she managed this, speaking at such a low and steady pitch. He himself was drowned out, every time. "Children? Oh, children," he would say, "couldn't you please—" Now Mary laughed, a rich soft laugh that carried effortlessly to every corner of the house. A few minutes later he heard her climbing the stairs. Dishes rattled gently on a tray. "Jeremy," she called, "I've brought your lunch up."

"Come in," he said, but she couldn't; he had absent-mindedly locked the door. First the knob turned and then she knocked. He had to put down his file and get off his stool and let her in—a task that seemed larger than it was, like having to rearrange every cell of his body within some thick dark sac of concentration. "Egg salad," she said. He stared at her dimly. She carried the tray in past him and began laying his lunch out on the table in front of the statue—a glass of milk, a salad bowl, a sandwich on a plate. Every time she set a dish down she had to move something of his out of the way. A glue bucket was pushed aside, a paintbrush was laid across the top of it (not where it belonged). A horseshoe magnet clanged to the floor. "Sorry," Mary said cheerfully. He felt that a long tail of noise and energy was pluming out behind her, brushing objects in his room as she turned. Although he had been thinking of her all morning, this seemed to be a different Mary from the one in his thoughts—clearer, sharper, more brightly colored. She changed the air in his studio, stirring up the center of it and making the corners look darker and dustier. The room appeared to be hers now. When she stepped back to look at the statue, he had the feeling that that was hers too. He imagined how efficiently *she* would make a statue: fitting it together in no time, without a wasted motion or a single revision, relying upon some rich lode of intuition that he did not possess. When she was done she would give the statue a loving smack on the rump, as if it were a child sent out to play after she had tied its shoelaces. "Very nice," she said now. "I like it."

She turned and kissed him. She wound her arms around his neck. He said, "I should get back to work, Mary."

But then when she was gone the other Mary returned, the silent floating one of his thoughts, and the image of her writing to her mother-in-law continued to pain him so much that he sat on his stool bent over and clutching his chest, like a man suffering a heart attack.

By early afternoon he had completed every last detail of the statue. Still, he didn't leave the studio. And when Brian came visiting—he heard his voice in the entrance hall—he refused to see him. "Jeremy, Brian's here," Mary called.

Jeremy didn't answer.

Then Brian's boots mounted the stairs, two steps at a time. His great hearty knock sounded on Jeremy's door. "Hey, in there. You feel like a visitor?"

Jeremy frowned at the ceiling. He was lying on the couch with his hands clasped across his stomach, trying off and on to think of another piece to work on. He didn't feel like seeing anyone at all. But while he was framing an answer Brian gave up and went away again, and Jeremy heard his voice and Mary's and then the slamming of the front door. He rose and padded over to a window. There was Brian crossing the street, weaving his way between cars stopped for a traffic light, arriving on the opposite sidewalk in a sudden burst of speed as if he had just made a daring escape. Jeremy watched after him for as long as he was in sight. It seemed to him that Brian's walk was lighthearted, nearly dancing; he might have been celebrating his return to freedom.

At suppertime, when Mary came with another tray, she said, "Why wouldn't you see Brian?"

"Perhaps tomorrow I will."

"You're not still angry about what happened at the gallery, are you? Jeremy, I honestly don't think—"

"No, it's just, you see, I'm busy with a new piece," he told her.

"Oh, I see."

Actually he never went straight from one piece to the next. It was necessary to have a regathering period, an idle space sometimes stretching into weeks. But Mary said, "I hope it's going well, then," and she took away his lunch dishes and left him his supper and a mug of hot coffee.

When she was gone he turned off the light and went back to the couch. By now the studio was in twilight—a linty grayness that he could almost feel on his skin. In spite of the warmth he wrapped himself in an afghan. It seemed to him that his heart had slowed, and his hands and feet were chilled. He stretched out on the couch and went to sleep, and the afghan made him dream of being held prisoner in some confined and airless place.

Long before dawn he awoke with a start. He spent several seconds wondering where he was. The doubt was more pleasant than disturbing. Even after he had found the answer, he kept trying to push it away again so that he could return to that floating, rootless state. Then he rose and ate supper in the dark—cold vegetables and meatloaf, a bowl of some sticky thick liquid that turned out to be melted ice cream. Every swallow gagged him but he ate the entire meal, and he finished the last of his cold bitter coffee with a feeling of accomplishment. Wasn't that what life was all about: steadfast endurance? In the dark, where his thoughts seemed more significant than they did in daytime, he decided that this was what made the difference between him and Mary. He saw virtue in acceptance of everything, small and large, while Mary saw virtue in the refusal to accept. She was always ready to do battle against the tiniest infringement. He considered those battles now with fondness; he pictured her tall, energetic figure fending off door-to-door salesmen and overbearing teachers and grade school bullies and household germs, all with the same enthusiasm. It seemed to him that his acceptance and her defiance made up a perfect whole, with neither more right than the other, although up till now he had always assumed that one of them would be proved wrong in the end. He worked through this idea with a feeling of relief. He even thought of going downstairs to wake Mary and tell her about it, but of course she would have no idea what he meant. She never wondered about the same things he did. (Did she wonder about *anything?*) She would only smile at him with sleepy, half-closed eyes and open the blankets and pull him in to her, her answer to all their problems. He dragged an armchair over to the front window instead, and sat there wrapped in his afghan watching the sky whiten over the city.

Was it possible that once, in the years before Mary, the house had been this still even in the daytime? He had trouble remembering it. He began pretending that this silence was permanent—that Mary and the children had gone away for some reason and left the house echoing behind them. Then he considered his work. What would he do if he were left all alone with his sheets of metal and blocks of wood? Would he still be successful if Mary were not standing behind him? He began twisting his hands together on his knees; something like anxiety or irritation tightened all his muscles. It was foolish to be asking himself such questions. He had been making his pieces all along, hadn't he? Long before *she* came here. He pushed back his armchair and flung scraps of cardboard off his worktable. He picked up a pencil and a sheet of newsprint, already drawing shapes in thin air while he planned his next piece. And when, just at dawn, Mary knocked on his door and asked if he were all right, he had trouble placing her. "What?" he asked, still frowning at his sketchpad.

"Are you all *right*, I said."

"Oh, yes."

He was going to make a statue of Brian rounding the corner—a man half running, glad to be gone. He chose that figure because it seemed the most solitary. No dogs, brooms, tricycles, or children accompanied him. He chose wood because it was slowest and took the most patience. Half the morning was spent selecting pieces from the lumber pile in the corner, lovingly smoothing them, arranging and rearranging them. Cutting and sanding the curve of a single shin took till noon. When Mary knocked with his lunch tray he called, "Just leave it outside, would you please? I'll get it in a minute." But in a minute he had forgotten all about it, and it was afternoon before the hollow in his stomach reminded him.

He ate while standing at the window, looking down into the street. The glare of sunlight on cement came as a shock to his eyes. He had to squint to see his children playing hopscotch on the sidewalk—their chalked game like an aerial view of a city, the tops of their heads gleaming, two stick pigtails flying out behind each little girl. The clothes they wore gave them a motley look. Plaids, ginghams, stripes, flowers, all mixed together. Hannah, spread-eagled on a skate-

board, looked like one of those dolls made up of
stacked felt discs all different colors: an orange scarf
around her neck, a puffy pink quilted jacket, a red
cardigan dangling below it and a plaid skirt below that,
bare white knees, and the cuffs of blue kneesocks rising
above floppy red boots. Their voices seemed too distant,
as voices had back when he was a child sick in bed—
words floating across some curtain of mist or water. He
used to think the change was caused by his being
horizontal, but here he was standing upright and still
they sounded like people in a dream. They were arguing about whether someone had broken a rule. Jeremy
could not figure out the point of this game. As far as
he could see it involved hopping down a series of
chalked squares. Was the pattern of those squares their
own? Was there some hidden, rigid set of regulations
that he knew nothing about? He was awed by their
ability to decide on their own amusements, to carry on,
by themselves, this mysterious tradition handed down
by an older generation of children. They lined up
efficiently, hopped with purpose, stooped for some sort
of glittering marker and tossed it to a new square before stepping smartly aside to await another turn. He
had never suspected that children on their own would
be so organized.

In the evening Mary knocked on his door and
said, "Jeremy, aren't you ever coming out?"

"In a little while, yes," he said. He blew sawdust
off a stick of wood.

"You're tying up the children's bathroom, Jeremy.
It's Abbie's bath night. Couldn't you just let her in that
long?"

"In a while."

He heard her sigh. He heard her whisper something he couldn't quite catch. "What?" he said.

"I said, you won't forget tomorrow, will you?"

"Tomorrow."

"It's Thursday tomorrow, Jeremy."

"Oh, yes."

"We're getting—"

"Yes, yes, I remember."

She set the tray outside his door. The familiar clinking of china on tin made him suddenly hungry, but he didn't go out to the hall. He waited for her to leave. He stood listening to her footsteps all the way down the stairs, and only then did he go to the door and open it. He didn't know why he behaved that way. The smell of her on the landing—warm milk and honey sprinkled with cinnamon, a drink that had comforted him all his life—seemed sickly-sweet. He picked the tray up and closed the door and locked it again. Standing just inside the room, holding the tray in one hand, he took bits of food in his fingers and wolfed them down. Behind him the sounds of the household crept up the stairs and seeped through the cracks around the door. He heard laughter and a thread of "Frère Jacques." Mary and Olivia were calling back and forth to each other between two rooms. Mary's voice was downward-slanting, definite, while Olivia's rose in an uncertain way at the end of each sentence. This might be a school for women; the thought had often occurred to him. In the old days he had assumed that what women knew came to them naturally. He had never suspected that they had to be taught. But listen to Mary, to the firmness of her voice, not issuing concrete instructions so much as showing Olivia how to *be;* listen to Olivia slowly and questioningly taking on her tone. To the little girls, even, cleverly coaxing Rachel to eat her carrots, Edward to try his potty chair—they were all being tutored. Jeremy set his tray down and stood beside the door in silence, eavesdropping, impressed and envious. Were there no such tutors for men? Was it only women who linked the generations so protectively?

But when footsteps climbed the stairs again—this time Olivia's—he scurried back to his work. "Mr. Pauling? Mary sent me with more coffee." He stayed quiet, a quarter-sheet of sandpaper frozen in one hand. After a while she went away.

By Thursday morning the framework of the statue was completed. Only he could have told what it was yet. There was just a skeleton, tied in odd places with strips from old sheets wherever gluing had seemed preferable to nailing. While he waited for the glue to dry he rummaged about for other materials—coarse fabrics and copper wire and a length of fine screen that he had been saving for something special. He overturned bins and drawers, blinking repeatedly to clear his eyes. (He had not had very much sleep the night before.) Under the sink he found a child's wool cap and sat down to unravel it, building a pile of crinkly red yarn in his lap. Later he would stiffen the yarn with his spray can, let it stream out from behind his figure's head. Whoever owned the cap would say, "Jeremy! Is that mine? You told us, Jeremy, you said you'd stop using all our stuff up, remember?" He remembered very well, but when he was in the middle of a piece some sort of feverishness came over him. He took whatever looked right, even the necessities of life. He broke or rearranged them as needed, fumbling in his haste, promising himself that he would replace the objects as soon as his piece was finished and he had the time again. Now he had no time at all. It always seemed likely at this stage that he might drop dead by nightfall, leaving his figure unfinished and his life in bits on the studio floor. What if his piece remained a skeleton forever, bound with rags at the joints and tipping in that precarious way he was planning to change, he knew just how, once he found the proper base for it? No one would ever guess what his plans had been. They would think the skeleton was what he had intended, with all its flaws. Surely, then, if ghosts existed he would have to become one; his restless spirit would be forced to return to haunt what he had left undone.

What he intended for this piece was the light, dissolving feel of Brian running, a splinter in a cold spring wind. He would be wrapped in matte surfaces. His face would be a thin blade of wood, cutting the air in front of him. He would trail curving tin streamers of motion. Tin? He looked for the sheet metal, the shears. It was hard to breathe. This certainty about what he was making had the same physical effect as fear: his chest tightened and his heart seemed to be rising in his throat, and he had a sensation of burning up his body's stores too rapidly.

When Mary knocked he didn't answer, didn't even bother keeping still for her. "Jeremy? *Jeremy!*" He bent tin, with a great hollow clang. Mary went away again.

On his lunch tray there was a note. "This is our wedding day. Do you still want to?" Something gave him a sharp stab of sorrow—the question mark, perhaps. The thought of Mary's low, even voice asking that question. For the first time that morning he listened to what was going on downstairs, sorting out the separate noises from the steady hum that was present all day long. Someone was playing a *Sesame Street* record and someone else was running the blender at high speed —Olivia, no doubt, fixing one of her peculiar meals of seed-paste patties or fresh-ground peanut butter. The blender ran at the level of a scream, on and on, spitting when it came upon nuts as yet unbroken. A child was crying, but not very seriously. He could not hear Mary anywhere. What time was it? He looked at the clock on the windowsill but it had run down, long ago. It occurred to him that he had not bathed or shaved or changed clothes in days. He had a musty yellow smell and his teeth seemed to be made of flannel. Well, when he had finished cutting the tin he would take care of all that. He would come downstairs newly washed, freshly dressed, and locate Mary among all those jumbled voices. He pictured himself descending into the noise as he would enter the sea—proceeding steadily with his hands lifted and his mouth set, submerging first his feet and then his legs and then his entire body, last of all his head.

The wool from the cap turned out to be a mistake. Too soft, too temporary. He had unraveled it for nothing. He tossed it into a corner and cut more tin instead, in tiny strips that he curled around a pencil and then stretched out again so that they would crinkle. It was a tricky job; he kept getting cut. Little seams of blood mixed with the paint and the gray rolls of glue on his fingers. Somewhere he had work gloves but he was in too much of a hurry to stop and look for them. The muscles at the back of his neck were stretched thin, and when he stood up with his bundle of tin strips he found that both legs were asleep. Now the strips had to be nailed onto the wooden head, which was the hardest part. First he had to find enough tiny sharp nails in his nail can and then he had to hammer them in absolutely straight or they skidded off the tin. His hands were sore all over, but the soreness was reassuring. He was merely getting used up, that was all. Like the lead of a pencil. Naturally the hands were the first to go.

At twilight Olivia brought his tray up. "Mr. Pauling? Could I come in?"

The thought of food gave him a sick feeling. He ignored her.

Something made working more and more difficult. It took him a while to realize that it was the darkness. The statue was only a glimmer before him. He walked over to the door on crippled, icy feet, but when he had turned the wall switch on the light hurt his eyes so much that he clicked it off again. He made his way to the couch and lay down, with one arm set across his aching forehead. As soon as he was comfortably arranged he felt a lurch like some gear disengaging, a ping! in his ears, and his mind floated free and he slept.

Even in his dreams, he worked. He cut, pasted, hammered, sanded. He had a feeling of pressure to finish, a sense of being pushed. Although he forced himself to ignore the pressure he went on working without let-up, and the closer he came to completing the piece the more he was filled with a sense of joy and light-headedness. When the last nail was hammered in he laughed out loud. He backed off across the studio with his eyes lowered, so that the finished statue could burst upon him all in one instant, and then he looked up to see what he had made.

A room. A corner of a room, a kitchen, to be exact. A counter with a loaf of rye bread and a bread knife on it, and a coppertone clothes dryer spilling out realistic wads of flowered and plaid and gingham clothes and a formica table with chairs set around it— oh, how he must have worked over that table! Its aluminum edge was grooved with three parallel bands; such attention to detail. The chairs were mismatched, a subtle touch. The wooden one alone must have taken him weeks to make, with its bulbous legs and the tie-on ruffled cushion on its seat and the Bugs Bunny decal on its back. He had even included, on the rungs, the scars of a hundred children's teetering shoes. Was this what he had labored over for so many hours?

He woke feeling dismal and empty and frightened. Sunlight flooded his face, a deep gold light casting long rectangles so that he suspected it must be mid-morning. What he wanted most was a cup of hot coffee, but all he found outside his door was last night's supper. A wilted salad, a glass of luke-warm milk, some peculiar brownish casserole that he could not identify. He ate it anyway, although it went down his throat in lumps. He swallowed the milk with narrow, dutiful sips and then set his tray outside the door again.

Now he saw that the statue was all wrong. What had he been thinking of, setting on each curl of hair that way? He might have been building a doll, or a department store mannequin. With a screwdriver he began prying the strips off, one by one. His hands hurt so much that he could hardly bend them. The statue's head showed nail marks down its back, but he was already thinking up ways to cover them.

At noon he checked for lunch, but found none. Later in the afternoon he checked again. There were only the supper dishes, crusty now. He stood on the landing and called, "Mary?" The word echoed back. There was not a sound in the house; only a clear, bell-like silence in which each of his footsteps fell too loudly. He descended the stairs, passing the empty second floor and continuing to where his children would surely be absorbed in a fairytale or some quiet table game. No. No one was there. In the parlor the baby's playpen was empty and the toys on the floor seemed to be coated with a furry film of stillness. In the dining room the face of the TV was sleek and blank; in the bedroom his and Mary's bed was made so neatly that it seemed artificial, something from a furniture store display. He had the feeling that no one had slept there for months, if ever. And the kitchen was strangest of all. The counters were absolutely clean and shining, like an advertisement for a linoleum company. No floury measuring cups, no cucumber peels, no stacked-up dirty dishes. The floor gleamed. The table was spotless. The clock ticked briskly and hollowly.

He felt that his sense of time, which was never good, had deserted him. Had he missed something? Had the days carried everyone else on by and left him stranded in some vanished moment? Maybe his family had just gone out to a movie. Maybe they had abandoned him forever. Maybe they had grown up and moved some thirty years before, had children of their own and grown old and died. He couldn't prove that it wasn't so.

Then, turning to the refrigerator for food and solace (fumbling at some new kind of double door where he had expected the old single one), he found a note stuck on with a teapot-shaped magnet. "Dear Jeremy, I have taken the children and left you. I borrowed Brian's cabin at the Quamikut Boatyard. I think it's best. Love, Mary."

He took the note off the door and read it over and over. It seemed that the air had gone out of him, so that the words striking his deflated chest jarred all the way through to his backbone. Finally he folded the piece of paper several times and tucked it in his shirt pocket. He headed through the house and back upstairs, fixing the image of his new statue very firmly in his mind like some magnetic star that would guide him through this moment. In the studio he resumed work immediately. He sanded the wooden head smooth again, at first so hard that the friction burned his fingers through the paper but then more slowly and then more slowly still. Like some clumsy, creaking wheel, he ground to a stop. He dropped the sandpaper and stood motionless, one hand upon his statue, staring numbly at the bare walls of the studio.

Deserted, he was like an old man who sees the last of the guests to the door and returns, stretching, and yawning, to an empty room. Now I am alone again, he says. Finally. We can get down to what I have been waiting to do.

What is it I have been waiting to do?

7

Spring and Summer, 1971: Mary

First it was like a picnic. I mean that I planned it with the same kind of bottled-up, excited energy. I lay awake all Thursday night making mental lists of what I would need for the children—just the essentials. We were finally getting down to the essentials again. I calculated the earliest time I could telephone Brian in the morning, and I decided on seven. Which was too early, as it turned out. I have forgotten the pattern of life without children. Brian answered sounding hoarse and sleepy, and he didn't seem to be thinking well. I said, "Brian, do you still have that house by the river?"

"Who is this?" he asked.

"It's Mary Pauling."

"Do I what?"

"Do you still have that house by the river. Where your boat is moored."

"Oh. Sure."

"Would it be all right if the children and I went out there for a few days?"

"Out—?"

"I wouldn't ask you this but you did say you never use it yourself. Didn't you?"

"Let me get this straight," he said. "You want to take the children there?"

"That's right."

"You and the children but not Jeremy?"

"That's right."

"But this is not a vacation house."

"No, I know that."

"It doesn't even have hot water. And it's filthy."

"Yes, we've been there once, remember?"

"Mary," Brian said. "Are you—I mean, is this—you're not *leaving* him or anything."

"Oh," I said, "you know Jeremy, he's just so caught up in his work right now and I thought it would help if we got out of his hair for a while."

Then Brian said, "I see. Well, of course. You can use it as long as you like."

I could tell that he was still puzzled. But how else could I have explained it? "Actually, Jeremy forgot to marry me, Brian, and of course I could have reminded him but that would have been the third reminder on top of my proposing in the first place, and what kind of wedding is that?"

By then I was packed. I had done that at dawn, while waiting for it to be time to call Brian. I tiptoed into the children's rooms as they slept and I felt for their things in the dark. All night I had been looking forward to it —I do like getting organized to go someplace—but it turned out not to be what I had expected. For one thing, the bare essentials for six children can fill a trunk in no time. You don't get the same feeling of purity as when you run away with one small child and her favorite doll. Clothes, vitamins, toothbrushes, baby aspirin, diapers, Edward's potty chair, Pippi's antihistamine, seven pairs of plastic pants . . . Also, I felt so sad. Hadn't I once sworn never to leave anyone ever again? Especially not Jeremy. Oh, never Jeremy.

I didn't tell the children until Miss Vinton had had her breakfast and left for work. I knew they would have passed it on to her; they can't keep secrets. Miss Vinton took an endless time buckling her mackintosh, smoothing the lapels down, checking on a little stain near the hem. I thought I was going to start screaming and shaking her, but instead I went on smiling. I looked steadily downward so she wouldn't notice any difference in my face. "Have a good day, Miss Vinton," I said. Then just as I was closing the front door after her I saw how straight she held her back, that rigid board of a spine marching off to deal with the world, those enormous Mary Janes flapping along, and I wished I had told her after all and given her a hug for goodbye.

Mr. Somerset sometimes slept till noon and Olivia even longer. She had a job now at a sort of leather shop. I never had figured out her hours, but I was fairly sure that she would sleep through our going. (The night before, making supper, setting out a tray for Jeremy, I started crying right in front of her. "Oh," I said, "I just can't go on with these everlasting *trays* of his," so she took over. She gave him part of her casserole—something organic, I believe. Later I was so ashamed. Haven't I been trying all this time to instill some sort of stability in her? This morning I didn't want to say anything to her at all. I couldn't face her. I wouldn't know how to explain.) I stood at the foot of the stairs for a moment, listening for any sounds from her room or Mr. Somerset's. Then I said, "Children?" They were still dawdling over breakfast. They thought they were going to school that day. I went out to the kitchen and leaned against the doorframe. "Guess what, children," I said. "We're taking a little trip."

They wanted to know where—all but Darcy. Darcy just got very still. She was feeding Rachel her Pablum, and she stopped the spoon in mid-air and didn't even notice when Rachel started shouting and grabbing for it.

"We're going to spend a few days at Mr. O'Donnell's cabin near the boatyard," I said. "Remember last summer, when he took you all to see his boat? We'll leave after breakfast; Mr. O'Donnell has kindly offered to drive us there."

"Something's gone wrong," Darcy said.

"Of course not, honey."

"But it's a school day. I have a math test."

"You can always make it up."

"It's going to count for half my grade."

"You can make it *up,* Darcy."

"Are we leaving Jeremy or something?"

Well, of course she would guess that. I suppose she remembers leaving Guy, although she has never said so or asked me a single thing about it. I said, "No,

Darcy, don't be silly. We're giving him a little peace and quiet, is all." Then I said, "Mr. O'Donnell is just providing the transportation."

Which I might not have needed to add, but I couldn't be sure. You never can tell what is going through that head of hers.

At nine o'clock Brian was supposed to be picking us up. (There *was* a city bus, but it didn't go the entire way and I was just as glad we weren't relying on it.) I gave each child a coat and a load to carry. "Hurry now," I said, "out to the vestibule. *Not* outdoors, just in the vestibule." I didn't want Jeremy to see us leaving. I was afraid that one of the children would suddenly decide to run up and kiss him goodbye, but nobody thought of it. Then too he might come down on his own. Why hadn't I taken him breakfast, so that he would have no reason to leave his studio? The fact is that if he did come, if he said a single word to keep me with him, I would gladly stay forever. I didn't *want* to go. Yet I kept feeling this pressure to get out of the house before he discovered it. I kept saying, "Move, Edward, we're in a hurry," and when Hannah wanted to run upstairs for her bear I said, "No! Stay down!" I scared her. She went immediately to the vestibule and stood sucking her thumb and staring up at me. I was like a burglar trying to escape without a sign, leaving behind me those gleaming countertops washed clean of every fingerprint. I made them all whisper. "Olivia's asleep, hush!" I said, and they stared. Hush for *Olivia?* She could sleep through nuclear warfare. We stood packed solid in that little cube of a vestibule, steaming up the front windows and keeping utterly silent. Yet if Jeremy would only come! If he would come and say, "What's going on, Mary?" and blink at me and put out one of his warm, pale hands to touch mine! Then I would herd everyone back in and lock all the doors and draw all the curtains, and Brian could wait outside our house forever.

His car was a powder-blue Mercedes. Well, I suppose he is quite rich. He drew up soundlessly and peered toward the house, and I pushed the children out before he could honk and attract Jeremy's attention.

"Hurry, now," I said. "Give me the baby, Darcy. Don't forget that basket. Where's my purse?" I was preceded by a parade of belongings, like some pampered movie star. Children, grocery bags, stuffed animals—I was *padded* with belongings. I felt I should apologize to Brian for having so many children, but during the first few minutes he was out loading things into the trunk and I was passing around Dramamine tablets. I had forgotten who was prone to car sickness; we so rarely drove. I gave Abbie a tablet by accident and then made her spit it out again. "Oh look," I told her, "*you* ought to know if you get sick or not—" All of which helped me get over being embarrassed in front of Brian. I knew that he must be shocked at me. I have a very clear picture of how I appear to others: I am so big and slow and unexcitable, and women like that don't act on impulse. They never *leave* people, certainly. Now when he was back in the car and maneuvering the rush hour traffic he kept throwing me sideways glances, maybe worrying that I would burst into tears or list all my grievances or spill some dark secret that he didn't want to hear. I didn't, of course. I kept the tears away by refusing to look behind me all the while that our house was in sight—that narrow, funny, lovable house with its potty bay window and the children's old tattered construction paper Valentines glued to the upstairs panes and the dead Christmas tree on its side in front, dripping tinsel, waiting all these months to be collected—and who knows, maybe Jeremy drawing back a frayed lace curtain high on the third floor and peering out, dim and cloudlike, trying to understand what I had done to him.

What was my purpose, sailing away in this ridiculous baby-blue car?

We headed out through stretches of Baltimore that I had only seen once or twice before in my life, rowhouses layered over with ugly new formstone, deadlooking saplings scattered along a divided street so wide and gray that looking at it seemed to bleach my eyes. Meanwhile the children said nothing. I had never known them to keep so quiet for so long. They sat in a row in back, each of them framed by stuffed-in bits and pieces that couldn't fit into the trunk. They gazed dreamily out the windows. Maybe they were in a state of shock, suffering through an experience I would never be able to erase. Maybe they were just admiring the view. Who knows? Children live in such a mist. I believe that most of what happens comes as a total surprise to them even when you think you've explained it. I said, "Abbie? Are you comfortable? Pippi?" They looked at me blankly, then looked away again. Hannah wet her finger and drew an H on the windowpane.

"In a week or so it will be spring," Brian told me. "*Then* would be a good time for you to be out there."

"It's a good time now," I said. "It's spring now."

"This morning I could see my breath."

"We're not made of glass, you know."

"Mary, that cabin is no better than sleeping out. Maybe you've forgotten. There's no heat, no—"

"I remember that," I said, "but it's the only place I know of to go." Then I saw his face close over, braced for me to begin my story. I said, "And I certainly do thank you. Last time we were there the children loved it."

The closed look didn't fade. He said, "Tell me this, Mary. How long were you planning to stay?"

"Well, I hadn't made any definite plans yet."

"I mean—"

"Probably not long," I said. I felt I had to help him out.

"I hope you don't mind my asking, but do you have enough money?"

"Oh yes," I said.

"Because if you don't, now—"

"Brian, you know better than anyone that Jeremy's just sold four pieces," I said.

Actually the little money Jeremy had made was still in the bank, and I had left the checkbook on his bureau, where he would be sure to find it. I wasn't a *genuine* burglar. What I took was my household-hints money, my money-back-offer money, my coupon money, which I had been saving against trouble all these years as I once promised myself I would. It had mounted up. Fifty dollars for telling how I use old bottle crates to make spice racks, twenty-five for the third-best recipe based on sliced pasturized processed cheese food and a dollar back for ten labels off canned beans. The money was in a plastic refrigerator container in my purse, and I reached in to touch it and felt strong and competent and too big for the car. Never mind, children; I might carry you away without ever saying why but at least I will be with you, and I will provide for you. I learned my lesson the first time around. Women should never leave any vacant spots for the men to fill; they should form an unbroken circle on their own and enclose each child within it.

We passed barren stretches now, where the fields had been peeled back and naked buildings sat on jagged slabs of concrete, looking as if they had recently been uprooted from some more crowded place. We passed long avenues of service stations and cut-rate tire dealers and machine shops, and then oil refineries and warehouses and strange mechanical monsters standing alone in tangles of dry grass—electrical objects on wiry, spraddled legs, tanks and cylinders, gigantic motors with bolts as big as grown men and twisted black pipes that could suck up a house, all silent and unused. The cars around us now were rusted and crumpled, fantastically finned, driven by gum-chewing men; we were close to the Bethlehem Steel Works. "Look!" said Pippi. "Country!" and she pointed to a matted gray line of tree branches far, far beyond an auto graveyard. "When we get to the river, can we swim?" she asked.

"Philippa Pauling! You'd get pneumonia."

"Typhoid, more likely," said Brian. "Bubonic plague." He looked over at me. I thought he might be about to smile, although it was hard to tell beneath that beard of his. And the children were perking up too—pointing out sights on the road and quarreling over whose turn it was at the window. The junkyards gave way to houses, all tiny and papery-looking but with signs of real people in them, at least. Wooden donkeys pulled wooden carts across the front yards, and there were bird baths and flowered mailboxes and silvery balls on pedestals everywhere we looked. Some people had set up housekeeping in trailers with cement bases built in under them. Now, why would anyone want to do that? All those temporary objects resting on permanent foundations? Well, maybe it was just my mood that made me wonder. I felt like a solid stone house, myself, jacked up on little tiny wheels when I had no business going anywhere.

Now the space between neighbors grew larger and we passed through woods—scrubby and meager, but woods all the same. We turned off onto a gravel road lined with more houses, most of them smaller than the boats that sat in the driveways. Cabin cruisers—ugly things. I never could see why some people like boating so much. I've never cared for the water at all, not one way or the other.

To get to Brian's house you go straight down to the river, through a cluster of bleak shacks and a store and a long shed where they do repair work in the wintertime. There were only a few boats tied up at the docks. The season had hardly begun. We went plummeting along a dirt road that ran alongside the water, and then Brian braked and we looked up to see his cabin: a gray weathered rectangle with a tin roof, and not a perfect right angle anywhere on it. Everything was sagging, leaning, buckling, splitting. The tops of both steps were missing; anyone entering would find himself stepping into wooden boxes, sinking down into cold black spidery caverns. I knew all that ahead of time, of course. I had meant what I told Brian. But still! There are some things you can't actually summon up in your memory—smells, they say (although *I* always could) and then the exact atmosphere, the weight and texture and quality of air, that exists in certain places. I knew that Brian's shack was dismal but I had forgotten how just standing next to it would make you feel dank and chilled, a *despairing* feeling, and how when you went in some heaviness would press down on your skin and cause your heart to sink. This is not just myself I am talking about. The minute we were inside Brian reached out and touched my arm, unnecessarily, as if the gesture had been startled out of him. "Mary!" he said. "You can't stay here."

The children climbed in one by one and fell silent, and stood in a huddle together shivering.

Part of it was the cold, of course. There is nothing so cold as air that has been trapped beneath tin all winter. Then there was the dirt. When Brian bought his ketch the shack came with it, automatically. The previous owner had stayed here whenever he was working on the boat or preparing for an early morning sail. Brian couldn't have cared less about the shack itself. He let the grit form a film on the table and the mildew grow on the swaybacked couch and the rust trickle down from the faucets in the kitchen sink. Boys broke windows, birds flew in and died after battering themselves against the walls. Why, I could have *shoveled* the dirt out! I pictured myself with a great garden spade, laboring over the cracked beige linoleum. Then I saw how I would rip down those tatty plastic curtains and scour the sink white again and cover the couch with some nice bright throw, and all my muscles grew springy the way they had the night before when I was planning the packing, and I knew that we would stay.

"You're not serious about this," Brian told me.

"Could you bring in our things, do you suppose?"

I set Rachel on my hip and took a tour of the house. Not that there was much to tour. There was a living room with a couch and an armchair, and the kitchen merely took up one end of it—a sink and hotplate, a table and three chairs. The bedroom held a concave double bed and an army cot and a highboy with one drawer missing. In a little cubicle off the bedroom was a toilet with a split wooden seat, its tiny pool of water a coppery color, set squarely beneath the biggest window in the house. Something about that window—the fact that it was curtainless, or the white scum on its panes—made the light passing through it seem cold and eerie. I stood staring out of it for minutes on end, although I knew I should be helping Brian. I watched the children carry things from the car, all of them ghostly behind that cloudy glass. They tottered beneath blurred objects that I could not identify, and in their midst walked Brian, stepping precisely in his narrow

Italian shoes, carrying the potty chair and something
pink. When they entered the house, they seemed to
have just that moment become real. Like people stepping off a television screen into your living room. I
heard their voices, warm and high-pitched and louder
than I had expected, and then Edward started crying
over a scraped shin and I went out to comfort him. I
was very glad to see their faces. Their noses were pink
from the fresh air and they were sniffing and puffing.
"Where shall I put this?" they kept asking. "What do
you want me to do with this? Where will we sleep?
What will we eat?" I bent to roll Edward's jean leg up,
tilting Rachel on my hip, but Rachel was used to that
and she just took a clutch of my blouse and went on
smiling in her sideways position, as adaptable as any of
them.

When I went out to say goodbye to Brian I could
tell that he was still worried. "Well, so long!" I said.
"And thanks again, Brian"—singing it out, hoping to
cheer him up. But he didn't seem to hear. "Mary.
Look," he said.

"We're *enjoying* this, Brian."

"Look. Why don't you tell me the whole story?"

"There's nothing to tell," I said.

He sighed and climbed into the car. He rolled
down the window to give me last-minute instructions
—"There's a phone up at the store . . . you can turn on
the water out back beside the . . . call me if you . . ."
—and I nodded and waved and smiled.

Then his car disappeared down the road, and I
turned back to see my children watching me anxiously
from the doorway. They were clustered at all heights,
smudged from the things they had been carrying,
framed by rotting wood with a great hollow blackness
behind them. I have seen happier pictures in those ads
appealing for aid to underprivileged children. I never
thought that any children belonging to *me* would look
that way.

From the little store up at the boatyard we bought
cleaning supplies and groceries, and we all cleaned un-

til dark but it hardly showed. Lunch was sandwiches and supper was canned spaghetti, and after supper we fell into bed. Bed: that was a problem. I put the three older ones in the double bed and Edward and Hannah at opposite ends of the couch. Rachel and I used the army cot. We didn't even have sheets—just the blankets I had brought and one musty old quilt we found in the highboy. The children were tired enough to sleep anywhere, but I lay awake for a long time wondering what I thought I was doing. I tried to call up a picture of Jeremy. Had he missed us yet? I imagined him sitting in front of the TV in the darkened dining room, keeping silent company with the boarders. Whenever he had something to think over he would stare at the television for hours on end. Maybe he was weighing us in his mind that very minute, stacking us up, listing our faults and our virtues. Or mine, at least. Surely he didn't need to think twice about the children. They might get on his nerves sometimes but at least they were mostly his own flesh and blood. I was the interrupter, the overwhelmer; nobody has to tell me that. I saw how he had to tear his eyes from his work when I climbed the stairs to ask him could he babysit while I went to a kindergarten conference? would he feed Hannah while I took Edward to the doctor? did he happen to have change for the diaper man? I knew these things weren't as important as his sculptures, but what did he expect me to do? This is what comes with having children. You don't just tie off their little navel cords and toss them on their way like balloons. You have to start thinking about adenoids and zinc ointment and the proper schooling, you worry about nutrition and germs, money begins to matter suddenly. Oh, hear how shrill my voice gets. Imagine what it would be like to be interrupted by such a voice just as you were conceiving your finest statue. As for my overwhelming him! Did he think I didn't know? I never spoke to him without a sense of holding myself in check, trying to keep the reins in. I didn't *want* to dominate. When I talked to him with big, wide gestures, with power and energy flooding out of me, I saw how he quailed and then

made himself stand firm. He was wishing that I would
shrink a little. He never guessed that I already *had*
shrunk, that this was as small as I could get.

I sent him messages through the dark: Come and
get us. Call Brian, call the boatyard. Make up some
excuse for missing your wedding, anything at all, I'll
believe it: you suffered a stroke or amnesia, you were
mugged in the studio, you would *never* have simply decided that you didn't want to marry me. I thought up
ways that he might get in touch with us. I pictured the
storekeeper banging on our door—"Lady? Man up
there on the telephone, says it's urgent, life or death."
Or he might come in person. No. Never. But couldn't
he, just this once? *He* wouldn't bang. His knock would
be so soft I would wonder if I had imagined it. I would
open the door and find him waiting, hidden in the dark,
recognizable only by the dear, sad hopefulness in his
stance and that hesitant breath he always took before
moving toward me. For that moment I would give up
anything, half the years of my life even, anything but
the children. I made a hundred silent promises, but
the night just went trailing on and on and the only
sound I heard was the murmuring of the baby in the
crook of my arm.

We finished shoveling the dirt out. We scrubbed the
floor and dusted the furniture, we replaced the broken
steps with cinderblocks that Abbie found down by the
water. Darcy washed the kitchen cupboards and the
mismatched dishes she found stacked in them, and
scoured the sink. The little ones polished the windows,
their favorite job. I taped cardboard patches over the
broken panes. We tore down the curtains and the great
meshy spiderwebs, we ripped the tacked-on oilcloth off
the table and the draggled calico skirt off the sink. From
the boatyard store we bought brighter lightbulbs, a
bucket of disinfectant, a flashlight for walks in that
deep, country dark that is so startling after a life in the
city, and finally—three days later, when I stopped
thinking we might be leaving at any minute—aluminum cots for the children to sleep on and more blankets
to cover them with. The store had no pillows except the

life-preserving kind. My children have always slept on pillows. "Never mind," I told them, "this way is good for the spine. You'll be healthier." Not that health seemed to be any problem. They worked hard every day fixing up the house, as if it were a game; they ate enormous meals and slept like rocks every night—pillowless and sheetless, crackling about on the red vinyl pads that came with the cots. I wondered what I would do with them if we had to stay here so long it stopped being a novelty. Should I put them in the local school? But it was so close to the end of the year by now—nearly May. The weather was getting warmer. We peeled off some of the layers of clothing we'd been wearing day and night. And as we slacked up work on the house the children simply took to the outdoors. They lugged Rachel with them through the tall grass and pestered the boatmen and hung around the docks. They weren't allowed to touch the water, even—it was foul and filmed with grease. "What about summer?" Pippi asked me. "Won't we get to go swimming?" I said, "Of course not. I'll get you a wading pool, if it's hot."

Summer! Would we still be here when summer came?

Brian stopped by almost every day. I told him not to but he said he had to come anyway—he had his boat moored out on the river, a little blue ketch bobbing in front of our house. "How are things in the city?" I asked him. "What's happening in Baltimore? Is the show going well? Do you have many buyers?" All except what I wanted to ask most: Why doesn't Jeremy miss us?

The only time he mentioned Jeremy was once during the first week, when it was still cold. I remember the cold because he asked me to step outside with him a minute, away from the children, just as he was leaving. I came in my sweater, with my arms folded across my chest for warmth, and he said, "*Not* like that, get a coat. I'll wait." Then out beside his car he said, "Mary, I feel I'm in an awkward position here."

"Do you want me to leave?" I asked.

What would I have done if he'd said yes?

But what he said was, "No, of course not, but I'd like to know what you expect of me. Am I supposed to be keeping your whereabouts a secret? Because if I am, now—"

"Oh no," I said. "Jeremy knows where I am."

"I wasn't sure that he did."

"He knows. I told him, I wrote him a note."

Then I thought, Suppose he never saw the note. Is that why I haven't heard from him? I said, "Did he *say* he doesn't know my whereabouts? Have you seen him? Did he ask you?"

"I saw him, yes. He didn't say anything. He didn't even seem to want to mention your going."

"Oh," I said. "Well, you can tell him, Brian."

"Of course I wouldn't bring the subject up myself. But if he asked, you see, I felt that I was in an awkward—"

"Bring it up, I don't mind. Tell him. It isn't as if this were a fight or anything."

"What is it, then?"

I pulled my coat tighter against a breeze.

"I don't want to pry," Brian said, "but is this something *permanent* you are doing?"

I didn't answer. I had questions of my own. I wanted to know how Jeremy had looked and whether he was getting enough rest and eating right. (He was always so fond of sweets and he didn't like meat.) But I knew those were housewifely questions that would make Brian smile, and anyway he wouldn't have been able to tell me. Oh, sometimes I think of other artists' wives, people that Brian must run into all the time. I picture them fragile and blond and hollow-cheeked, the kind that model in the nude and lead unscheduled lives in garrets and never, never complicate things with children and plumbers. When I used to come clumping into the gallery every month, wearing my nursing bra and my best black dress with the spit-up milk down one shoulder, I imagined that Brian looked stunned. He would stare at me, and if he happened to be talking with other women they would hush and stare too. I suspected that they were feeling sorry for Jeremy. "An artist—married to *her?*" Then I would pull my stomach in and stuff the straggles of hair back behind my ears, and when I was looking at paintings I spent longer before each one than I wanted to, just showing I could appreciate art. I wouldn't have been caught dead mentioning anything domestic. And now all I allowed myself to say was, "I hope he's making out all right."

"Oh, you know Jeremy," Brian said. I had no idea what *that* was supposed to mean. He smiled down at me and said, "Don't worry, Mary. I'm sorry I brought it up. Go back inside now before you catch a cold."

The next time he came he didn't mention Jeremy at all, and I was afraid to ask.

Now more and more boats were tethered at the docks and bobbing on moorings. Weekdays, when not many people sailed, I could look out over a stretch of black water prickling with masts, and I like to pretend that I was some fisherman's wife living in a hut at the edge of the ocean. The river did have the feeling of an ocean. There was no opposite shore in sight; from this boatyard you sailed due east into the Chesapeake Bay, which looked like white veils at the limits of our vision. Late Friday afternoon the city people would begin to arrive from Baltimore and Washington—couples dressed for yachting, carrying ice buckets and windbreakers and Hudson Bay blankets. My children would crowd along the dock to stare at them. We saw their sails scudding away all Saturday, converging on us again all Sunday evening like birds flocking home. While we ate our supper doors would be slamming in the parking lot, motors revving, voices calling goodbyes. By Monday morning all that remained were their tire tracks in the gravel and those naked masts lined up again beside the docks. A few people drove in during the week to sail on their own or make minor repairs, but they were quieter and the only time I was aware of them was when I ran into them at the store. Then their solid, confident city voices startled me, and I would stand gawking like any country woman as they read off their long extravagant lists. Ice, they wanted, and a Phillips screwdriver and a can of rust remover and a sack of potato chips. Luxuries, every one. *We* took our food unchilled, or bought it from the store refrigerator just before time to eat; our tools we borrowed from neighbors or made ourselves from scraps; we stripped that everlasting salt-air rust off them with the Coca-Cola left in discarded cans. As for potato chips! I made the children eat protein foods instead. I have never liked being stingy with food but what else could I do? I fed them lots of eggs and cottage cheese and powdered milk. I gave the baby bits from my plate. Gerber's was too expensive. Even doing the laundry was expensive. Once a week I carried the dirtiest things to the store washing machine and dropped my quarter in the slot and sprinkled on the detergent, rationing every grain. I lugged the clothes home wet and hung them up to save fifty cents, even if it was rainy and I had to drape the living room with them and bat my way between damp blue jeans for a day and a half till they dried. Then here came this city man with his list so long that it filled two separate pages of his memo pad, not to mention what he idly tossed in from the counter displays as he wandered about the store whistling through his teeth. I doubt if he noticed me. If he did he probably thought I came from one of those shacks beside the store, where the boat mechanic lived or the carpenter or the old retired steelworker and his daughter. Poor white trash with dusty paper flowers before the madonnas on their windowsills and cotton balls on their screen doors to keep the flies away. *That* was what I had become. My children ran in and out between counters with their faces dirty and their dresses unironed, their feet bare and callused even before the summer had set in.

When Brian came he almost always offered to take us sailing, unless he had brought a girl along or a group of his friends. I was afraid he felt he *had* to offer. "Brian's here! Brian's here!" the children shouted when they saw his car, and I would say, "Stop, now! Hush. I want you to stay in here with me." They couldn't understand that. They always crowded around the windows and cheered when he knocked. To make up for them I kept my back to the door and was slow answering and pretended to be surprised when I saw him. "Just stopped by to see what you were doing," he would say, and usually hand me something—a little patterned rug he had been keeping in storage, towels he said were cluttering up his apartment, most often a sack of some kind of candy for the children. "How about it, kids?" he would say. "Feel like a sail?" He said he needed the help on deck. I didn't believe him. I was afraid he felt responsible for us in some way. I didn't want to say no to the children—what other treats did they have?—but usually I stayed home myself and kept the baby. I only went sailing twice all spring. The first time was the first sail I had had in all my life, and I didn't think much of it. I don't like to be *floated* to places, willy-nilly. But I stood on the deck with Rachel on one hip, pretending to enjoy myself, and he didn't keep us out too long. The second time was unplanned. It was in July, after several days of rain. He came late one afternoon when the little ones were off playing somewhere. "I wanted to see if you'd do me a favor," he told me. "Oh, anything!" I said. I was so glad to have *him* asking *me* for something.

"After rainy spells, if I don't have a chance to get down here myself, would you row out to the boat and dry my sails for me?"

"Do what?"

"Come out; I'll show you."

So we left the baby with Darcy and pulled the dinghy out of the weeds in front of the house, and he showed me how to row. Well, *that* much I more or less knew already, having been to Girl Scout camp on a muddy pond the summer I was ten. But then we reached the ketch and I felt so clumsy. I hated that clambering up the side, wondering if I might kick the dinghy out from under me or tip Brian into the water when he offered me his hand. Up on deck I shook myself out and smoothed my skirt down and gave a little laugh. "Well!" I said. "Now tell me what to do." He taught me how to unfurl the sails and run them up. It didn't look hard. "Let them stay awhile, an afternoon or so," he said. "Bring the kids if you want." Then he said, "Let's take her out, shall we?"

"You mean right now?"

"Why not?"

"But it's—now it's almost *evening*," I said.

"We won't be long."

"All right," I said. I was getting nervous. I felt fairly sure that he wanted to talk about Jeremy. Why else take me away from the children, and suggest a sail in that artificial voice that meant it wasn't so spur-of-the-moment after all? I wondered if Jeremy had fallen ill, or died, or found somebody else. I felt my hands growing cold, but I didn't tell Brian to break the news because I was too scared. I just sat there freezing to death on a warm summer afternoon, and Brian started the motor and steered us slowly out past the other moored boats.

When we reached open water he cut the engine. The quiet rolled down over us like a bolt of silk. I could hear water lapping, ropes creaking, Brian doing something complicated to tighten the sails. Oh, everything was so unfamiliar! I felt that this entire scene was foreign and bizarre, some trumped-up substitute for the world where Jeremy lived. Every move that Brian made, even the tone of his voice and the way his beard ruffled and parted in the wind, was *makeshift;* nothing like Jeremy at all. When he came to sit down beside me the sheen in the unknown fabric of his shirt made me want to go home. He laid an arm across my back and his hand rested on my shoulder—a big, wiry hand, as unlike Jeremy's as a hand can get. Now, I thought, is when he will say it. They shield you and brace you before they tell you, as if the blow they are about to deal is a physical one. I know all about it. (Don't ask me how.) I swallowed and waited, and hoped that he wouldn't feel me shudder when he started talking.

Only he didn't. He didn't talk at all. First I thought he was waiting for me to prepare myself, and then I thought he was having trouble finding the words. And then, when the silence had gone on for several minutes, I gave him a sidelong glance and saw him sitting perfectly relaxed in the orange light, one hand loose on the tiller and his eyes on the mainsail. He wasn't looking for words at all.

Well! I was too surprised to be angry. Where were all those thin blondes that came visiting at the gallery or sauntering down to his dinghy in their crisp white bellbottoms? Or was he, perhaps, just laying an arm around me out of bachelor's habit? I am not the type to jump to conclusions. I moved away, rising to peer off the stern of the boat as if I had seen something interesting. "Come here and sit with me, Mary," Brian said. I was afraid I might laugh. He seemed so sure of himself, giving directions that way—it was a tone I wasn't used to. It didn't seem to have anything to do with me. I stayed where I was, staring at the streamers of the sunset in the water and fighting back the laughter and the tears that were swelling in my eyes. "Well," said Brian finally. "Shall we head back?"

Going home, he used the motor all the way. Then when he had tied the boat to the mooring again he furled and bound the sails in silence. I wondered if he were angry. The only friend I had nowadays. And with all that I *owed* him! There suddenly seemed to be so many complications to life, so many tangles and knots and unexpected traps, that I felt too tired to hold my head up. I dropped like a stone into his dinghy, pretending not to notice the hand he held out to me. I sat slumped over with my elbows on my knees while he rowed us ashore. Then as we touched land, as I was stepping past him while he steadied the dinghy, he said, "Mary."

The sun had set by now. In the twilight his voice seemed closer than it was, a little furry behind the beard. Whatever he was planning to say, I didn't want to hear it. I spun around and smiled, giving him a good brisk handshake. "I certainly do thank you for the boat ride!" I said. "And I'll be sure to tend to those sails, Brian, if we happen to have a rainy spell."

But he held onto my hand and looked straight into my eyes, not smiling back. "Don't worry, I'm not going to rush you," he said. And after a minute: "Good night, Mary."

That's what they say in soap operas: Don't worry, I'm not going to rush you. The romantic, masterful hero with the steady gaze. People don't say it for *real*. There are no heros in real life.

I went back into the house and found the children

grouped around Rachel, who was standing. Not unsupported, of course—she had two fistfuls of the couch cover—but it was the first time she had managed it and they were all excited. "Come watch," they told me. "Sit, Rachel. Sit down. Show mom how you do it." They uncurled each of her fingers and tried to fold her up, but she wouldn't bend. She stiffened her legs, refusing to return to her old floor-level existence. I had forgotten how desperately babies struggle to be vertical. Always up, away, out of laps and arms and playpens. Why, in no time she was going to wean herself! All my children lost interest in nursing once they could walk. They took off out the door one day to join the others, leaving me babyless, and for a few months I would feel a little lost until I found out I was pregnant again. Only now, it wasn't going to be that way. I hadn't considered that before. I stood staring at Rachel, my very last baby, while she fought off all those grubby little hands that were trying to reseat her. "Look, Rachel," they said, "we just want you to show Mom. Sit a minute, Rachel."

For the first time, then, I knew that Jeremy was not going to ask us back.

Now it was deep summer, and the air under the tin roof was so hot that we spent most of our time outside. I bought the younger children an inflatable wading pool. They stayed entire days in it, splashing around in their underpants, but Darcy was too old for that kind of thing and she had trouble amusing herself. I would find her sitting in the scrubby brown grass, under the glaring sun, frowning at the river. She was so *serious*. "Why don't you take a walk, honey?" I said. "Pick us some flowers for the dinner table." Then she would look straight at me, narrowly, as if she were trying to figure something out. I thought probably she wanted to ask what we were doing here. She was old enough, after all, to see how strange it was. She had been yanked out of a school she loved; she had been separated from Jeremy without even telling him goodbye, and in some ways she was closer to Jeremy than any of the others were. But it was the others who asked the questions—

when would they see him, and what was he doing that kept him so busy, and could they bring him back a present of some kind? Darcy kept quiet. "Why don't you head over to the boatyard and see what's going on?" I asked her. But if she did she took Rachel with her, as if she couldn't imagine doing anything purely for her own enjoyment. She set the baby on her little sharp hip and walked off tilted, with her head lowered, plodding along on dusty bare feet. The knobs on the back of her neck showed and her legs were all polka-dotted with mosquito bite scabs.

Coming here was the most selfish thing I have ever done.

In the evenings I heated kettles of water on the hot plate and sponged off the little ones. Then I dressed them in fresh underwear—I hadn't brought anything so inessential as pajamas—and sent them to bed. Darcy sat up reading movie magazines borrowed from the steelworker's daughter. The whole house had the sharp smell of insect spray. Moths were pattering against the sagging screens and I felt as if I were coated with a thin layer of plastic, I was so salty and sweaty. It was the hardest time of day for me. "I believe I might go for a walk," I would tell Darcy. "Will you keep an ear out for the baby?" Then I would step into the dark and go down to the water's edge, and slip the dinghy from its tangle of weeds. All alone I would row out to the ketch—me! so landbound! It was the only place I could get free of the cramped feeling, those masses of hot little bodies tossing in a tiny cube of space, sticking to the red vinyl mats. To escape from that I was even willing to cross the black water and make the climb from the dinghy to the deck, trusting my weight to this mysterious object that somehow managed to keep itself upright fifteen feet above solid earth.

Now there were fat little orange life vests heaped all over the deck—six of them. Brian had brought them out one Saturday, laying them before me one by one like an Indian warrior laying skins before his maiden's tent. Five would have been bad enough, but six! That

implied we would be here until Rachel was old enough
to sail too. "Oh, Brian," I said. "Well, I—that's very
nice of you but I really think the regular life preservers
were fine, it's not as if they go with you all that—"
You would never have guessed how often I pictured five
of my children drowning simultaneously. At the moment all that worried me was Brian, his brown eyes so
gentle and amused above the beard—so *confident*.

Jeremy's eyes were blue. Brown eyes didn't seem
right any more.

In the Gothic novels Guy used to buy me the
heroine was always marrying for convenience or money or safety from some danger, and when she was proposed to she took pains to make that clear. "I must be
honest, Sir Brent, I do not love you." "Oh, I understand
that perfectly, my dear." Then later, of course, she did
begin loving him, and everything ended happily. I wish
I had been honest. I accepted Jeremy because it was
all I could think of to do at the time, and although I
believe he knew that we never discussed it in so many
words. I was trying to be so *delicate* with him. My first
mistake. One day he said, "Mary, do you love me?"
He said, "I need to know, do you?" And I said, "Yes,
Jeremy. Of course I do." Well, I did have a sort of fond
feeling. When he brought me that first bouquet of chicory and poison ivy my heart went right out to him, but
not in that way. Then after we had been together a while
it seemed as if something crept up on me without noticing, and one morning I watched him stooping to fum-
ble with Darcy's broken shoelace and the love just
came pouring over me. Only by then, of course, there
was no way to tell him. He thought I had been loving
him for months already. Was that why things went
wrong?

For we never got it straightened out. When I tried
to show how I felt it seemed I flooded him, washed him
several feet distant from me, left him bewildered and
dismayed. Sometimes I wondered, could it be that he
was happier when I didn't love him back? It seemed all
I could do was give him things and do him favors, and
make him see how much he needed me. The more he
depended on me the easier I felt. In fact I depended

on his dependency, we were two dominoes leaning against each other, but did Jeremy ever realize that?

Once he made a piece showing a white cottage with a picket fence and roses on trellises, set on a green hill. At first you might think it was a calendar picture. The hill was so green, the cottage so white. "Oh!" I said when I saw it. "Well, it's very—it's not exactly *like* you, Jeremy, is it?" Then I came closer, and something disturbed me. I mean, it was *too* green and white, and the sky was too blue. The hill was too perfect a semi-circle, and the pickets of the fence marched across the paper like gradations on a ruler. I felt that he had twisted something, and yet I couldn't say what. I felt that in some way he was insulting me, or protesting against me. Yet I don't think he knew that he was. "Jeremy—" I said, and turned to look at him, but I found him punching red paper circles to make perfect flowers, and I could tell from his frown that that was all he was thinking about.

He has no sense of humor but I never understood why that should be important. He has always been either too much removed from us (shut away in body and in spirit, cutting burlap) or too much with us (smack underfoot from dawn to dark, when other men are busy in some office). And I won't try to convince anyone that he is handsome. Nor that he has what they call "personality"—watch some visiting neighbor woman stammer when he fixes her with his worktime gaze, as if he were wondering why she doesn't leave when in fact he is not even aware that she is there. On top of that we are separated by years and years, although with Jeremy that never mattered as much as it might have with someone else. He is not really a product of his time. When I was a toddler, for instance, other men his age were fighting World War II, but Jeremy wasn't I don't have any proof he even knew about the war—not that one, or the one we are going through now. Nothing outside touches him. Sometimes he seems younger than I am, as if *events* are what age people. I remember when his sisters came to meet me. We were having tea in the parlor and they were discussing dead friends and relatives. I couldn't take my eyes off them. They were so old! They had that reverence for the past—forever returning to skate back around its edges, peering down, fascinated by its cold and pallid face beneath two feet of water. Repeating all they said in that doddery, old-lady way. (Jeremy did that too but I had never noticed before.) I looked from one to another. I felt like a very small girl at a tea party with three ancient relatives. I began to be shy and tongue-tied. What was I doing here? How could I have anything to do with this elderly man? But when they left he stood hugging himself at the door with his face all forlorn and I felt he was a two-year old in need of comfort. "There now," I told him, "won't you come back in? Have another cup of tea." And I laid my hand on his soft limp home-clipped hair and pressed my cheek against his, and felt far older than he would ever be.

When I first came here, I would have laughed aloud at the thought of loving him. Yet it is only now that I think to be surprised at myself. While it was coming about I hardly noticed. We have such an ability to adjust to change! We are like amoebas, encompassing and ingesting and adapting and moving on, until enormous events become barely perceptible jogs in our life histories. All I know is that bit by bit my world began to center on him, so that my first thought in the morning and my last at night was concern about his welfare. "Are you all right?" I used to wake and ask him out of nowhere. "Are you—is there anything you need?" I would move to his side of the bed and feel him seep away from me somehow, backing off from my everlasting questions and my face too close to his and my perfume, which—even if it was only the hand lotion I had put on after finishing the dishes—suddenly seemed too rich and full now that I was next to him. "Oh, I'm sorry!" I wanted to say. "I never meant to—I don't want to *overpower* you in any way, believe me!" But then he would only have backed off further; saying that would have been overpowering in itself. There was no way I could win. Or I could win only by losing—by leaving bed, reluctantly, to sit up with a sick child or a colicky baby, and then he would come stumbling through the dark house calling my name. "Mary? Where'd you go, Mary? I can't find you."

He changed. I changed. He gathered some kind of stubborn, hidden strength while I became more easily touched by anything small and vulnerable—changes that each of us caused in the other, but they were exactly the ones that have separated us and that will keep us separate. If he calls me back he will be admitting a weakness. If I return unasked I will be bearing down upon him and plowing him under. If I weren't crying I would laugh.

One day in August Rachel started fussing at breakfast time, and she kept it up without a single pause. She wouldn't eat or sleep. She was flushed and her breath had an ether smell that my children usually get with fever, but no one in the boatyard owned a thermometer and I was too hot myself to be able to gauge the temperature of her skin. By afternoon I had decided I would have to find a doctor. I was going to ask for a ride from Zack—the boat mechanic, a slimy man who whistled whenever he saw me, but still he did have a pickup truck—and then I saw Brian's car pulling up in our backyard and out he stepped, looking very steady and reliable in his old jeans and a fresh-ironed shirt. "Brian!" I said. "Will you drive me to the doctor? Rachel's sick."

"Of course," he said, and turned on one heel without a second's pause and went back to the car. I felt better already. I grabbed up Rachel and my purse, called out instructions to Darcy, and slid into the front seat. "Her doctor is on St. Paul," I said, "just a few blocks away from us. Away from Jeremy."

"What's the matter with her?" Brian asked.

"I don't know. I just don't know."

Rachel was quieter now, maybe from the shock of being in a car, but she still whimpered a little. Brian said, "Could be a tooth."

"Oh, no, she wouldn't make this much fuss."

"Are you sure? It's my understanding that—"

"Will you please just *drive?*" I said.

He stopped talking. We sped down the gravel road I had nearly forgotten, between rows of neat little flower-decked houses and trailers. After a minute I said, "Sorry, Brian."

"That's all right."

"It's just that I'm afraid he'll close his office soon, you see, and then I wouldn't know how to—"

"Sure, sure, I understand."

We turned onto the main highway. It seemed to me that Brian was driving faster than I had ever gone before. Fields and factories and junkyards skimmed past, and then came the first gray buildings of the city and the long unbroken walls of rowhouses. Brian dodged in and out between slower cars, honking like an ambulance, scarcely ever putting on his brakes. I felt that I was in good hands.

In front of the doctor's office, he double-parked and got out of the car. "Oh, don't come with me," I said. "You'll get a ticket, Brian." I was expecting him just to drop me off and then pick me up later. But he had already opened the door on my side and reached for the baby, and I let him take her. Freed of her weight, I felt light and cool. I floated behind him across the sidewalk, which seemed very crowded, through the revolving door of a surprisingly tall dark building. In the lobby I was hit by the cold smell of marble, which I had forgotten about. I had also forgotten the doctor's office number. Imagine, after ten years of school checkups! It was as if I had been away for decades. My eyes had trouble focusing on the tiny white letters in the showcase. Even my hand, skimming a straight line between his name and his number, looked like a stranger's hand, brown and chapped, bigger-boned. "Four thirteen," I told Brian.

"We won't wait for the elevator."

I followed him up the stairs. Rachel peered at me over his shoulder; all this speed had startled her into silence.

In the waiting room Brian told the nurse, "We don't have an appointment, but it's an emergency. This baby is very ill."

The nurse looked at Rachel. Rachel grinned.

We were shown into a cubicle at the front of the building. Above the examining table was an enormous, sooty window overlooking the street. I could peer down and see cars threading their mysterious paths below us, stopping and starting magically. I felt I was observing them from another planet. "You can undress her now, I'll send the doctor in immediately," the nurse said. But all Rachel wore was a diaper, a damp one. I left it on her. I stayed at the window, remembering other, happier times when I had come here with three or four children for their shots. Then my only worries had been how to keep them out of the cotton swabs, and how to calm the one who was scared of tongue depressors, and what to fix Jeremy for supper that night.

The doctor came in with his white coattails billowing—a young man, dark-skinned. "Now! Mrs. Pauling," he said. "What seems to be the problem here?"

"I think Rachel's sick," I said, "but I can't tell what's bothering her."

He gave Brian a short nod and stretched the baby out on the table. She frowned at him. He prodded her stomach, felt her neck, looked into her nose and mouth and ears and listened to her chest. I held my breath. The skin on my scalp ached from waiting. Then, "Ear infection," he said. "Both sides."

"Oh! Are you sure that's all?"

"It's all I see. She been pulling at her ears lately?"

"No, she hasn't."

"Usually that's a sign."

"Well, *I* know that," I said. Relief made me snappish. I felt he was accusing me of something. Did he think that after six children I wouldn't notice a thing like ear-pulling? *All* my children have been susceptible to earaches. I wondered if he disapproved of Rachel's single, grayish diaper. I became aware suddenly of what I must look like in my dirndl skirt and rubber flip-flops, one shoulder strap slipping out from the sleeveless blouse that I had fastened shut with a safety pin. My purse was patched with a flesh-colored Band-Aid. I turned it to its good side while he was bending to write out a prescription.

When we were back in the car, loaded down now with penicillin and decongestants and a brand-new thermometer, Brian turned east although it would have been simpler to continue due south. I suppose he thought it would disturb me to pass near my old neighborhood. "Wait," I almost said. "Let's go back, can't we?" What I wanted to do was just confirm that the house existed; it wasn't that I planned to walk inside or anything. But Brian looked straight ahead and chewed on his pipe, pretending that this route was a natural one, and I didn't say anything after all.

His car was air-conditioned—something I hadn't noticed when I was so upset. For the first time in weeks I could stop fighting the heat, and Rachel actually went to sleep in my lap. "Must be fast-acting medicine," Brian said. (We had given her the first dose back in the drugstore.) When I told him I thought it was the coolness he frowned. He said, "Now will you believe that shack is no place for children?"

"Well, I don't see how the *shack* comes into this," I said. "We're perfectly comfortable there. The children get earaches any old place; it's something to do with the twists in their ear tubes."

"In summer, even?"

"Any time."

"I don't believe it," Brian said. "And if they're sick in summer, what will winter be like? The place is not insulated, you know. There's no heat, and you will have to turn the water off every night, and I won't show up just in the nick of time this way."

"No, I know that," I said. Actually I had thought about winter several times lately, but then I put it out of my mind again. I said, "We'll work it out when the time comes. I'm sure that everything will—"

"It's August, Mary."

"I'm aware of that."

"Could you tell me what's going on with you and Jeremy?"

"Well, I don't know exactly," I said.

"Do you still love him?"

"Oh yes," I said. Which was easier than describing

the exact combination of love and hurt and anger that I had been feeling about Jeremy lately.

Brian looked over at me for a second, and then back at the road. "I don't want to step on Jeremy's toes," he said, "but I wish that if you've really left him you would make it final and get a divorce. Are you considering that?"

I don't know why my life always seems more confusing than other people's. First Jeremy proposed marriage when I wasn't divorced and now Brian was proposing a divorce when I wasn't married. I said, "I'm sorry, I really don't want to think about anything right now."

"All right, then. I'm just letting you know that I'm here, Mary, and sooner or later you're going to want *someone* to turn to."

Did he suppose I hadn't thought of that?

My poor, pathetic store of money, which once had seemed the answer to everything, had almost disappeared. I lay awake nights trying to think of people who might help. On the trip home now I dreamed up ludicrous solutions: I could take up with the slimy boat mechanic, I could suddenly reappear at Guy Tell's front door. I pictured the string of children trailing me like ducklings, Guy's startled face, his new wife peering out behind him. "I've come back to you, Guy!" "Uh, who are all these people with you, Mary?" I nearly laughed, but then I grew serious. I began to see how every move I had made in my life had required some man to provide my support—first Guy when I left my parents, then John Harris when I left Guy, and Jeremy when John Harris left. Now I couldn't imagine any other way to do it. I had come here on my own, certainly, but it began to look as if I couldn't keep it up. Underneath, Jeremy and I were more alike than anyone knew. Eventually I would give in and find someone, Brian or someone else, it all came to the same thing. I could see it ahead of me as clearly as if it had already happened. I couldn't think of any way out. I felt drained and weak suddenly, as if I had shriveled.

I looked over at Brian, but he had dropped the

subject when I told him to and now he was just driving along puffing quietly on his pipe.

In the evenings I tell fairytales, the same old fairytales over and over. The children curl against me, clean and warm in their fresh white underwear, smelling of milk. I close my eyes and take a deep breath of them. I could tell these stories in my sleep. "Another, now another," the children say. Don't they ever get tired?

I see myself on a sagging couch beneath a warped tin roof, braced on each side by my children for lack of firmer support. I understand that from outside I seem to have been leading a fairly dramatic life, involving elopements and love children and men stretching in a nearly unbroken series behind me, but the fact is that when you proceed through these experiences day by day they are not really so earthshaking. All events, except childbirth, can be reduced to a heap of trivia in the end. When I die I expect I will be noticing a water ring someone left on the coffee table, or a spiral of steam rising from a whistling teapot. I will be sure to miss the moment of my passing.

Rapunzel. The Princess and the Pea. Rumpelstiltskin. My voice grows croaky. My mind runs ahead of the words. I play silent games with the tired old plots, I like to ponder the endings beyond the endings. How about Rapunzel, are we sure she was really happy ever after? Maybe the prince stopped loving her now that her hair was short. Maybe the Genuine Princess was a great disappointment to her husband, being so quick to find the faults and so forthright about pointing them out. And after Rumpelstiltskin was defeated the miller's daughter lived in sorrow forever, for the king kept nagging her to spin more gold and she could never, never manage it again.

8

Spring through Fall, 1971: Olivia

You know how I knew she had left him? I found him
smoking a cigarette. I went up to his studio on Friday
night to ask where the others were, it felt so weird
downstairs. I knocked and stuck my head in, and
there he sat on this purple velvet couch holding a cigarette between his thumb and index finger and blowing out a long careful funnel of smoke. "Mr. Pauling?"
I said. "Jeremy? Where's everyone gone to?" But then
I guessed for myself, right while I was asking. Something about the way he was holding the cigarette. I
don't know why. "Good Lord, she's left you," I said.
He nodded. I wouldn't say that he looked upset. Just
stunned, sort of. He cleared his throat but didn't say
anything, and then he switched the cigarette to a new
position between his index and middle fingers and sat
there staring at it, and I closed the door again.

Well, it shouldn't have surprised me. Actually she was
a very ordinary woman, not at all what you'd expect of
an artist's wife. The wonder of it is that she ever had the
good sense to marry him in the first place. So *earth-
bound*, she was. Always nagging and tidying and
bringing him her little domestic problems. Knocking
on the door: "Jeremy, the storm window man's here
with an estimate and won't take any signature but
yours. *Won't* you please come out. Do you have any
idea what goes into the running of this house?" If they
ever start a men's liberation movement, I'll join it in a

flash. Though of course it's taken me a while to see her so clearly, I admit it. At first I was just glad to get a roof over my head, someone watching out for me and making me wear my raincoat. But I left a mother just like her up in Pennsylvania, went through all the bother of running away only to end up here in the same kind of stewpot. It's lucky I finally got wise. When I think how close I came to going over to her side!

All the same, it was sort of a shock at first to discover she was gone.

I went downstairs to make a peanut butter sandwich. By then the senior citizens were in the kitchen scrounging for supper. The two of them got on my nerves, shuffling around the way they did. They seemed to be weaving a net across the kitchen floor. "Listen," I said. "Mary's taken the kids and left." *That* shook them up. Mr. Somerset's mouth sagged open and he forgot to watch the frying pan. Old lady Vinton went on stirring her eggs but I could tell she was surprised. Her spatula went slower and slower. She kept her eyes on what she was doing. "Took to her heels," I said. "Didn't you know?"

"Perhaps she's off visiting," Miss Vinton said.

"Who would she visit?"

"Well, now, we don't know the whole story. I'm sure there's an explanation."

"Like what, for instance."

"I'm sure it will all work out in the end."

People say that when they mean that life will get back to the way it was before. It never occurs to them that a change might be for the better.

I said, "I think I'll take Jeremy a peanut butter sandwich."

"I don't believe Jeremy eats peanut butter," Miss Vinton said.

"He's never had mine, then. I make it myself."

Mr. Somerset said, "Yes, yes, we all know that." Mr. Somerset doesn't like me. His voice when he spoke to me was all cracked and peevish. "Don't think I haven't heard you," he said, "running that blender to death the minute I set my head on my pillow for my afternoon nap."

I ignored him. I spread peanut butter on a slice of whole wheat bread. "At *least* I imagine he could use the company," I said.

"Perhaps he would like to be left alone," said Miss Vinton.

"That's for him to tell me, isn't it?"

"People can't always say what they feel, Olivia. I imagine he might like to think things through a while, and when he gets hungry he'll come down and—"

I know her type. Always so virtuous about keeping out of the way, letting others be. It's an excuse, of course. Aloofness is the easy way out, I believe in plunging right ahead. Slamming the sandwich on a tray and adding an orange (artificially colored, but what could I do?) and marching straight upstairs to Jeremy. Knock-knock. "It's me, it's Olivia. You hungry?"

No answer. I went in anyway. He was smoking another cigarette. "Here," I said, setting the tray down, and then I went over to a half-finished piece and said, "I like it." I pretended not to notice how deserted it looked. I pretended he was just carrying on with the making of it no matter what, which in my opinion is what he should have been doing. "It's got a good flow to it," I said. To tell the truth I didn't have the vaguest idea what comments were required, but I was going to learn. I have the deepest respect for artists. I said, "When are you planning on finishing it?"

"I don't think I will ever finish it," Jeremy said.

"Nonsense."

He put the cigarette to his mouth again. You could tell he wasn't used to smoking. The filtered tip barely touched his lips, and he sucked in very quickly and let the smoke out without inhaling it. The pack in his lap said "True"—Miss Vinton's, then. A namby-pamby brand. "Look," I said, "do you mind if I just stay a while and see how you work?"

He stopped watching his smoke and looked at me. His eyes were wide and his mouth fell open. I wasn't expecting so much attention so suddenly. I

smoothed my hair back and said, "Of course, if I would
distract you in any way—"

But then he suddenly got to his feet, he *lurched*
to his feet, like someone pulled by strings, and set his
fingertips to his mouth and stood swaying there. After
a moment he turned and ran to the bathroom and I
heard him throwing up. It seemed to go on forever. I
sat down on the couch and wound a strand of hair
around my finger, waiting for him to come back. I wasn't
in any hurry to leave. I had all the time in the world.

Once last winter when I was on my way to work I
looked across a street and saw Mary walking her kids
home from school. She was heading toward a very busy
corner where a crossing guard usually stands, but that
day for some reason the crossing guard was absent. A
crowd of school children milled about on the curb
looking scared. At the moment I happened to glance
over, Mary was just arriving in their midst. She carried
the baby and held Edward by the hand, and her little
girls were around her in a circle. Then the light changed.
Down she stepped, into the street. Little hands reached
out from all directions; strangers' children clutched
at the hem of her coat or the edge of her sleeve or the
corner of her purse or even the baby's one dangling,
bootied foot; and if they couldn't reach her they hung
onto the coat of a child who could, and off she sailed
with her beautiful white face looming high above them
keeping watch on all sides for runaway cars and rough
boys on bicycles and any other unexpected dangers.
What do you suppose it feels like to be so certain of
your role? To have such a clear sense of place? I'd been
waiting a long time to learn what *my* role was. I kept
going to different towns, as if what I looked for were a
physical object. At night I dreamed eerie dreams. Voices
floated in and out, offering solutions and promises and
answers, but when I woke up I could never remember
what they had said. Every morning I took Jeremy
some nuts and fruit for breakfast, and at noon a sandwich, and at suppertime another, and although he
didn't appear to notice me I stood waiting anyway,
hoping to be defined.

I went in one day with a bowl of granola and an apple, and I found him nailing boards together into a sort of box. He was working very slowly, and not on the statue he was on before. That surprised me a little. Mary told me once that he always finished everything he started, even if it wasn't turning out to be what he wanted; he seemed to think pieces came out of him like olives out of a bottle, and he had no choice but to let the first one out before he could get to the second. Well, I don't know, maybe this particular olive was only a fragment all along. I set his breakfast down and he said, "Oh. I'll be with you in a minute."

"You will?"

"Just find your things. Where are your things?"

"What things?"

He straightened up and looked at me. "Aren't you here for a lesson?" he said.

I didn't know what to think. As far as I knew he didn't even *give* lessons. I wondered if he were losing his mind. "Wait, now," I said. "I'm Olivia. Remember?"

Then his whole face got pink and he began fumbling with the hammer. "Oh," he said. "I'm so—I'm sorry."

"That's okay."

"I must have been—you appear to be somewhat the student type, you see."

"Well, I'm not," I said. "I'm not at all."

Then he said, "No one is purely what they seem on the surface."

It was the first real thing he had ever said to me. Well, all right, it wasn't much. But it was a beginning.

He gave me a list of supplies to buy for him at an art shop. The shop bowled me over, I'd never been in such a good place before. It was very small and cozy and it smelled of glue and wood and canvas. The old man behind the counter came about to my waist. He said, "Yes? Can I help?"

"I'd like half a dozen cans of spray adhesive," I read off the list, "and two tubes of liquid solder and five pounds of scrap stained glass." I had no idea what

I was ordering, but it seemed to make sense to the old man. He kept scurrying around, coming back to set things on the counter. "This is for an artist friend of mine," I told him.

"Yes," he said.

"Maybe you know him. Jeremy Pauling, he had a one-man show at the O'Donnell Gallery."

"Pauling, yes," the man said. He started penciling a column of figures onto a sheet of brown wrapping paper. "We often see his wife," he said.

"You do?"

"I'll just put this on the account, shall I?"

"Account?"

He stopped adding the figures and looked up at me.

"Oh. Okay," I said.

I don't know why I was so surprised. Sears and Roebuck doesn't carry *everything,* after all; she'd have had to run errands for him now and then. Still, it sort of spoiled my mood. Especially when the man gave me the package and said, "I hope Mrs. Pauling isn't sick. She's *such* a lovely person."

Of course, he was only a salesman. Salesmen always have to sound complimentary.

By the time I got home again I was feeling better. I climbed the stairs pretending to be in a movie. Maybe someday there *would* be a movie made, right in this house. Some Hollywood actress pretending to be me would bring supplies to an actor pretending to be Jeremy. An American Toulouse-Lautrec. What theme music would they choose? I made up something and hummed it as I went. I was only a side character but powerful, a major influence, and the last scene would show me holding his head as he died. Some major transformation in his art would be dated from the time he met me. I tried to imagine what that transformation would be. When I walked into the studio his new piece was the first thing I looked at, but to tell the truth it didn't seem much different from anything he'd done in the past. Complicated. Involved. Like one of those poems you give up on after the first couple lines, because even though you know it must be good it takes so much work to read it. He had stood his box construction on end and set in boards horizontally and vertically, as if he were making a cabinet with lots of different-sized cubbyholes, and now he was painting the inside of each cubbyhole a different color. Oh, well. Still in the movie, I put a hand on his shoulder and said, "I think you've hit on something this time." He shied away and blinked up at me. "Anyway," I said. "Here's the stuff I got you."

When he went through the art supplies he knew exactly what he was doing. For the first time he seemed perfectly sure of himself. He held a sheet of blue glass to the light and squinted at it and then set it in a sort of vertical rack beneath a counter; he shook a can of adhesive next to his ear; he rotated a ten-color ballpoint pen I'd lifted on impulse from a display card on my way out of the shop. I liked the way he held it in both hands, so respectfully, as if he understood it in some deeper way than ordinary people could. Oh, he was really getting to me. "That's on the house," I said. He looked over at me. "I mean it's a present, it's from me to you." He set the pen down on a table. Maybe he didn't like getting presents. He wiped his hands on his trousers and stood there a minute, frowning at the pen, before he turned and picked up his brush again. Not very good movie material. They could make this a silent film and never miss a thing. "Tell me, Jeremy," I said. "Don't you ever go to bars or cafés or anything?"

"What? Oh, no."

"Seems to me you'd want to go *someplace* like that."

He finished painting a cubbyhole gray. He switched brushes and started on another: yellow. Every little crack covered completely, the brush prodding a knothole over and over with patient, stubborn, whiskery sounds until it was filled in.

"Look, where are all those mad happy artists I'm always hearing about?" I asked him. "Don't you ever go drinking or anything? Don't you have any artist friends? Don't you ever dance with them or get drunk or sing songs?"

His eyes when he looked up were so pale and empty, I thought he would sink into one of those staring spells, but he surprised me. "I believe," he said, "that the last happy artist was a caveman, coming back from the hunt and dashing off a picture of it on a stone wall."

"Oh," I said. "Well, what about—"

"Or maybe not," said Jeremy. "Maybe not, even that far back. Maybe he was lame, not allowed to hunt, and he stayed home with the women and children and drew those pictures to comfort himself."

"How do you figure *that?*" I said. "How do you know the caveman didn't stay home because drawing took so much out of him, he *couldn't* hunt?"

It wasn't for nothing I asked him that. Sometimes it seemed to me that Jeremy got up looking like other men and then faded away as he worked, as if art erased him somehow. As if each piece were another layer scraped off him, when already he was down to the quick. But if he heard me, he didn't take me seriously. He was off on some track of his own. "I often dream that I'm a caveman," he said.

"Oh, *do* you?" I said. I love to talk about dreams.

"It's always back before men could make fire, you understand. They observed it, yes, but only when lightning struck and forests caught fire by accident and burned themselves out. In my dreams I sit all night watching the treetops, hoping that within my lifetime something will be set on fire for me to see."

"Maybe it's a message," I said.

"Pardon?"

"Something supernatural."

"Oh. Perhaps."

I said, "Oh, Jeremy, don't you just love talking this way? You never did, before now. I was beginning to wonder about you. Don't we get along beautifully together?"

"What? Oh. Surely," Jeremy said.

Then he set the yellow brush down and chose an

ivory one, and when he looked up at me a moment later I might as well not have been there, his face was so slack and his eyes so transparent.

I went to O'Donnell's Gallery, looking for some clue to Jeremy. This was in July, but I wore my white trenchcoat with the belt ends stuck in the pockets because that always makes me feel more in control of things, and I didn't take my sunglasses off even inside. Galleries tend to make me go to pieces. I told Mary that once, when she asked if I wanted to see Jeremy's one-man show, and she laughed. She thought I was speaking figuratively. *Mary* never goes to pieces. I don't believe she is capable of it

Now Jeremy's show was over and I was sorry I had missed it, but there was still plenty of his work around. All lamplit against white walls. Displayed like that, it didn't appear to have been made by human hands. I found collages of his, a few small early statues, a more recent one standing in the middle of the room. I looked at the recent one first. I was counting on some chink of light to open for me, but it didn't. What was I supposed to make of this? A man pushing a wheelbarrow, webbed around with strings and pulleys and chains and weights. He was mostly plaster, but you could find nearly every material in the world if you looked long enough. It seemed as if Jeremy had thrown it together in some kind of frenzy. Painted sections faded suddenly into carving, carving into découpage, and down the man's chest I found words hurriedly etched with some sharp instrument—"A heavy cup of warm . . ."—trailing off where he ran out of space, as if he had thrown his knife away in some fit of impatience and had reached blindly for what came to him next, a sheet of burlap or a glue bottle or a coil of wire. I didn't get it. I moved backwards in time, past the smaller pieces, on to the collages. I took off my sunglasses, but that didn't help. Besides, my neck was beginning to ache. That always happens when I get frustrated. So I gave up, but I did have one last thing to do before I could leave. I went to the owner, who sat in a little office at the rear. He was riffling through a sheaf of papers on a clipboard. Good-looking man with a beard. "Hi," I said.

He smoothed the papers and looked up at me. He said, "Well, hi."

"I noticed you have some pieces by what's his name, Paul? Pauling? Now I'm not buying just this *moment* but I did want to say that I hope you know how good he is. He's the best guy you've got. How come you price him so low?"

"It's Olivia, isn't it?"

"What?"

"I saw you once in Mary's kitchen when I was carrying out a piece," he said. "Good to see you. I'm Brian O'Donnell."

"Oh," I said. I put my shades back on. "Well. Sorry. I just thought I'd throw in a vote for him while I was here."

"Good idea. How is he?"

"He's fine."

"I saw him last week but he said he didn't have any pieces ready."

"No, but he will," I said. "Really, he's going to have a lot, very soon now. Very different from his other stuff. It's a transformation. You know his wife left him."

"Yes."

"Now *I* am with him."

"You are?"

I pulled the belt ends out of my pockets and buckled them. I stuck out my hand and said, "Well, good seeing you." He stood up and leaned across the desk. His palm was stippled from the back of the clipboard. He held onto my hand even after I had started to pull away. "You're with Jeremy?" he said.

"Oh yes."

"You're—are you—?"

"You must come and see us sometime," I said.

"Well, all right."

"Only not right away, of course. He still has a *few* tag ends to finish up. See you later."

"Sure thing," said Mr. O'Donnell.

I slung my purse over my shoulder and left. I could feel him staring after me. Outside it was about ninety degrees, but still I was glad I'd worn my trenchcoat.

I am not as disorganized as I look. I see the patterns, I can put two and two together as well as anyone. And what I'd figured out so far was that if I went on being Jeremy's link with the outside world, buying his glue and fixing his breakfast, I was going to turn into another Mary. That's how these things happen: inch by inch. What I had to do was get *inside,* somehow. Get in his little glass room with him, where it would just be the two of us looking out. Mary never did that, but I was going to. All right, I knew he was old. The first time I saw him he seemed ancient, and peculiar besides. Shaking hands with him was like taking hold of a warm pastry. But that was before I saw him clearly. I saw him clearly as soon as Mary left. I started to feel some pull on me, something in that situation, that artist sitting alone three storeys off the ground, that woman who could leave a man in crumbs just by removing herself from his world. Why, she *was* his world! Why couldn't I be? Only better, closer, more understanding. How do you get into a man like that? Where is the secret button?

I said, "Your whatchamacallit is going well, Jeremy." Though all I could see was that he had finished painting the cubbyholes and started putting bits of junk in them. "It's quite, it's really something," I said.

"But is it unique?"

This wasn't the first time he had asked me that.

"Would you say it was unique?"

"Well, of course," I said.

"Is it—you don't see anybody else in it, do you?"

"Huh?"

"Mary, for example."

"Mary?" I said. What he had added in so far was a bicycle bell, a square of flowered wallpaper, and a wooden button.

"I keep having the feeling that Mary is coloring things in some way."

But the color *I* saw was actual, a sheet of blue glass he was cutting up with a little thing like a pizza wheel. I felt like laughing. Then I got depressed. When was I going to figure out what his work was all about? I had expected it would just come to me—that one day I would walk in the studio door and suddenly understand what he meant. But it hadn't happened yet.

"As if I were seeing through her eyes," he said.

"Seeing—?"

"But of course that's not true. I see for myself."

"Of course."

"I see for myself."

"Sure. All right."

"There's no one else in it, there's not a fragment, there's not a single other person."

"All *right*, Jeremy."

I stopped going out. I stopped answering the phone. I let mail stack up on the sideboard. Mealtimes Jeremy and I went down to the kitchen together and ate an entire box of chocolates or Miss Vinton's liverwurst or nothing at all, it didn't matter. If he was working I lay on the couch in the studio and swung one foot in the air. I looked at the skylight. I knew all the cracks and dead leaves on it. He didn't work very much, though. I had thought he would go faster than he did. Some days he just doodled on a scrap of paper, or sat in his armchair chewing his fingernails, or walked around and around his piece without ever once looking at it. If I spoke, he wouldn't answer. I stopped trying. I lay back and watched brown leaves scuttle across the skylight in the wind.

What we did most was watch television in the dining room. Of course that wasn't what I'd expected to be doing, but I was trying to see things through his eyes, after all. I sat beside him and watched from morning to night. I'd never guessed how caught up you can get in television programs. On the soap operas people's lives were ruled by some twisted design underlying everything, something we were too ignorant to see. On the panel shows they talked back and forth so courteously, their faces so cool and untextured. Look how they waited for one speaker to stop before another began! Look at the way they chose their tones without a second's faltering—a cheerful tone after a dark one, a question, a trill of laughter, a note of sudden firmness. All so perfectly orchestrated. How well behaved they were! I turned toward Jeremy and opened my mouth. I wanted to see if I had the same effect when *I* spoke, but unfortunately I couldn't think of a thing to say. He wouldn't have heard me anyway.

In the afternoon there was *Sesame Street,* I was afraid it would remind him of his children, but it didn't seem to. He watched it like a child himself. When the numbers zoomed out at him he started and then relaxed. He always hoped today's number was a high one that took a lot of singing. He laughed in all the funny places, and bounced a little in his seat. Well, they *were* kind of comical. There was one skit in particular—a thing where a little puppet complains that nothing but a skinned finger has happened to him all day. Then it turns out he skinned his finger running from a dog and the dog was running from a lion who was let loose by a monkey when the fire engine hit the monkey's cage . . . well, I don't remember the exact events but Jeremy certainly did enjoy it. They must have showed it about twenty times over, and every time he sat forward in his seat to peer and nod, and when it was done he would sigh and look down at his knees.

In the evening there were the adventures, a lot of chases and escapes. Jeremy watched everything but the shows where innocent men were suspected of some crime. Then he would say, "No, no, that's no good" —he didn't like feeling anxious for people. He would ask me to locate a comedy, or some medical show where the only deaths were preordained. When the commercials came on, the senior citizens used the time to get a sweater or a bite to eat but Jeremy and I sat still. These things can grow on you after a while. You admire the actors' faces. You get fond of the background music. That funny little chewing gum dance. The Coca-Cola song where everybody seems to like each other.

When bedtime came Jeremy went without saying good night. I might as well not have been there. First he would blink and then rub his eyes and then he would wander off, sort of aimlessly, and a little while later I would hear the water running in the downstairs bathroom. Then I would go to bed myself. I didn't sleep well. I lay curled on my side for hours, listening to the house settle down and grow quiet as if it were folding itself up, huddling inward away from the world outside. Or if I slept I might suddenly awake, at two or three or four in the morning. I sat up strangled in bedclothes, much too hot, dry-throated. It was September now and some nights the steam heat came on. The radiators warming up smelled dusty and bitter; the house seemed like an old person, all rattling bones and coughs and stale breaths.

Other painters have blue periods and rose periods, but Jeremy didn't. His changes were in depth, not color. A flat period, a raised period. A three-dimensional period. What comes after three-dimensional? Four-dimensional. "You're making a time machine," I said to him.

"Hmm?"

"That explains all those weird thingummies you're sticking in."

"Weird? I don't understand why you say that."

But there he went, gluing a plastic banana from Pippi's toy grocery store into the lower right-hand cubbyhole. Next a curly-handled baby's feeding spoon. Poor Rachel. Objects sat jumbled in every cubicle, most of them metallic. The whole thing had the makeshift look of some mad inventor's scale model. Is it any wonder I thought of time machines?

"Time must be the explanation for everything," I told him. "Time loops. Little tangles in time that get knotted off from the main cord. You, for instance," I said, and he looked up. "Do you know why you make your pieces? You're in a time loop."

"I am?"

"You're cut off from the main cord. That's how you see clearly enough; you have more distance. Maybe this statue is a sort of notation, like what archeologists jot down when they're on a dig. You're just visiting. But are you aware of it?"

I didn't expect him to take me up on that, but he did. Not to the *point,* exactly, but, "I've often thought," he said, "if I went back, you know, back in time somehow, I would never be able to show anyone how to make a radio."

"Why would you want to?" I asked him.

"What I mean is that the twentieth century has been wasted on me, don't you see."

"Of course. It's not your time."

"I wish it were," Jeremy said.

"No, Jeremy! Don't you get what I'm saying? If you weren't off in a time loop you wouldn't be making pieces the way you do."

"I *still* wish," Jeremy said.

Then he sat down on the floor and began peeling dried glue from his fingers, like a surgeon stripping off his rubber gloves. Usually that meant he had finished work for the day. His schedule was so peculiar —three hours walking around and around the piece giving it quick shy glances, then ten minutes' work and down he would go in this sodden heap on the floor. I slid off the couch and squatted in front of him. "Ghosts, now," I told him. "I've just figured out what they are. Do you know?"

"No."

"They're people from the past, our ancestors, come to visit us in a time machine. Well, of course! Maybe they're here by accident. Maybe they don't even know what's happened to them. They *wander* in. 'Good heavens,' they say, 'what's going on? How'd I get here?' Then they step back into their time loop, try another period. That's why they keep fading away like they do. I bet you've haunted a lot of places, Jeremy."

"I feel so hungry," Jeremy said.

"Martians, take Martians. How come we think

they're from another planet? They're from *our* planet,
Jeremy, twenty centuries in the future. Wearing helmets
against our outdated atmosphere and looking a little
different on account of evolution. Our descendants,
come back to do a little historical research."

"Well, perhaps," said Jeremy. "You may be right."
He gathered glue peelings into a little heap on the
floor. He said, "Do you know how to make waffles?"

"No." I took the glue peels from him and rolled
them around in my hand. I had so much I wanted to
say to him, and it wasn't very often he would let me
get face to face like this. "Have you ever had something just vanish, with no explanation? And you never
found it again?"

"Oh yes."

"Maybe your descendants took it."

"They did?"

"The Martians, so-called. Maybe it's their weakness, sticky fingers. Some of our belongings, you know,
will be priceless antiques someday, and of course the
Martians know exactly which ones. Know what we
should do when we find something missing like that?
Buy about twenty more. Like an investment. Why,
right now I've lost my belt with the fringe. I've looked
everywhere for it. In the fortieth century they may not
even *wear* belts. Shouldn't I buy a whole stack and
save them up?"

"I'm so hungry, Olivia," Jeremy said. "Aren't
you?"

"Yes, but wait, I want to ask you something."

"I don't believe we had any breakfast."

"Listen. Which are you, Jeremy? A descendant, or
an ancestor. Do you know?"

"What?"

"Do you know what time you're from? Do you?
Think, Jeremy. I want to find this out."

But all Jeremy said was, "I wish you could learn
how to make waffles."

Then I slammed my hand down on his, which
was resting on his knee, and he started and drew back.
But instead of removing his hand he left it there, and

after a long motionless minute he said in a faraway
voice, "How cool you are."

I thought he must be trying to sound hip.

He slid his hand away. Still leaning back, he
reached out and touched the end of a strand of my
hair with one fingertip. "You're so cold," he said.

Then I understood. It seemed I understood all
about him now. "I am always cold," I told him. "Never warm. Mary was warm."

"*You're* not," he said.

We stared at each other, not smiling at all.

He liked me in the colors of ice, pale blues and grays
and whites, everything smooth, preferably shiny. He
never said so, but I knew. He never had to say anything at all any more. Sometimes we went days without speaking or looking at each other, and we never
touched, even accidentally. We just moved about side
by side, in step. We sat in identical dusty green chairs
in the dining room, watching housewives win electrical
appliances. When they won they screamed and hugged
the emcee and took his face hard between their hands
to kiss him on the lips. "*I* used to win things," Jeremy
said. One woman jumped up and down and landed
wrong on her spike heels and twisted her ankle. Jeremy
and I watched without changing our expressions, like
two goldfish looking out of a goldfish bowl.

I saw that other people were forever rushing
somewhere, and nine-tenths of what they did would
have to be redone the next day. Cleaning, bathing,
making conversation. I thought about it a long time,
but I didn't mention it to Jeremy. I didn't need to. Half
of the idea I caught from him, by osmosis; the other
half I concluded for myself and passed back to him
just as silently. He quit shaving. His whiskers grew out
half an inch and stopped. How much time he could
have saved all these years, if he had known they
would do that! We quit going upstairs. His studio vanished; so did my bedroom. Look at stairs, we thought,
silently, together: what a perfect example of point-
lessness. They go up and down, both. If you go up you

must come down. You undo everything and start over. After *The Star-Spangled Banner* we fell asleep in our chairs, or out in the living room, or in the downstairs bedroom, side by side on top of the spread. I followed him everywhere but without asking a thing, an un-Mary sharing a pool of chilliness. I taught him to sleep late. Waking, finding me beside him, he would struggle up. "Be still," I said, and he lay down again and stared, as I did, at the towering white ceiling while noon approached and rolled over us and rumbled away again. Now I was an artist too. In my mind I colored the ceiling with the jagged lightning bolts you see when you squinch your eyes tight; so did Jeremy. We did it together. No strings snagged us to the rest of the world. "Good Lord in heaven!" Mr. Somerset said, shuffling up, stopping in the bedroom door-way. "Look here! What do you two think you're up to here?" I didn't answer. Jeremy didn't hear. Jeremy was farther along, he was nearly out of touch al-together, but I was catching up with him as fast as I possibly could.

I wouldn't eat, but Jeremy did. He devoured all the food that belonged to Miss Vinton: a loaf of bread, a quart jar of mayonnaise, a pack of wieners. Watching him eat made me feel stuffed. I saw that my fingers were getting knobby and my jeans were loose, but I felt so fat. He stopped chewing and looked over at me. I closed my eyes. He went on eating.

Once he said, "My mother died and so did both my sisters."

"Oh," I said.

"Also my father."

"Your father."

"Then her. Everybody left me."

"I haven't left."

"Everybody *outside* me left."

That was the way he let me know how he felt about me.

I was lying on the bed listening to the pigeons tearing at the ivy on the outside wall. It must be fall. Berries on the ivy. Jeremy was asleep beside me, he had been sleeping for hours while I kept watch. Then Miss Vinton came. She was wearing navy. Such a harsh color. She stood in the doorway a minute, and then she walked into the room and bent over me. She took hold of me by the chin and turned my face to her. "Olivia," she said.

I just looked at her.

"Olivia, do you hear me?"

Now Jeremy sighed and muttered. He was dreaming of horses, flocks of wild horses in muddy colors.

"I want you to listen, Olivia. You must pull yourself together. Do you hear me?"

The older you get the more you censor what comes into your head. Big blank spaces grow where you have snipped things out. You get like Miss Vinton and Mr. Somerset; you speak very slowly, spanning all those gaps. "I want . . . you to take . . . a good look at yourself, Olivia."

I just went on looking at her.

"Answer."

Her hand was like a vise on my chin, like grownups forcing you to confess. "What do you want me to say?" I asked, but I kept my voice flat, to show I wasn't scared of her. Her hand loosened a little.

"I choose you to speak to because I think you're more in touch than he is. Surely you must see what you're doing to yourself. Have you bathed lately? Look at your hair, your lovely long hair! You're skin and bones, you don't seem healthy. There's something funny about your eyes. What is that you're wearing?"

I wish they would break for commercials in real life.

"I can't stand watching you harm yourself, Olivia. And you're making Jeremy all the worse, you know that, don't you?"

A lie. See, I wanted to tell her, how faithful I am when all others desert him? The last believer left in the church. *I'm* making him worse?

"I think you are losing your mind, Olivia."

The vise on my chin again.

"Well, yes, I suppose I am," I said, "but it's nothing I can't bounce back from."

"Do it, then. Bounce."

"You don't believe I can."

"Oh yes. I believe it. That's why I'm telling you to do it."

"I don't see any reason to," I said, and then I wrenched free of her hand and turned away from her.

"How about Jeremy, then? Olivia?"

"How about him."

"He hasn't worked in weeks. You've let him get too removed. Doesn't that bother you?"

I didn't answer.

"Olivia?"

She left. I heard her clacking into the kitchen, sighing, clacking out again.

When Jeremy woke up I said, "Why aren't you working?"

"Working."

"I didn't cause you to stop."

Something made him raise his eyes, maybe some tone in my voice. I was so hurt. I couldn't understand what had happened.

"I finished the piece," he said.

"Oh," I said. "Oh, then."

He didn't say when he was planning to start another.

It must have been a weekday. Miss Vinton was gone and I couldn't see Mr. Somerset. The cat was hunched on the drainboard in the kitchen, turning his flat green eyes on and off. I felt sick to my stomach. "I don't want breakfast," I told Jeremy. "Let's go look at your piece."

He was finishing the little finicky toast rims that Miss Vinton had left in her cereal bowl. "Another time," he told me.

"I want to see it now."

"Olivia?"

"Now, Jeremy."

We climbed the stairs. It was like returning to

your childhood home—everything looked smaller and dingier. Clothes were overflowing a hamper in the upstairs hallway and on the windowsill was a vase containing a single brittle flower, stone dead. The closed door of my room seemed pathetic. We went on climbing. I was out of breath and darkness kept swooping in on my eyesight. When we reached the studio I said, "All right," but all Jeremy did was go straight to his armchair. I had to look at his piece on my own.

Imagine a wooden soft drink crate, only bigger, standing on end. A set of compartments, and in each compartment a different collection of objects. Like an advertisement showing a cross-section of a busy household. Was it the telephone company that used to do those? Yes, Bell Telephone, demonstrating why you need an extension in every room. Or maybe some other utility. Flameless electric heat, maybe. I ought to remember; I certainly pored over them enough as a child. In one room would be Junior with his stamp collection, in another Sis was dressing for a date, in the bathroom Dad was showering and Mother stood over the stove in the kitchen. Only in Jeremy's piece, there were no people. Only the *feeling* of people—of full lives suddenly interrupted, belongings still bearing the imprint of their vanished owners. Dark squares upstairs full of toys, paper scraps, a plastic doll bed lying on its side as if some burst of exuberance had flung it there and then passed on, leaving such a vacancy it could make you cry. Downstairs food, wheels, a set of jacks, a square of very bare green carpeting. Other things too fragmented to make out. I had to lean forward and squint, and give up finally, and settle back on my heels and shake my hair off my face.

"Why not just go on and make a dollhouse?" I said.

He rocked in his armchair, staring out the window.

"What do you call it? 'Ode to the Suburbs'? 'Hymn to Mary'?"

He kept rocking.

" 'In Praise of the Good Life'?"

I went around to the front of his armchair, where he would have to look at me. "Finally I get to where I understand, and then this is the piece you show me," I said. "But *you* I don't understand. Never. Jeremy? Wasn't I what you needed? Surely you're not going to say *she* was. Are you? Was she?"

But even when I stood directly in his line of vision, it didn't seem that he saw me. His eyes were as flat as that cat's eyes in the kitchen. He saw beyond me, without even having to try. There was a small trembling smile at the corners of his mouth. Only crazy people smile like that.

All I had to pack were the few things I'd brought in my knapsack—jeans and T-shirts, two of each. I left behind my ice-blue blouse and my shiny white Mexican dress and my white trenchcoat and my gray smock with the shimmery embroidery across the yoke. I packed some fruit and a box of granola. I was starved. I slid into my sandals and went out into the street.

How did it get so cold? All the leaves were down. The wind blew straight through my shirt and I had to hug the knapsack against my chest to keep warm. What I had planned was to walk out a ways and then hitch a ride on some larger street. I was thinking of going south. I didn't want any two-block errand-runners picking me up. But it was so cold that I started right in thumbing where I was, walking backwards down a line of parked cars. People whizzed past staring sideways, as if they didn't know what to make of me. Then the traffic light at the end of the block turned red and the cars started coming slower, preparing for the stop. I saw a Cadillac with tinted windows, one lady driving it all alone. A plump cheerful lady wearing a hat. I thought surely she would stop for me. I held my thumb higher, so that the cold air prickled all the little hairs on my arm. I looked straight at her through the windshield as she rolled closer. Please, lady! I'm only eighteen and a girl to boot, and it seems much brighter and colder out here than I had expected. I didn't know the sky would be so *wide* today. Won't you please give me a lift? But the car rolled past. I was so sure she would stop I had already turned, ready to reach for the door handle. She didn't even look at me. Just slid on by, leaving me standing there with my mouth open and my teeth chattering and my heart about to break. Now, why couldn't she have let me in? She had so much space! She seemed so nice! Her car looked so warm! Would it have hurt her any just to reach across and give me a smile and open the door? Why did she leave without taking me along?

9

Fall, 1971: Jeremy

First he tried making a woman seated at a sewing machine, but the curve of her back kept coming out wrong and after a while he gave up. Then a child with a cat, but he lost interest halfway through. Then a girl braiding her hair, which he finished because he made himself, but he knew it wasn't right. Lines came out knotty, angles awkward, flat planes lumpy and uneven. He kept ripping things out and then neglecting to replace them, sitting instead on a stool beside the piece while his hands went on working at useless tasks, at picking a cuticle or creasing the material of his trousers. Why couldn't I have been a musician, he wondered, and played what other people have already written down? Why not a writer, just giving new twists to words I already know? Yet Miss Vinton, bringing him cocoa, smiled at the statue of the girl and said, "Why, it's Darcy!" He was only modeling the people he had seen in real life, wasn't he? No. There was no way to sum people up; he was making new ones. An imaginary family. He stroked the imaginary Darcy's hand with a touch like a feather. Then he shook his head. "Sorry," Miss Vinton said. "I thought—here, I brought some cocoa. I won't keep you from your work." She went out on tiptoe, protecting his concentration. All she saw of him was the seamless exterior—Sculptor at Work. She never guessed at the cracks inside, the stray thoughts, tangents of memory, hours of idleness, days spent leafing through old magazines or practicing square knots on a length of red twine or humming under his breath while he tapped his fingers on the windowsill and stared down at the people in the street. A morning of half sleep on the couch in the corner, five minutes changing the slant of the statue's eyes, an afternoon playing with a tube of Christmas glitter powder.

He had heard that suffering made great art, but in his case all it made was parched, measly, stunted lumps far below his usual standard.

In his sleep he worked so hard that sheer exhaustion woke him up. He dreamed of cutting scraps of moonlight, strips of rain-spangled air, long threads of wind. Arranging them took such effort that he could feel his brain knotting. It seemed that he was aiming for some single solution, as in a mathematical problem. "Is this it? Is this it?" No answer. No click in his head to tell him he was finally right. He awoke feeling strained and damp, hoping that morning had arrived, but it hadn't. He always found himself in an opaque darkness, behind drawn shades and closed curtains, swaddled in grayish bedclothes. His life, he thought, was eye-shaped—the tight pinched corners of childhood widening in middle age to encompass Mary and the children, narrowing back now to this single lonely room. The silence hummed, and sometimes voices leaped out of it and startled him. He knew they were not real. They were accidental, something like the cells formed by molecules colliding and combining. He heard his sister Laura praising a friend's needlework, Pippi talking to a ladybug, a long-forgotten medical student requesting a new study lamp—all those separate eras weaving themselves together in his head. Mary asked if he needed new pajamas. Had her voice really been that young, once upon a time? Why, when they first met she must have been barely twenty-two. He had never thought much about that before. To him she had always been calm and stately, ageless, classical. Only now he remembered her flashing laughter and the pounding of her feet up the stairs and the whimsical, pigtailed paper dolls she used to make for Darcy. Her easy tears, her tempers with the children and the sudden way those tempers would disappear in swift, impulsive hugs that reminded him of reunions after journeys. How had he managed to overlook all that? He had loved her for the wrong qualities, the ones that were least important or that perhaps she did not even possess. He had ignored the ones that mattered. "How's your supply of socks?" she asked him. Behind her words he heard sparks and ripples, maybe even laughter, maybe directed at the absurdity of the subject they were discussing.

In the dark his mother's voice was thinner than a thread, weaving its way through a tangle of other people's words. "Oh, Jeremy, you were always so . . . I really and truly don't . . ." She spoke with that whispery sigh that meant he had done something wrong—a sigh not of anger but of disappointment. Well, of course. Lying here on his back, watching his mistakes roll across the ceiling, he felt he had done *everything* wrong. "Why, Jeremy?" she used to say (when he spilled his milk, or wrinkled his clothes, or failed to make his bed). "Why are you treating me this way? I've been as good to you as I know how to be. Now I see that being good is not enough." It occurred to him that she had spoken truer words than she knew. Being good was not enough. The mistakes he reviewed were not evil deeds but errors of aimlessness, passivity, an echoing internal silence. And when he rose in the morning (having waited out the night, watching each layer of darkness lift slowly and painfully), he was desperate with the need to repair all he had done, but the only repairs he could think of were also aimless, passive, silent. He had a vague longing to undertake some metaphysical task, to make some pilgrimage. In books a pilgrimage would pass through a fairytale landscape of round green hills and nameless rivers and pathless forests. He knew of no such landscape in America. Fellow pilgrims in leather and burlap would travel alongside him only long enough to tell their stories—clear narratives with beginnings, middles, ends and moral messages, uncluttered by detail—but where would he find anyone of that description? And think of what he would have to carry in the rustic knapsack on his back. The tools of his craft; Epoxy glue in two squeeze tubes, spray varnish, electric sander, disposable paintbrushes. Wasn't there anything in the world that was large scale any more? Wasn't there anything to lift him out of this stillness inside? He fumbled for his clothes and picked his way downstairs. He made his breakfast toast and ate it absently, chewing each mouthful twenty times and gazing at the toaster while he tried to find just one heroic undertaking that he could aim his life toward.

On a Saturday morning early in November he went into the older children's room on the third floor. He braved the tumult that seemed to go on filling the air with noise and movement even this long afterward—circus paintings and laughing dolls and plastic horses and coffee cans overflowing with broken crayons—and he found Abbie's pink nylon backpack at the bottom of the closet. In the kitchen he made two cheese sandwiches and a thermos of coffee, and he put them into the backpack along with an apple, a flashlight, and all the rent money from the cookie jar. He located a city bus map in the front of the telephone book, and after studying it for a moment he carefully tore out the entire page and folded it over and over and put it in his shirt pocket. Then he was ready to go.

Outdoors he was swept by a sudden coolness that he was not prepared for. He was wearing light-weight clothes, and a cotton windbreaker and his gray tweed golf cap. For warmth he kept his arms tightly folded and he walked with short, brisk steps, with the backpack whispering and bouncing behind him. He traveled several blocks, barely hesitating as he came to street crossings. Someone watching very carefully might have seen him swallow, or brace his shoulders, or look a few too many times to the left and right when a traffic light turned green, but otherwise he seemed no different from anyone else. At one corner he stopped and peered up at the street sign a moment, and then he made a turn and kept walking. He was among crowds now. Women sped past carrying dress boxes and string-handled paper bags, looking purposeful. A stroller with two children in it ran over his left foot. At the doorway of the dimestore, teenagers stood around shoving each other and popping their bubble gum and combing their hair and beginning dance steps they never finished. "Excuse me," Jeremy kept saying. "Oh, I'm sorry. Excuse me, please." They didn't listen. He threaded his way among them, his arms down at his sides now, trying to avoid touching anyone.

The inside of the dimestore smelled of wooden floors and popcorn. It seemed to him that there were far too many people in the aisles. "Excuse me," he kept saying, but as if he were transparent, no one noticed. He had to make his way to the toy department inch by inch, indirectly. When he finally reached it, he found a girl in a wrinkled smock filing her fingernails behind the counter. "Excuse me, I am going to need six toys," he told her. She looked up, still filing away. "I need toys to take to my children."

"Fine with me," she said.

"Do you have six toys I could take to them?"

She waved the nail file toward the toys, which spilled down not one counter but several and were made up of far too many colors. His eyes began blurring. "Well, I—do you possibly have any suggestions?" he asked her.

"Just look around, is what *I* suggest."

Rubber, paper, painted tin, plastic in phosphorescent shades of pink and chartreuse. Everything he saw seemed to make him hungry. He felt hollow and weak. "Perhaps—" he said. His hand hovered over a tiny wind-up metal tricycle, ridden by a metal boy, but when he looked up at the salesgirl she only filed a thumbnail and stared past him, refusing even a hint of encouragement. He sighed and moved on. He traveled down the rows of toys and then beyond them, up other aisles, pausing at a rack of coloring books and then again at infants' wear but still not buying anything. A terrycloth bib bore a painted picture of a baby who reminded him of Rachel, but the words beneath it said "I'm Daddy's Little Angel" and none of his children had ever called him Daddy. He wondered why not. He wondered if it were too late now for them to begin. But still, he didn't buy the bib. He imagined that Mary might give him an odd, considering look when she read the words on it, and the thought of that look made him feel foolish.

At the stationery counter he became fascinated by party favors. They hung on hooks, in little cellophane packets—clusters of tiny paper parasols that really opened, plastic cradles no bigger than walnut shells, tin horns with tassels and decks of cards the size of his thumbnail. He hung over then open-mouthed, reverently touching first one packet and then another. "Help you?" a woman said, but he shook his head. He made himself leave the favors and think of children's things again—masses of balloons in a plastic bag, striped paper hats, then stationery with pictures of little girls in the upper left-hand corner. Stationery? He wasn't sure which of his children were literate. He returned to the party favors, and found beneath them a section containing small white spherical packages tied with blue ribbon. "Excuse me," he said to the woman. "I was wondering what was in these."

"These here? Surprises."

"I mean—could you tell me what the surprises *are?*"

"Now, if I knew that," she said, "they wouldn't be surprises, would they?"

"No, I suppose not."

They were sold in packs of three. He could buy two packs and they would come out even. Also he thought it would be exciting to have gifts that were so mysterious. Who knew what might be hidden inside? Perhaps occasionally they filled a package with a real treasure, something worth far more than the price. As soon as he thought of that, choosing became difficult. He didn't want to make any mistakes. He picked up a pack and then dropped it, picked another, burrowed deep down to find the bottom-most one. From time to time he looked up at the woman and gave her a small friendly smile, but she never smiled back at him. Still, he felt he was making the right decision. When he had paid for them he took off his backpack to put the surprise balls inside, and the smooth way they fit between his cheese sandwiches gave him a feeling of competence. He had chosen well, unerringly, with all his instincts working for him. He was still smiling when he left the store.

Now he pulled the bus map from his pocket and checked it one last time, although he had already memorized where he should go. It was very important to find the corner where his particular bus stopped. If he forgot, or had misread something, he could be lost for days. He might never get home again. Perhaps he should not have attempted this. But the surprise balls rustled crisply in his pack, and the map pointed out his bus stop very clearly, and if he went home now he knew that he would despise himself forever, he would spend the rest of his life chewing the bitter knowledge that he hadn't a single spark of courage in him. He set out toward the bus stop, walking more slowly now and holding the map in front of him, blindly folding and unfolding it.

At the corner he wanted he found four people already waiting, which was encouraging. They stood below a blue sign bearing the number of his bus. He checked the number against the map, thought for a moment, and then checked it again. Everything was in order. He smiled at the other people. They looked around him, through him, above him. There was a woman in elastic stockings, a teenaged boy, a soldier, and a younger boy with his hands in his pockets. For some reason their skin appeared to be all the same shade of rough, dry pink and their hair straggled down in identical brown wisps, although they stood separate from each other and were obviously not related. Jeremy felt chilled by them. He thought of his sculptures, in which people like these so often appeared—standard representatives of what Brian called simple humanity, but any time Jeremy went out he was forced to see that humanity was far more complex and untidy and depressing than it ever was in his pieces. The old ladies were rude and sniveling, the men lacked solidity somehow, and the children seemed to carry a threat of violence. Jeremy spent the rest of his wait standing sideways to them—not confronting them but not facing totally away, either, for fear of giving offense—and like them he kept his eyes fixed on an empty spot in the distance.

When finally the bus came, it seemed almost as familiar as home. He climbed into a smell he had remembered without realizing it from thirty years in the past, from the days when he rode to art school or went shopping for clothes with his mother. The air was warm and slightly stuffy. Although he had to ask the driver what the price of a ticket was nowadays, he noticed that the seats still braced his spine at the same unnatural angle, and the doors still pleated themselves open and shut, and the back of the driver's neck still gave the impression of kindliness and reliability. Jeremy relaxed and looked out the window. He held Abbie's pack on his lap now, so that he could sit more comfortably, and as he rode along he kept stroking the slippery pink nylon as he had once stroked the satin binding on his blanket, long ago in childhood, waiting to be borne off to sleep.

Two ladies behind him were discussing someone's drinking problem. The soldier was whistling. A husband and wife were arguing over a woman named LaRue and up front a tiny black lady was talking to the bus driver. "You ought to seen him when they told him," she said. "He jumped up and shouted, 'Where's my gun? Where's my gun?' Planning on shooting his self. Later he wanted to jump into the grave. They had to hold him back by the elbows." "Is that right," the driver said. "Well, I expect he felt mighty close to her." Jeremy nodded over and over, impressed by the strangeness of what he heard and by the driver's easy acceptance of it.

Now the landscape outside his window was more open and barren, and the streets were less crowded. He was not sure that he had ever been here before. The scrubby trees far at the edge of the horizon had a desolate look, but in his present mood, when he was so proud of this trip and so hopeful at the thought of seeing Mary again, even desolation gave him the feeling of happiness swelling and unfolding inside him. He thought of things that had not occurred to him for years, some of them sad. He thought of his grandmoth-

er Amory, whom he had loved very much, and of the
gilt-framed picture that hung in her parlor. A crowd of
people in a faded forest. "See that forest?" his grandmother said. "Every bit of it is real. It is made of dried
plants, the pines are dried ferns and the flowers are
dried violets." "How about the people?" Jeremy had
asked, not thinking. "Are they dried too?" He thought
of Mrs. Jarrett, his mother's old boarder. Why, he had
never properly mourned Mrs. Jarrett's passing! Grief
flashed through him like a sharp white light. How
elegant she had been, with her plumed hats and her
white gloves! How hard she must have worked to keep
up her appearance! He looked around him at the inside of the bus, at the people nodding and agreeing
with each other and the soldier whistling his tripping
little tune. Then down at his hands, cupping Abbie's
pink backpack. Even his hands seemed dear and sad,
and gave him cause for joy.

Now here was the narrow rutted road to the boatyard,
pointed out to him so patiently by the driver. A line
of cottages and trailers dotted the wild grass. Jeremy
plodded along in the herringbone prints of some truck
or tractor, keeping his head bent against a cold breeze
that was blowing up. The soil was very soggy, as if
it had rained not long ago, and soon his shoes and
trouser cuffs were damp. He thought the dampness
was pleasant—two cool hands pressing the soles of his
feet. After rounding each curve he looked for a glimpse
of the boatyard. He had no idea how far it was. But
when he failed to find it he trudged on without mind-
ing. Some kind of rhythm had been set up, and his legs
swung forward in a steady trundling gait that seemed
to require no effort. He felt he could have gone on till
nightfall and still not have tired.

   Then up sprang a cluster of gray shacks and a
sheet of water beyond them—silently, eerily. He almost thought he had caught them moving into place
just out of the corner of his eye. Above the largest
building, which was plastered with soft drink signs, a
tin chimney seemed suspended from a thread of smoke.

There were several shabby cars scattered about, and a rusty flatbed truck beside a shed, and boats lining the dock and moored out on the water, but he saw no sign of humans. He approached the largest building as slowly as possible. Still, he felt he brought more noise and motion than the rules of this place would allow.

"Al's Supplies" the sign outside said, with Coca-Cola circles at either end like giant red thumbtacks. Jeremy climbed the hollow wooden steps and went inside. He found a man sitting beside a pot-bellied stove, reading a tabloid. All around him were display cases full of astonishing objects, things made of brass and wood and leather. Coils of very white rope hung from the rafters. In the dimness beyond he saw tinned goods on shelves, and he could smell cheese. "Excuse me," he said. The man folded his paper very carefully and creased the fold with his thumbnail before he looked up. "I was wondering if you knew where Brian O'Donnell's house is," Jeremy said.

"O'Donnell, No such fellow *here* by that name."

"But—but there has to be," Jeremy said.

"Nope."

"Isn't this the Quamikut Boatyard?"

"Yes, but there ain't no—"

"He has a house here. His name is O'Donnell, a man with a beard."

"Well, I never seen him and I know everybody roundabout, Mister."

"But surely you—and there's a woman there now with six children, staying in his house."

"Oh! You're talking about Mary Pauling."

"That's right, that's who I mean."

"*She's* here, but I never heard of no O'Donnell before."

"Well, um, could you tell me how to find her?"

"Sure. You just go on a ways down that road you come in by. Pass the boatyard, you'll find her place the very last thing. Her and the kids ought to be there right now, it's Saturday."

"I see," said Jeremy. "Well, thank you."

"You a friend of hers?"

"Friend?"

"I don't want you going down there if you're not welcome, now."

"No, please, it will be all right," Jeremy said.

He had to endure a long, silent inspection. The man tipped back in his chair and looked him up and down and chewed on his lower lip. Then he said, "Well, okay, get on."

Jeremy hitched his backpack higher on his shoulders and walked out again. Some of his confidence had faded. Mary's house was stamped with her name already, her schedule was familiar to people Jeremy had never laid eyes on, her safety was guarded by total strangers. And all in such a short time, a period he would have called sufficient for merely a visit. What was her secret?

He continued down the road past the shacks, alongside the water, across a gravel parking lot. What he was looking for was a vacation cottage, perhaps one of those shingled A-frame things that he had often seen advertised in the resort section of the Baltimore *Sun.* Instead he found a tipsy gray shanty with cinderblocks for a doorstep. Not *here,* surely. He moved around it, hoping for something more suitable just beyond. On the other side, standing on a wooden crate beneath a window, he found Mary. She was humming a cheerful, meandering tune and rolling up a sheet of newspaper. The wind whipped her skirt around her knees, and in spite of the cold she wore no sweater. While he watched she laid the tube of newspaper along the lower crevice of the windowframe, reached down to her feet for a wheel of masking tape, and taped the tube in place. Then she bent for another sheet of newspaper, which was anchored beneath her foot. As she straightened she caught sight of Jeremy. She stopped humming. He thought her face grew pale, but her voice was perfectly calm. "Hello, Jeremy," she said.

"Hello."

He shifted his weight to the other foot.

"Well!" she said finally. "Have you come for a visit?"

"Yes, I—no. I thought—"

His awkwardness made him feel overheated. From one pocket he pulled out a handkerchief to wipe his forehead, and while he was doing that she stepped down off the crate and came over to him. "Jeremy?" she said. "Are you all right?"

"Yes, certainly."

"How'd you get here?"

"By bus, and then I walked," he said.

"Walked! You poor soul!"

She laid a hand on his arm. "Really, it was nothing," he told her. "I'm not at all tired." Then he was sorry he said it, because she let go of him and moved away again. He felt he had lost some opportunity that he had noticed only too late. Where her hand had rested, his arm seemed to have become more sensitive. He concentrated on it, re-creating the pressure of her fingers, wishing that his arm possessed some sort of magnetic power. All he saw of her now was her back, the springy tendrils of hair escaping from her bun and her skirt whipping and flattening in the wind. "You'll want to see the children I guess," she called back.

"Why, yes, I—"

She led the way to the front of the house. He still couldn't believe that she would live in such a place. The cinderblocks made a gritty sound beneath his feet, the doorknob was a globe of solid rust and a bald patch in the linoleum nearly tripped him as he entered. At first all he could see was layers of diapers hanging up and down the length of the room. "Sorry," said Mary, "we've had a rainy spell lately, I had to hang them inside." She went ahead of him, parting diapers. He felt like a blind man. It was impossible to tell what kind of room he was in. He smelled laundry detergent and cold, stale air. He heard the children's voices but could see no sign of them. "Seven of hearts," one said. "Eight." "Nine, ten." "Jack? Anyone got the pack?" "Children, Jeremy's here," Mary said. Then they broke the last diaper barrier and stood in a doorway, looking into a tiny bedroom. The four oldest girls were playing cards on a caved-in double bed. Edward sat beside them stirring up a deck of cards of his own,

and over by the window stood Rachel—could that be
Rachel? standing?—holding onto the sill and turning
to smile up at him, wearing unfamiliar pink overalls
and showing several teeth that he had never seen before. "Jeremy!" Darcy said. They piled off the bed and
came to hug him. He felt a tangle of arms around his
chest, another pair around his knees. Everywhere he
reached out, he touched heads of hair so soft it seemed
his fingers might have imagined them. "What are *you*
doing here?" they asked him. "Did you come to stay?"
"Did you miss us?" He was amazed that they were so
glad to see him. After all, they might have forgotten
him, or never even noticed his absence. "Well, now,"
he kept saying. "Goodness. Well, now!"

"How come you're wearing my backpack?" Abbie asked.

"Oh, I hope you don't mind, I borrowed it to
carry my supplies."

"No, that's okay."

"Also some gifts, I believe," he said. "Let me see,
here." He hunched his way out of the backpack and set
it on the bed. From between his two sandwiches he
pulled the surprise balls, and then took forever trying
to break into the plastic wrappings. In the end he had
to chew through them with his teeth in order to start a
rip. He distributed the balls in a great hurry, one to
each child, one even to Rachel. "Open them," he said.
"Go on. They're surprises, no one knows what's in
them." He was so anxious for the gifts to turn out all
right that the children's fumbling fingers strained his
nerves. He reached into the backpack for one of the
sandwiches, unwrapped it and took great tearing bites
of it, chewing steadily as he watched the long ribbons
of white crêpe paper unwinding onto the floor.

The first to find anything was Pippi. A little ping
sounded at her feet. "Oh!" she said, and bent and
picked up a flat tin whistle the size of a postage stamp.
She turned it over several times. "It's a whistle," she
said finally. She blew on it, but the sound that came
out was whispery and toneless. She turned it over
again. "Never mind," said Jeremy, "go on unwrapping.
I'm sure there's more." He took another bite of his

sandwich. He looked over at Darcy, who had just found her surprise—another whistle. Everyone had whistles. Some had one, some two or three. The only difference between them was the colors. The gifts' round shape was formed by a cardboard center, something like the core of a ball of string. The centers fell to the floor and rolled around with hollow sounds. Crêpe paper ribbons rose like mounds of spaghetti around everyone's feet. One by one the children lifted the whistles to their lips, blew them, lowered them, and looked at Jeremy. They seemed not so much disappointed as puzzled. Their faces were courteous and watchful, as if they were waiting for some explanation. When Rachel cried out, holding up her own ball, which was still unopened but damp where she had chewed it, Mary said, "Here, Rachel, I'll help," and those faces swung toward Rachel all at the same second, as if they thought *she* might provide what they were waiting for. While Mary unwound the ball Rachel reached out with both hands, catching tails of crêpe paper. At the very end two whistles fell to the floor—one yellow, one blue. She crowed and stooped to pick them up, but Mary was too quick for her. "No, honey," she said. "You might swallow them." Over her shoulder she called, "Darcy, find her something. Hand her my keys, will you?" But the keys were no good. Rachel threw them away and started crying, still straining toward the whistles in her mother's hand. "Rachel, they'll *hurt* you," Mary told her. Then she said to Jeremy, "I'll just save them till later, shall I?"

"Oh. Surely," he said.

"As soon as she's old enough I'll give them to her. I know she'll love them."

Never mind, the last thing I need is *tact,* he wanted to tell her. I know they don't care for whistles. And I know it doesn't matter all that much anyway; I'm not a child, after all. But there was no way to say it out loud without bringing on *more* tact—reassurance, protestations. "*I* think these gifts are lovely," Mary said. "Aren't they, children? Wasn't it nice of Jeremy to bring them?"

Murmurs rose up too quickly, on cue. "Thank

you, Jeremy." "Golly, these sure are nice, Jeremy."

"Oh, well," he said.

"You know how fond children are of things that make noise," Mary told him.

He looked at her helplessly, at her kind, protecting, understanding eyes, and for lack of words he finished the last of his sandwich with a single chomp and wiped the crumbs off on the front of his shirt. Chewing gave him a good reason not to speak. He gazed straight ahead of him, chewing hard, conscious of seven faces turned in his direction and frozen there.

"How is your work going?" Mary asked him.

He chewed on. He couldn't seem to finish. The bread and cheese seemed to have molded together like soggy newspaper.

"Jeremy?" she said. "Aren't you working any more?"

Her face was so *concerned*. She was being so careful of him. He swallowed hard and cleared his throat. "Of course I am," he said.

"You are?"

"My work is going *very* well. Very well. I am very pleased with it."

"Oh," said Mary. "Well, that's wonderful."

"In fact, it's going better than it ever has before," he said.

"That's nice."

She turned and went out of the bedroom. Following her, he had to bat his way between the damp diapers. The children came behind him in a shuffling, whispering line. When he located Mary again—just easing herself onto a dingy mound of a sofa and arranging Rachel upon her lap—Jeremy sat down too, but at some distance from her. The children settled themselves on the floor, all facing their parents, completely silent now. He winced to see them on that cold, blackened linoleum. He noticed how shabby and unattractive they looked—ragged children with reddened noses and chapped hands and lips, their sleeves short enough to expose their wrists and their shoes muddy and curling at the toes. And the house filled him with despair. At each gust of wind outside the cold burst in upon him like little knives from several directions. The furniture seemed untrustworthy—infested or disease-ridden. He sat gingerly on the edge of the couch. He kept his eyes averted from the miserable attempt at a kitchen that he had glimpsed across the room. Why must she choose the very *worst* house to live in? Why had she gone husbandless to the hospital that time, no doubt calling down all the nurses' pity and indignation? Was it purposeful? Was it aimed at him? Yet the next thing she said was, *"We're* doing very well, too."

He stared at her.

"We're doing beautifully," she told him.

Yes. She would do beautifully anywhere. There was no defeating her. He felt tired at the thought of her.

"I have a job now, you know," she said. "I work at a day nursery in one of those cottages up the road. You probably passed it."

"Do—but what about the children?" he said.

"Well, the younger ones I take with me. The others go to school."

"School? Is there a school out here?"

"There are schools everywhere, Jeremy. They can walk out to the highway and catch a bus that takes them right to the door."

He imagined them in a huddle at the bus stop, shivering in their thin, patched dresses, their bare legs blotchy with cold. "Mary, I don't think—it sounds so—"

"The day nursery lets out the same time school does. I'm home before they are. And I like my work."

Yes, but what about me? he asked silently. Are you saying you won't consider returning? Have I come all this way for nothing?

"You know, Jeremy," Mary said, "I'm managing on my own now. I'm not depending on a soul. I'm doing it on my own."

Well, of course she was. Mary had *always* managed on her own. Why did she even bother mentioning it? The answer was simple: she was telling him she had no place for him. He turned to meet her eyes and found her glowing and confident, as beautiful as ever, *more* beautiful. "I've even started paying Brian rent money," she said. "I don't want to be beholden to him."

"Mary, haven't you used any of the money in the bank?"

"That's *your* money, Jeremy. I'm trying to manage on my own."

"But the children! I mean—"

"How are things at home? Is Miss Vinton helping you out?"

"Oh, Miss Vinton, yes."

"How's Olivia?"

"Why, she left," he said. "She didn't even tell us goodbye."

"Left? Where'd she go to?"

"I'm not at all sure. And toward the end she didn't seem to be herself, I do hope—"

"Oh dear, I've thought of her often," Mary said. "I should have taken her with me."

"Where, here?"

"Certainly here."

"I don't understand how you have room for the number you *do* have," he said, looking around.

"Really, we're very comfortable. Also I'm planning to buy an oil stove," she told him. "That will help when it gets colder. And Darcy and I are winterizing the place ourselves, did you notice?"

"Um—"

"Sealing off the windows and everything."

He thought of the rolled-up newspapers. "Ah, yes," he said. "No, I know what winterizing *is*, I just thought—"

"We're doing a pretty good job, don't you think?"

"Yes."

"Most people would have to ask some man to do that."

"Oh. Well, I think *I* had better take care of it now," he said.

"You?"

"I'll go tend to it right away."

"But Jeremy," she said. "Wouldn't you like to—"

"Do you think I don't know how?"

"No, of course not. I don't think that for a minute. I'm sure you know how."

"Well, then," he said. "I expect I'd better get started."

"Do you mean right this minute?"

"Why, yes."

"Wouldn't you like to sit here a while? I could give you a bite to eat."

"I've already eaten."

"You could sit and talk, maybe. Don't you want to?"

If they talked, she would say what he dreaded to hear, and once said it could never be taken back. He rose hastily, draping his bald spot with the sudden coolness of a diaper. It was important to take action at once. To surround her with efficiency and authority. "I'll do it all, you see to the children," he told her. And he had clapped his cap on and was out the door before she had time to rise to her feet.

He had to do a better job of it than she and Darcy could. That was essential. Instead of folding tubes one by one as he needed them he did them all at once, and weighted them with a stone. He cut off lengths of masking tape and fastened them by their tip ends to the sills of the various windows. Only then did he climb up on the crate and begin the actual task. It seemed that his fingers could not make a wrong move today. Everything proceeded so smoothly, in such a well-ordered fashion. Why, there was nothing to this sort of work! He could have been taking care of it all these years. The wood was rotten and it crumbled beneath the tape but he managed anyway, locating the most solid places, feeling a sense of patience and tolerance for this pitiful world that Mary thought so much of. He could win her back in no time, it wasn't impossible. Wasn't he managing this windowsill well? Wasn't he finally in control?

Mary came out of the house carrying a mug of coffee, balancing Rachel on her left hip in a familiar way that hurt him to see. She still had not put on a sweater, and the baby's feet were bare. "She'll get sick, Mary," he told her.

"Why do you say that?"

"It's much too cold out here."

"Cold?"

She looked up at him, at where he stood teetering on the crate. "Jeremy, it's not cold," she said. "This is the warmest fall in anyone's memory. It's November and people still have their boats out."

"But the wind," he said.

She turned and looked out toward the water, as if the wind would be visible there. She looked at him again. "But it's not a *cold* wind, Jeremy," she said. "It's just a cool breeze. Are *you* cold?"

"No, no." He felt beaten. He was sorry he had mentioned it. Mary smiled up at him with her face bright and suntanned and her eyes very certain, her bare arms showing not a single goose bump. When she handed him the mug of coffee she touched his hand with hers, and even her fingertips were warm. She let her hand rest there as if proving the warmth, gloating over it, but Jeremy slipped out of her reach immediately and then she went away.

As soon as the windows were done he went back in the house. He carried his stack of newspapers and roll of tape. "Oh, good, you're finished," Mary said. "Won't you sit down with me and have some more coffee? Children, will you get out from underfoot, please?" But Jeremy said, "No, no, I want to do this properly. I'll have to seal the insides, too."

"You mean, right now?"

"I want to get this done the way it ought to be," Jeremy told her.

"I see," said Mary. "Well, goodness. You certainly are fixing it so we could stay all winter here."

"I can manage everything. I don't want you to have to bother yourself at all."

"I see," Mary said again, and then she sat down in a kitchen chair and let him get on with his work.

"What next?" he said when he was done. Mary was in the kitchen, slicing carrots. There were so many children around her that he had to shout to make himself heard, but as soon as he had spoken they fell silent. He had never known such a silence. He couldn't understand what they were waiting for. Mary turned and looked at him, but her face was blank and he wondered if he should repeat the question. "What next?" he said. "What else needs doing?"

"Why, nothing I can think of, thank you."

"Nothing? There must be *something*."

"No."

"You said you were doing things to winterize."

She turned very suddenly back to the cutting board. She began slicing the carrots with a clipped, definite motion.

In the silence one of the children said, "We were going to air the sails, remember?"

"We can do that later," Mary said without looking around.

"Do what?" said Jeremy.

"Air the sails," Abbie told him.

"I don't understand."

"We do it for Mr. O'Donnell. After a rainy spell we go out and run up his sails to dry them. Mom *hates* doing it."

He looked at Mary. Still only at her back.

"Oh," he said finally. "Well, then. It seems that's something *I'd* better take care of."

Then she did turn. She said, "Never mind that, Jeremy, I can see to it later."

"But I—Abbie says you hate it."

"Jeremy, please. Can't you stop *doing* things a minute?"

"I'm not at all overtired," he said.

"No, I know you're not."

"Then what are we waiting for?"

He was out the door and six feet away before he realized that he didn't know which boat was Brian's. When he turned, he found a whole cluster of children watching him from the steps. They advanced on him,

all talking at once. "It's the blue one, the ketch."
"There it is." "You have to row out in a dinghy."

"A dinghy. Oh," he said.

"There's the dinghy."

He followed Hannah's pointing finger and found a
dinghy nearly hidden in a clump of weeds down by
the water. An enormous thing. He cleared his throat.
"Ah, yes," he said.

"You run the sails up the masts and let them dry
a little while."

"Yes, I see."

"Can we come too?"

"Come—surely your mother must need you at
home," he said.

"No, she doesn't."

The thought of the children alongside him, rocking the boat and swarming everywhere, falling over-
board and requiring him to jump in after them when
he couldn't swim, was even more terrifying than the
thought of rowing alone. "Perhaps another time," he
said.

"Why can't we? Mom always let us."

"She does?"

"She takes the bunch of us and the baby too."

"I see. Well, then," said Jeremy, "I suppose you
may come."

The children cheered. Jeremy walked toward the
water with very small, firm steps, fixing his eyes upon
the dinghy and praying for it to turn out to be more
manageable than it looked from here. It wasn't. It
seemed gigantic. It's peeling, weathered surface had the
same depressing effect on him as gray-painted machinery or factory buildings. There was a pool of scummy
water in the bottom. Wasn't that a danger sign? The
oars looked too long to handle. Even the rope that tied
it presented a problem; it was fastened to a post with a
clever, casual-looking knot. "Here," said Darcy, when
he had taken too long loosening it. "Let me." She
slipped it off easily and handed it to him. While he
waited, numbly keeping hold of it, she helped the children pile in. *"Not* Pippi, Pippi went first last time. It's
Eddie's turn. Who's going to sit next to Jeremy?"

"Wait!" they heard. Jeremy turned and saw Mary flying down the slope toward them with the baby bouncing on her hip and her face pale and her eyes dark and wide, almost without whites to them. He thought something terrible must have happened. He had never seen her look so frightened. When she came up beside him she was breathless. "Mary?" he said. "What is it?"

"Jeremy, I—please don't take the children."

He felt as if she had hit him in the stomach. While she gasped for breath he did too, clenching his end of the rope. "I'm sorry," Mary said. "It's just that I—well, I was just about to feed them. Why don't you leave them with me? You'll only be gone a *little* while."

Of course he shouldn't take them. He knew that too. But to have her stand there telling him that, saying she was willing for him to go himself but not to take the children! She thought his silence meant that he was simply being stubborn. "Or, I know what," she said, trying a new tone. "I'll come along. How will that be?" She smiled up at him. The children murmured encouragement. She laid a hand gently on his arm. "Wouldn't that be nice? Wouldn't it be better if we all went out together?"

"Get away from me," he said.

Her hand dropped. Her smile vanished so suddenly it seemed to have broken and shattered.

"Just leave me alone, leave me be," he said. "And you," he told the children. "Get out."

They came awkwardly, stumbling over each other and keeping their eyes on him instead of the ground. "Jeremy?" said Mary. Her voice was thin and choked, but he didn't look at her. As soon as the last child was on dry land he bent over the boat, gave it a long shove, and then hopped in, as neatly as if he had done it all his life. The only thing that gave him away was the violent trembling of his knees as he bent to sit down. The whole boat trembled. He pretended not to notice. He reached for the oars, fitted them into the oarlocks, and after a few dry swoops hit water and pulled. The dinghy set off with a start. But was he facing in the right direction? He thought of Winslow Homer's paintings; he tried to remember which way the men in dinghies had been pulling. It would be just like him to perform this entire task sitting backwards. He splashed himself a few times, then plowed too deep and took a while to realize which oar to lift when he veered to one side. The dinghy kept jerking ahead and then losing half the gain before he could manage another stroke, but when he looked over his shoulder he saw that he was making progress. He knew he would get there eventually. He turned to look at the shore again and found Mary and the children lined up, watching. Their faces were small and white and featureless. The only sound that came from them was the shrill tweet of Edward's whistle, which he blew in an absent-minded way as he faced out toward the water. Then Hannah's whistle, copying Edward's, but hers was softer and the creaking of the oars nearly drowned it out.

He thought it took about half an hour to reach Brian's boat. Maybe more. Another man could no doubt have done it in five minutes. He felt the nudge and scrape of the dinghy against painted wood, and he turned and reached for the ledge that ran around the deck. But how would he secure the dinghy? Slowly, now. He mustn't rush. He thought for a long time, then passed the end of the dinghy's rope very cautiously around a cable that rose from the deck of the ketch. Above all, he worried about falling into the gap between the two boats. He would not even stand to fasten the rope. He remained seated, straining upward, tying knot upon knot until he had a long chain of them that would certainly not slip out no matter what. Then he clung to the side of the ketch and rose by inches. He took a deep breath, hoisted himself upward, and there he was—kneeling on the deck of a sailboat, alone, with no more ill effects than the loss of his golf cap to the black greasy water and a tingling echo of fear in the palms of his hands and the soles of his feet.

He rose and made his way toward the sails. Walking on a ketch was no trouble at all, nothing like standing in a dinghy. He felt he could breathe freely again. Still, he didn't turn to look at his family. The sound of their whistles trilled in his ears—four or five whistles, now, so he knew they must still be there, but he kept his back to them and pretended they were gone. For him, they were gone. He had never felt so isolated. Gulls slid through the air about him as white as drifting ashes, and the water dabbled softly around the edges of the boat while the dinghy scraped rhythmically against its hull. He found ropes twined around the sails, holding them furled, but it wasn't hard to loosen them or to figure out how to raise them. First the biggest one, then the middle-sized one, then the little triangular scrap out front. They fluttered and flapped and crackled. Jeremy sat down on a deckseat to wait for them to dry. Every time a gust of wind blew up the sails would fill and the boat would move, but it seemed securely moored and Jeremy didn't worry. He was beyond worry. The boat scudded around its mooring in wider and faster circles and the children on shore piped it on its journey with tin whistles while Jeremy, slumped on his deckseat, blinked his tears away and watched his gray golf cap bob off across a wave and grow dark and heavy and finally sink.

10

Spring, 1973: Miss Vinton

This house is back to its beginnings now. Lonely boarders thumb through magazines in the kitchen while they wait for their canned soup to heat. The television runs nearly all night, hissing its test pattern to a fat man asleep in an armchair. There are yellowed newspapers stacked on the window seat and candy wrappers in the ashtrays, and this morning when I came down to breakfast I removed a pair of dirty socks from the bottom stairstep and laid them on the newel post, where I suspect they will stay forever.

The house is the same but the street is changing. Getting younger. Old people are dwindling. The few that are left pick their way down the sidewalk like shadows, whispering courage to themselves and clutching their string shopping bags full of treasure. There goes the lame lady who lives above the grocery store in a room full of cats and birds and goldfish. There goes our boarder Mr. Houck, who thins himself to a pencil line when passing a black harmonica player. Miss Cohen, with her widowed mother. The bald man with the ivory-handled cane. All flinching beneath the cool eyes of the boy in dungarees who sits on a stoop fiddling with his ropes of colored beads.

Sometimes I invite Jeremy to come to the grocery store with me. I tell him it will do him good. I call him down from his studio, from his great towering beautiful sculptures, and help him into his jacket and offer my arm for support. We go very slowly. He is not used to walking much. He tends to whisper instead of speaking out, and even once we are inside the grocery store he whispers to Mrs. Dowd. What would be good to buy today? Her day-old pies? Anything will be all right. We head toward home again, arm in arm. We trundle down the sidewalk like two clay ducks, and the boy on the stoop yawns and reaches for a beer. If he looks at us at all he sees only an elderly couple, together no doubt for centuries, arriving at the end of their dusty and unremarkable lives. The woman's cardigan is drab and frayed. The man wears crocheted bedroom slippers. He seems peaceful but distant, detached from his surroundings. The boy starts whistling a lighthearted tune, and he goes on whistling long after the elderly couple has turned in at the house near the corner and locked the door and drawn the window shades.

Books By ANN BEATTIE

_CHILLY SCENES OF WINTER　　*(A31-108, $3.50, U.S.A.)*
　　　　　　　　　　　　　　　(A31-109, $4.50, Canada)
　　　　　　　　　　　　　　　　(Available May 1983)

A remarkable writer's highly acclaimed first novel. "The literary debut of a mesmerizing, exalting, uncannily unsettling talent."
　　　　　　　　　　　　　　　　　　　—*Washington Star*

"CHILLY SCENES OF WINTER thaws quite beautifully."
　　　　　　　　　　　　　　　　　　　—*The New Yorker*

_DISTORTIONS　　　　　　　*(A31-110, $3.50, U.S.A.)*
　　　　　　　　　　　　　　　(A31-111, $4.50, Canada)
　　　　　　　　　　　　　　　　(Available May 1983)

Here is a collection of the dazzling stories that have made Ann Beattie one of the most celebrated new voices in American fiction. "Miss Beattie is very young and immensely talented, and she seems to have jumped out of the head of an autumnal Samuel Beckett."
　　　　　　　　　　　　　　　　　　　—*John Leonard*

_FALLING IN PLACE　　　　　*(A31-112, $3.50, U.S.A.)*
　　　　　　　　　　　　　　　(A31-113, $4.50, Canada)
　　　　　　　　　　　　　　　　(Available May 1983)

The setting is suburban Connecticut, and the story turns on the fortunes—and misfortunes—of one family and the people around them. "People like Cynthia and John and Peter and Nina; Cynthia who teaches John's daughter in summer school and lives with Peter, her lover, who used to be Nina's lover, the same Nina who is John's lover and might be his wife if he ever divorces the one he has now."
　　　　　　　　　　　　　　　　　　　—*Harper's*

_SECRETS AND SURPRISES　　*(A31-114, $3.50, U.S.A.)*
　　　　　　　　　　　　　　　(A31-115, $4.50, Canada)
　　　　　　　　　　　　　　　　(Available May 1983)

A collection of stories by "the best new writer since Donald Barthelme...She is a writer for all audiences, combining a remarkable array of skills with material of wide popular appeal."
　　　　　　　　　　　　　　　　　　　—*New York Times Book Review*

Also By ANNE TYLER

__EARTHLY POSSESSIONS

(A31-171, $2.95, U.S.A.)
(A31-172, $3.75, Canada)

Charlotte Emory...a youthfully vital woman in a marriage that has grown old. A runaway from respectability on the perilous road to freedom, joined to a man who is at once her total opposite yet uncanny mirror image. "One of today's most talented and mesmerizing authors is at her best in EARTHLY POSSESSIONS...She makes you laugh and cry and share intensely in the feelings of all her people." —*Publishers Weekly*

To order, use the coupon below. If you prefer to use your own stationery, please include complete title as well as book number and price. Allow 4 weeks for delivery.